•aka•
McGuire

To Judy & Joe,
It's been great
re-uniting —
Enjoy the read!
Janet Eutyel
4/5/08

·aka· McGuire

Janet Entzel

Beaver's Pond Press

www.beaverspondgroup.com

ISBN 10: 1-59298-192-5
ISBN 13: 978-1-59298-192-2

Library of Congress Control Number: 2007930887
Printed in the United States of America
First Printing July 2007
11 10 09 08 07   6 5 4 3 2 1

Beaver's Pond Press is an imprint of
Beaver's Pond Group
7104 Ohms Lane, Suite 216
Edina, Minnesota, 55439-2129
www.beaverspondgroup.com

This book is dedicated to my mother, Jean Blomquist Hoff

Janet Entzel

Janet Entzel was elected to the Minnesota House of Representatives in 1974. During her tenure, she served on the Criminal Justice Committee. In 1984, she left elected office and accepted a managerial position in the administrative office of the Minnesota Department of Corrections (DOC). Having developed an interest in the criminal mind, she requested and received a mobility assignment at the adult, male prison in Lino Lakes, Minnesota. There she worked inside the walls and had direct contact with both staff and inmates.

Upon her return to the administrative office of the DOC, Ms. Entzel was the Assistant Commissioner of Legislative Relations and Juvenile Services. Her focus was crime prevention and early intervention programs. She retired in 1999 and is living with her husband in Coon Rapids, Minnesota.

Acknowledgements

To Beavers Pond Press; Milt Adams, Judith Palmateer, and Renee Ketchmark, thank you for accepting my manuscript and for mentoring me through the publication process. To my editor, Jennifer Manion, you are absolutely the best. Chris Fayers, thank you for making the book design process seem easy, when it's not. The cover is spectacular!

For expertise and advice, I am indebted to the following people: Lieutenant "LT" Pratt, Commander, Green Valley Patrol District, Arizona; Dr. Fulginiti, Medical Examiner, Pima County, Arizona; Jim Robideau, Arizona Department of Corrections; Dave Simone and Tom Smith, Florence, Arizona; and to the employees and patrons of La Gitano, Arivaca, Arizona

Thanks to Orville Pung, former Commissioner of the Minnesota State Department of Corrections, and Assistant Commissioner Lurline Baker-Kent, for having the courage to hire a legislator; and thanks very much to department experts, Ken Carlson, psychologist; Pat Orud, psychologist; Connie Roerich, warden; and Dan O'Brien, assistant commissioner.

To Gothriel "Fred" LaFleur and Dennis Benson your vision and department operational knowledge is amazing. Thanks for serving as my mentors.

Phil Puscuzzi, Hennepin County Medical Examiners Office, thanks for the lesson on bugs and crime scenes; and to my son-in-law, Dan Hamann, for technology support.

A special thanks to William Kent Krueger my instructor and mentor.

To all my experts, I apologize for any liberties I may have taken with the information you so willingly provided. I did so only if I felt it made the plot more interesting.

And to those who read, edited and critiqued my manuscript in various stages: Jean Hoff, Nancy Schafer, Cynthia Entzel, Norene Hoftiezer, Shirley Hokanson, Shari Burt, Betty McMahon, Peggy Stoks, Jo Erhart, Judy Thurston, Nan Morris and my writers group. Your contribution to this effort is very much appreciated.

Arnie Entzel, your constant support and encouragement kept me from becoming discouraged and throwing in the towel. Your willingness to read and critique my manuscript several times was extremely helpful.

Author's Note

The town of Empalma is fictitious. Descriptions of the Empalma cemetery and cantina came from the town cemetery and the cantina, La Gitano, which are located in Arivaca, Arizona. La Gitano is where this novel took root.

Although I have toured the prison complex in Florence, Arizona, the prison described in AKA McGuire is fictitious, as are the warden, employees and inmates. Any similarity to people, living or dead, is purely coincidental.

My thanks to the employees and patrons of La Gitano, Gibby's and the L&B Inn for the hospitality extended to me, and my family, during our visits to Arivaca and Florence.

•aka•
McGuire

Prologue

DR. CHARLES McGUIRE closed the case file he was working on and glanced at his watch. It was seven o'clock on Friday evening, and he was alone in his office. Tomorrow morning he would be flying from Michigan to San Diego. From there, he would rent a car and travel up the coast of California to Oregon. It would be a retracing of the honeymoon trip that he and his wife had taken nearly twenty-five years ago, but this time, Charles would be making the trip by himself. Marie had recently lost her battle with cancer. McGuire hoped that by taking the trip up the coast, he would have the time he needed to grieve. Then, maybe, he would be able to let Marie go. Dr. Sobel, his good friend and associate, had agreed to fill in while he was gone.

Dr. McGuire took off his glasses and rubbed his temples. He heard the outside door to the clinic office open and close. McGuire had been so preoccupied with getting his things in order that he had forgotten to lock the outside door after the other staff left for the day. He stood up and walked out into the reception area.

"Hello," said the tall, handsome, dark-haired man. He was wearing a warm winter coat and leather gloves. The man looked familiar, but Dr. McGuire couldn't place him.

"You don't remember me, do you, Doc?" the man asked, voice tinged with sarcasm.

"I'm sorry, but I can't remember your name."

"Well, we haven't seen each other in over two years; I guess that's to be expected. I'll give you a clue. I'm no longer wearing prison issue clothes."

Prison clothes. Now McGuire remembered the man. It was Sean Byrnes, a prisoner who had been incarcerated in the Saginaw Correctional Facility when McGuire had contracted with the Michigan Department of Corrections to provide mental health services for inmates. After his wife was diagnosed with breast cancer, McGuire had terminated his contract with the prison so he could spend more time with her.

"What are you doing here, Mr. Byrnes?" McGuire asked.

"No greeting? No 'nice to see you' or anything? Just 'What are you doing here, Mr. Byrnes?'" Sean snarled.

McGuire watched as Byrnes slowly pulled off his gloves, one finger at a time, and opened his coat. Then, without warning, Byrnes pushed the psychiatrist back into his office and kicked the door shut.

"Sit down over there, Doc," he said, pointing to a chair on the far side of the room. Byrnes helped himself to the doctor's plush leather chair. He dug the heels of his hiking boots into the carpet and rolled the chair over to block the doorway. He swiveled around once, and then glared at Dr. McGuire.

"What do you want?" the psychiatrist asked, realizing he couldn't leave the room unless he went through the inmate.

"I got released last week, no thanks to you." Byrnes' pale, ice blue eyes narrowed. "Now you shut the hell up and answer my questions."

Byrnes' tone was unnerving. "What do you want to know?" the doctor asked, in as calm a voice as he could muster.

"Why did you tell the parole board I shouldn't be released until my expiration date?"

A shiver ran across Dr. McGuire's shoulders. The psychiatrist had testified before the Michigan Parole Board. When asked about Byrnes' potential for success if he was to be granted an early release, McGuire had testified that he felt the inmate was a poor risk because of his psychopathic tendencies.

The doctor looked directly into the pale eyes glaring at him. "To be honest with you, I didn't think you were ready to be released. I felt that you would benefit from more anger management therapy."

"Excuse me? Did I hear you say more therapy would benefit me?" Byrnes' began bouncing his left leg. "Let me tell you how much those extra years benefited me. When my girlfriend found out I wasn't getting released early, she left me. As if that wasn't enough, my mother moved to Arizona because of her arthritis. I didn't have any visitors coming to see me. Do you really think the extra time in prison helped me become less angry?"

The psychiatrist knew it would be pointless to try to reason with Byrnes. "I'm sorry you feel that way," he said, "but if I can do anything to help you now, let me know."

"You know what, Doc? I'm going to take you up on your offer."

Byrnes, with eyes locked on McGuire, stood up. He reached back under his coat and pulled out a large Bowie hunting knife he had stolen shortly after his release. A moment later the knife was poised at the doctor's throat. A feeling of impending doom coursed through McGuire's veins but he knew he needed to stay calm.

"Stand up slowly and turn around. Don't do anything stupid; I'm right behind you," Byrnes ordered.

Standing up, Dr. McGuire felt the tip of the knife slide from his throat, past his neck to the middle of his back. "Why are you doing this?" he asked.

Byrnes ignored the question. He noticed the doctor's leather briefcase on the floor beside the desk. "Get your briefcase. We're leaving."

The doctor did as directed. "Can I get my coat?"

"Yeah." Byrnes was glad McGuire had mentioned the coat. It would look suspicious if the coat were hanging in the closet while the doctor was out.

Holding McGuire firmly against him, Byrnes moved them both into the hallway. It was deserted. Byrnes pushed McGuire through the building's back door and into the cold night air. A black Lincoln Continental was the only car in the dimly lit parking lot.

"That yours?" Byrnes nodded in the direction of the car.

"Yes."

"Must cost some big bucks to buy a car like that. I bet you have a bunch of poor suckers paying you lots of money to cure them."

The night air was frigid. Large snowflakes drifted gently to the ground. Ice and snow crunched beneath the feet of the two men as they walked towards the Lincoln. Through his winter overcoat, McGuire could feel the constant pressure of the knife against his spine and ribs.

His mind was racing. Should he make a run for it and risk being stabbed? No, he decided. Byrnes was younger, stronger and in much better shape. There was no way he could outrun him. He'd have to wait for a better opportunity.

"Give me your wallet," Byrnes demanded after they reached the car.

He's going to rob me, the psychiatrist thought, somewhat relieved. He took the wallet out of his jacket and handed it over.

"And your watch."

The doctor reluctantly pulled off his Rolex and gave it to Byrnes.

"Now the ring."

"This is my wedding ring. I can't. . ."

"Stop whining and give me the damn ring."

It took a few tugs before Dr. McGuire slide the ring off of his finger.

"Open the trunk of your car," Byrnes directed.

McGuire fumbled for the keys and unlocked the trunk. As he straightened up and turned around, the ex-convict tightened his grip on the knife and threw a vicious blow with his right fist, hitting the doctor squarely under the chin. Off balance, the psychiatrist tumbled backwards and Byrnes moved in, pushing Dr. McGuire into the trunk.

Byrnes looked down at the semiconscious, quivering psychiatrist. He grabbed the doctor's legs and spun him face down into the trunk.

An army blanket lay folded neatly in the corner. "Here, I'll tuck you in and make you all cozy," he said, as he reached for the blanket.

Byrnes jerked Dr. McGuire's head up by the hair and with one stroke of the knife slashed the doctor's throat. Blood spurted from the jugular vein. He shoved the blanket around the doctor's neck to stem the flow of blood.

With a gurgling sound, blood ran out the corner of the doctor's mouth.

Byrnes quickly swiped the bloody knife on the blanket and returned it to the leather sheath tucked inside the waist of his Levi's.

"I guess that's a wrap, Doc." He slammed the trunk shut, took the keys and unlocked the car.

Byrnes rummaged through McGuire's wallet and briefcase. He found a driver's license, social security card, several major credit cards, an honorable discharge card from the United States Army, six hundred bucks in cash and the roundtrip plane ticket showing McGuire had planned on being gone a month. *My lucky day*, Byrnes thought. *Too bad Dr. McGuire can't say the same thing.*

Byrnes started the engine and the car lurched out of the parking lot. It had been a long time since he had driven. He drove cautiously. If he had an accident and anyone poked around, it would be difficult to explain the body in the trunk of the car.

Byrnes pulled into the long-term parking lot at the airport and took a parking stub from the machine. The gate opened. After pulling into a space near the back of the lot, he grabbed the briefcase and put the wallet in his coat pocket. "Thanks for the help, Doc," he sneered as he stepped out of the car.

Byrnes sauntered out of the parking lot and hailed a taxi. "Take me to the bus station," he directed the cabbie.

1

THE DRIVE TO SONOYTA went quickly. In a few minutes, Kitt would be leaving Mexico and returning to the United States. She pulled up to the border crossing and handed the officer her passport.

He studied her face for a moment, then asked, "How long have you been in Mexico?"

"Four days," Kitt replied.

"Where you headed?"

"To the prison complex in Florence." Noting a surprised look on the guard's face, she explained, "I'm the warden there."

"Well, if you're headed for prison, you have permission to enter the United States," he said with a smile.

Kitt laughed, put the car in gear and entered Arizona. She slipped a Waylon Jennings CD in the player and sang along in her low, alto voice, "I've always been crazy but it's kept me from going insane."

She was delighted with her decision to take a different route back to Florence. By driving the back roads, the return trip would be slower but more scenic.

It was only the first week of March, but the desert was in bloom. The barrel and prickly pear cacti were covered with brilliant pink, yellow and purple blossoms. A forest of saguaro cacti populated the desert as far as the eye could see. Kitt had read somewhere that a saguaro could grow to be fifty feet tall – or more – and live for over two hundred years. One saguaro with large, round limbs looked like Mickey Mouse. Another, with two round limbs beside each other, resembled a buxom female. Some had long, slender branches that twisted into strange positions. Those reminded her of Gumby, the rubbery child's toy.

The past four days in Puerto Penasco, Mexico with Louise had been very relaxing. Louise had flown there from Minnesota. The first afternoon, Kitt and Louise sat on the balcony outside their room and chatted until the sun was low and bright orange on the horizon. They stopped talking to watch the sun drop into the ocean and disappear. Ocean sunsets always gave Kitt a sense of the awesome power of the universe.

She smiled when she thought of the fishing trip they chartered on the second day of their vacation. The crew consisted of three handsome Mexican men, all of whom were in their early twenties and about a foot shorter than either of the two women. Kitt and Louise enjoyed flirting and laughing with the men, and they had felt more like teenagers than grandmothers in their mid-fifties. For their lunch the crew made delicious fish tacos from the morning's catch.

Kitt swerved to miss a roadrunner crossing in front of her car.

Her thoughts drifted to her husband, Cordell. He had flown to Chicago for the International Transit Union convention the same day she left for Mexico. Even though Cord was retired, the national union leadership had invited him to be their guest at the convention, a thank-you for his hard work and dedication to transit issues. He would be in Chicago for a week. Kitt would get home several days before Cord returned to Florence.

With a start, Kitt realized she had been daydreaming. She shook her head. *Where am I?* Feeling hot, she reached down to adjust the air conditioner and saw that the instrument panel was lit up like a red light district.

Kitt maneuvered the car to the side of the narrow road just before it took its last gasp and stalled. Deciding the eighty-seven-degree temperature outside would be cooler than the inside of her car, she got out and opened the hood of the Chrysler. *Don't panic,* she thought as steam poured from the engine. Realizing the situation was out of her control, Kitt walked over to a large, flat rock about fifteen feet away. She sat down and ran her hand through her short, auburn hair and thought about her unforeseen predicament.

She looked down at her arms. Her freckles had popped out while she and Louise had been sitting by the pool, soaking up the sun and drinking margaritas. Cord would have more freckles to count. He had begun trying to count her freckles after their marriage twenty-seven years ago.

The desert was silent except for the constant hum of the cicadas. Kitt looked up and saw the wrinkled, red heads of turkey vultures circling above her. They were considered the garbage men of the desert. Did they sense a meal?

Out of the corner of her eye she noticed movement. A huge orange and brown lizard, at least eighteen inches long, was lumbering towards her. Was she hallucinating? No such luck. She recognized it as a Gila monster. She sprang from the rock and ran back to the car, barely noticing her leg had brushed against a Teddy Bear Cholla cactus.

Safely back inside the car, Kitt stretched her long, slender leg across the passenger seat.

"Damn it to hell, anyway," she said aloud, slamming her fist onto the dashboard. She took a deep breath and began plucking out the prickly, needle-like cactus quills from her leg. A stream of sweat trickled down her forehead and into her eyes. She wiped her forehead with her sleeve.

Glancing around the passenger seat, Kitt noticed her cell phone but it was of no use to her; she had forgotten to recharge the battery. "Stupid idiot," she mumbled.

Kitt glanced at her watch. It was three o'clock. Looking back at the road, she saw a speck on the horizon. Was it a car or a mirage? Slowly the object came closer and took shape. It was an old, red pickup covered with dust. She jumped out of her car and stood in the middle of the road, frantically waving her arms.

The pickup stopped and a man wearing a pair of faded blue jeans, a baggy plaid shirt and dusty boots got out. He started across the road towards her. The gray cowboy hat covering his hair, which was pulled back into a ponytail, had sweat stains at the base of the crown. His skin looked like it had been over-exposed to the sun for many years. She guessed he was about sixty-five years old.

"Thank the Lord," Kitt said as she started across the road to meet him. "I'm Katherine Logan. My friends all call me Kitt."

"I'm Eddie," he replied cheerfully, "and my friends call me Eddie." His smile was warm and friendly. He was more soft-spoken than she expected. Believing herself to be a good judge of character, she quickly decided Eddie was not a homicidal maniac.

She looked into the man's hazel eyes and said, "I've never been so glad to meet anyone in my whole life. Thanks for stopping."

"No problem. You having car trouble?" Eddie asked as they walked back to Kitt's car. After peering under the hood for a moment or two, he stood up and wiped the sweat from his forehead. "I'm no mechanic, but it looks like you have a major problem. Hop in the pickup. I'll take you into town. We'll see if Clyde has time to come out and get your car." They walked back across the dusty road.

"How far to the nearest town?" Kitt asked, as she climbed into the pickup.

"It's about eight miles to Empalme," Eddie responded. "Not many people left there anymore. A few miners are still hoping to strike it rich, but most have moved on. Ranchers stop by the cantina to say hello and have a shot of whiskey every now and then, but other than that, Empalme's pretty quiet. If you don't mind my asking, what brings you down our way?"

"I've been in Mexico spending some time with a friend. She and I used to work together at the Minnesota Department of Corrections, but I moved to Florence last year. I'm the warden at the prison complex."

There was a short pause in the conversation. "Do you mind if I give you some advice?" Without waiting for an answer, Eddie continued, "I wouldn't mention the fact that you are a warden to the folks in Empalme. We have a few shady characters around town, and they might not take kindly to your line of work."

"That's good advice, thanks."

The road curved, and the small town of Empalme came into view. A tumbleweed blew across the road and hitched a ride under Eddie's pickup. Many small, vacated adobe homes had broken windows and desert plant life encroaching to the front doors. Other yards showed signs of life; faded blue jeans and ragged towels hung on clotheslines strung from the side of one small house to a nearby mesquite tree. Kitt smiled when she saw some chickens chasing each other around the front yard of another abandoned house.

Eddie pulled up in front of the only gas station in town. It was a small adobe building with a rusty, corrugated metal roof. The crooked, weathered sign in front of the establishment read CLYDE'S. A short, muscular, middle-aged man with a brown crew cut walked briskly towards the pickup.

"Howdy, Clyde," Eddie called. "I picked me up a stray out on the highway. This here is Kitt Logan."

Clyde glanced at Kitt, grunted and looked back at Eddie. "What's her problem?"

"She needs a tow. Her car is about eight miles outside of town." Without a word, Clyde went back into the garage, got in his tow truck and backed out. He pulled up on the passenger side of Eddie's pickup. "You come with me, Eddie," he yelled.

"Should I come, too?" Kitt asked.

"No, you wait inside," Clyde growled.

The only amenity inside the cluttered station was an air conditioner, which was secured tentatively in the small window. Kitt brushed off the dirty, leather chair near the window and sat down to wait for Eddie and Clyde to return with her car.

They were back within the hour. Eddie poked his head inside the door and said, "You're in good hands with Clyde. I'm going over to Carlita's Cantina for a beer. If you care to join me later, I'll let you buy me a drink."

Kitt watched as Clyde unhitched her car and opened the hood. She gave him a few minutes to look things over, then asked, "How serious is it?"

"For starters, you got a busted alternator and your battery exploded. There's acid all over your engine," he responded gruffly, without looking up. Clyde offered no information about the length of time it would take to get her car running again.

Kitt was beginning to lose her patience with Clyde but realized she needed to maintain her composure. Clyde was her only chance to get back on the road.

"How long will it take to get my car repaired?" she asked, summoning up as nice a tone as possible.

"Two to three days. If you didn't drive such a fancy car, it wouldn't take that long. As strange as it may seem to you, I don't have an extra Chrysler alternator lying around."

The more Clyde said, the more Kitt wished he'd shut up. "So now what?" she asked.

"I could call a dealer in Phoenix and order one." He gave her a condescending look. "Well," he drawled, "what do you want me to do?"

"Order the damn thing," she hissed, all civility gone from her voice.

The corners of Clyde's mouth turned slightly upward. "Okay." Kitt started down the street towards Carlita's Cantina. A couple of beers might help take her stress level down a few notches. The cantina was in a fort-like building, its adobe archway opening into a courtyard. The south wall was lined with cushioned seats, which had been removed from cars. A black Labrador was stretched out on one of the partially shaded car seats, taking a siesta.

She walked across the brick patio toward the door of the cantina. Two men were playing cards at a table by the door. One of the men had long, dirty hair; tattoos covered his arms. His most notable tattoo was a large skull and crossbones, just visible below the sleeve of his dirty shirt. *He fits the stereotype of an outlaw*, Kitt thought. The other man was very large. He wore huge red suspenders that hiked his pants up above his waist. Neither seemed to notice her as she neared the table.

I wouldn't want to run into either of these guys in a dark alley, she thought. *They've probably done time in the slammer.*

A faint smell of marijuana hung in the air near the two men. As she walked past the table, the outlaw yelled, "Hey Sal, where's our beer?"

Startled, Kitt let out an audible gasp.

"A little jumpy, ain't ya?" the outlaw sneered.

Kitt looked him squarely in the eyes but did not respond.

A stocky woman with a long, blond, thick braid down her back came through the door carrying a couple of beers. The two women nearly collided.

"Sorry," both women said, as they passed within inches of one another.

When Kitt walked into the cantina, all conversation stopped. The people seated at the bar turned to stare. It took a moment for her eyes to adjust to the dark, smoky room. Other than the squeak of Kitt's sandals as she walked across the wooden floor, there was total silence.

"Hey Kitt, come on in," Eddie called from his barstool. "Everyone, meet Kitt Logan. She's had a run of bad luck and will be in town for a day or two."

A couple of people murmured greetings but most ignored her and went on with their conversations.

Sal, the braided woman, stepped behind the bar and pointed

to a sign on the wall which read ALL GUNS MUST BE SURREN-
DERED TO THE BARTENDER. In a raspy, cigarette voice, Sal
asked, "Are you packing?"

Kitt hesitated for a moment, then took the snub nose 38 special Smith and Wesson out of her purse, placed it on the bar and
sat down.

Sal picked up the gun and added it to her collection behind
the bar.

"Well, lookie there, a starter pistol," said a thin man perched
on the bar stool beside her.

Kitt gritted her teeth. "Very funny," she said, "but it's no business of yours what kind of gun I carry."

"Never mind Jeb. He has a strange sense of humor," Eddie
said with a wink.

Kitt looked at the man beside her. He had the longest gray
beard she had ever seen. His sharp nose was set in a leathery,
tanned, wrinkled face. Jeb's eyes, which were the color of chocolate drops, sparkled as he said, "Aw, relax, Kitt. I'll buy you a beer
to prove I don't mean you no harm."

"Well, thanks, I could really use a beer. Sorry I snapped at you,
Jeb."

Kitt suddenly realized she was hungry. Looking around, she
saw a popcorn machine against the wall. She walked over and
filled a bag. The metal sign above the machine read, "I AM A
PROSPECTOR 83 YEARS OLD. SOME SON OF A BITCH
SHOT MY BURRO. SIGNED C.E.N."

As she turned to go back to her seat, she noticed a man sitting
at the far end of the bar. He was staring at her. He was a good-looking man with black, wavy hair. Not a native of Empalme, she
decided, noticing his smooth, pale complexion. His piercing, crys-
tal blue eyes seemed to see right through her and contributed to
his striking good looks. He had just a hint of a smile frozen on his
lips. He gave off an air of confidence and superiority.

Kitt broke eye contact with the man and returned to her seat
between Jeb and Eddie.

"Are you a rancher, Jeb?" she asked.

"Nope, I'm a miner. I got a claim staked up in the hills outside
of town. Dug out enough to live on, but I ain't hit the mother lode,
so to speak. Don't know what I'd do with the money if I did."

Jeb reached inside his pocket and pulled out a pouch of

tobacco and a cigarette paper. Kitt watched with interest as he filled the paper with tobacco, rolled it and licked the end of the paper. He struck a match, carefully lit the cigarette and took a drag.

"How do you keep your beard from catching on fire?" Kitt teased.

"Well now, it only happened once many years ago; had one too many beers. I've been careful ever since." Jeb gave his beard a loving stroke.

Kitt turned on her stool to look at the stuffed head mounted on the wall, a javelina. She chuckled at the cap and sunglasses someone had put on the ugly beast's head. The sign below the javelina read NO SNIVELING.

Sal leaned back against the bar and asked, "Anyone going to old Buster's funeral tomorrow?"

"Hell, no," Jeb said. "Buster deserved what he got. It's like the old saying goes, 'What goes round comes round.' Earl just made it happen, that's all."

Eddie explained to Kitt that Earl Jenkins had stopped by, unannounced, to see his sister. When he got there, he found his sister all bloodied up from a beating her husband, Buster, had given her. Earl picked up an ax lying by the front door and threw it at Buster. The ax hit him in the chest, killing him immediately.

A perfect example of frontier justice, Kitt thought. *This place is just like an old western.* "So what's going to happen to Earl?" she asked.

"He's in jail," Eddie said, "but I got a feeling they'll go easy on him. Buster had a history of assaulting people."

Sal walked over and picked up the empty bottle in front of Kitt. "Want another one?"

"No thanks. I need to get something to eat."

"So do I," said Eddie. "How about I take you over to the best and only eating establishment in Empalme?"

"Sounds good."

"Don't forget your piece," Sal said, reaching under the bar.

"Thanks," Kitt said as she put the gun back in her purse and followed Eddie out the back door of the cantina.

The remains of a small adobe building stood about fifteen feet from the door. "What was that building?" she asked Eddie.

"That, my dear, was a brothel. It was a busy place during the early mining days in Empalme. The ladies not only accommodated the town folk, they also provided their services to black soldiers who served in the Indian Wars on the western frontier, the Buffalo Soldiers."

"Buffalo Soldiers?"

"The Apache gave them the name because their curly hair reminded the Indians of a buffalo's mane."

Eddie continued to explain that the black soldiers had also fought in the Revolutionary and Civil wars and that the all-black regiments were disbanded in 1952 after the army was desegregated.

A few minutes later they passed through the front door of a small café.

2

A WAITRESS PUSHED through the swinging doors that led to and from the small, smoky kitchen.

"Hi Eddie," she said.

"How you doing, Josie? This is Kitt Logan," he said, nodding in Kitt's direction.

Josie had long, straight, blond hair. She was of medium height and very thin – *too thin*, thought Kitt. She was pretty, but her slumped shoulders indicated not only fatigue, but probably a lack of self-confidence as well.

"I hear you're having car trouble," Josie said, her shy, melancholy smile revealing a missing bicuspid. "Word travels fast when a stranger is in town," she added.

"Car trouble is an understatement," Kitt said, "but Eddie assures me I'm in good hands with Clyde. It's nice to meet you, Josie."

Eddie and Kitt settled into a booth, looked over the menu and ordered.

After finishing her last bite of roast beef, Kitt glanced out the window and noticed it was getting dark. She hadn't thought about where she would be spending the night.

"Do you know where I can find overnight accommodations, Eddie?"

Eddie laughed. "No such thing in Empalme. My house is small but I have an extra bedroom. You're welcome to stay with me." After seeing the surprise on Kitt's face, he added, "It beats sleeping in your car."

Kitt wondered if Eddie had a hidden agenda. She hadn't learned if Eddie was married or not.

Realizing she had no other options, Kitt's decision was easy. "If you're sure I'm not inconveniencing you, I'll take you up on your offer. You've already done so much for me." She reached for the check. "The least I can do is buy your dinner."

Once outside, Kitt found the evening air cool and refreshing. A full moon shone brightly above the eastern horizon.

"It's a short walk to my house," Eddie said pointing to the west, "and with a little luck, the javelina won't be running down the arroyo the same time we're cutting across."

"I know what javelinas look like but I don't really know anything else about them. Do they wear sunglasses so they can remain incognito?"

Eddie laughed. "No, they don't wear sunglasses. Some people call them wild pigs, but they are really in the peccary family. They are hoofed mammals with dark bristled hair and razor sharp teeth. They stink to high heaven and are very nasty tempered. Nervous?"

"Frankly, I'd rather not run into one tonight. I've had enough excitement for today already."

As they passed the gas station, Kitt realized her luggage was still in the car. She gave Eddie's arm a tug.

"Hang on a second, Eddie. I need to get a suitcase out of my car."

When she entered the garage, Clyde was standing by the cash register. "Just getting my suitcase, Clyde."

Clyde jerked his head towards her, nodded and turned his attention back to the cash register.

"What's up with Clyde?" Kitt asked when she rejoined Eddie.

"He's an ex-Marine; tough as nails on the outside but good-hearted on the inside where it counts. Don't worry about him. He's just a little hard to get to know."

That's an understatement, Kitt thought. She didn't care if she ever got to know Clyde. All she wanted was for him to get her car fixed so she could get back home.

"Well, here we are," Eddie announced after about ten minutes. He turned and walked up the path towards the door of a small, tan-colored adobe house. "It's not the Ritz, but it's a roof over my head."

Kitt took notice of the well-manicured yard and its many inter-esting desert plants. Several covered wagon wheels were attached to the fence that surrounded the house. Vertical black bars enclosed the glass panes of the windows.

Kitt looked up at the elevated water tank standing beside the house.

"That's the shower," Eddie explained. "Water is scarce out here, so I catch rain in the tank and use it for bathing. You'd be surprised how well it works. The water will be plenty warm, so help yourself if you want to give it a try."

She smiled and nodded. "A shower sounds good."

Unlocking the door and gesturing to Kitt to go in, Eddie fol-lowed and turned on a light in his small living room. In one cor-ner was a display of Apache burden baskets. Several Navajo rugs were scattered on the wooden floor. A dark brown leather couch and an old rocking chair faced the small brick fireplace.

"Your home is nicely decorated, Eddie."

He smiled with pride. "Your bedroom is over there, and the bathroom is just down the hall. I'll put out some clean towels. Do you want a robe?"

"Please," Kitt said as she walked down the hall and into the room.

A couple of minutes later Eddie returned with a woman's bathrobe. "I'll take you out and show you how the shower works when you're ready." Eddie stepped out of the bedroom and closed the door.

Kitt put the robe on the bed, again wondering if Eddie was married. Maybe he was a widower. He hadn't mentioned a wife. She put her suitcase on the wooden table near the bed and slipped out of her clothes and into the robe. She started toward the bath-room. All of a sudden she heard a loud, hoarse voice crying out, "Hello, Eddie. Hello, Eddie."

Someone else was sharing space with Eddie. Maybe it was his wife. Whoever it was had a terrible case of laryngitis.

"Who's that?" Kitt called to Eddie.

"It's Pete. Come and meet him," Eddie said from another room.

Not knowing what to expect, Kitt walked cautiously towards Eddie's voice. Eddie was standing beside a very large birdcage. It housed a beautiful parrot. The bird had brilliant plumage, a long saber-shaped tail and a powerful curved bill.

"Pete is a ten-year-old macaw," Eddie said proudly. "Macaws can live to be seventy or eighty. I'll have to make provisions for someone to care for him after I'm gone. Would you be interested?"

Eddie was teasing. Kitt smiled and shook her head, "Thanks, but no thanks."

"Didn't think so, but just thought I'd ask. If you're ready, I'll take you out and show you how the shower works." The two went out the patio door and into the warm night.

Kitt listened attentively as Eddie explained how to pull the chain to release the water.

"There's soap and shampoo over on that little shelf. Enjoy." Eddie went back inside the house.

The shower felt wonderful. When she was done, Kitt put on the robe Eddie had given her and was towel-drying her hair as she walked backed into the house. Her jaw dropped as she stared, in shock, at Eddie. The graying, long brown hair, which earlier had been pulled back into a ponytail, now hung loosely around Eddie's face. Gone were the dusty cowboy boots; in their place were pink slippers. The low-cut robe Eddie was wearing revealed cleavage and the soft fabric of the robe hugged what seemed to be breasts. Kitt couldn't believe her eyes. She tried her best to hide her astonishment. Eddie was a woman.

Eddie smiled broadly and, with eyes twinkling, said, "Sleep well."

3

"HELLO, MAMA," PETE CROAKED from the room across the hall. "Hello, Mama."

Kitt awoke with a start. She looked at her watch. It was eight thirty.

Hopping out of bed, she took a peek out the small bedroom window. The sun was bright and the sky cloudless. She noticed Eddie's nicely landscaped backyard. Several varieties of cactus were in bloom around the patio. A cardinal was enjoying his morning ablutions in the birdbath under a Joshua tree.

She put on her robe and padded down the hall. The smell of freshly brewed coffee wafted in from the kitchen.

"Mornin' sunshine," Eddie called from Pete's room.

"Mornin' sunshine," repeated Pete.

"Good morning, Eddie. Good morning, Pete. I bet you thought I was going to sleep forever."

"You had a rough day, yesterday. I'm glad you were able to sleep in. Pour yourself a cup of java. By the way," she added, "everyone who stays with me has to do chores before breakfast."

"I'll be glad to help with chores. What do you want me to do?"

"Feed the quail. There's a can of birdseed beside the door in the kitchen. Sprinkle a handful on the patio. The quail will be making their daily appearance anytime now." Eddie turned her attention back to Pete.

Stepping out on to the patio, Kitt threw the birdseed around the patio then stood for a moment, breathing in the fresh morning air. Feeding the quail now reminded her of the many times she had fed quail while visiting her mother, who lived in Globe, Arizona. She smiled, remembering the time one of the birds had flown into her mother's glass patio door. She and her mother watched the unconscious bird for a while, but it didn't move. After a few minutes, her mother had walked out on the patio, picked up the bird and wrung its neck. Kitt had assumed her mother didn't want the bird to suffer, but that wasn't the case. Her mother cleaned the bird, and they ate it for dinner that night.

Kitt went back inside, poured herself a cup of coffee, and sat down at the kitchen table. Within minutes the patio was filled with quail. One adult male perched atop an Ocotillo, which was fully blooming with beautiful red flowers. He stood guard over the others while they dined. Adult females with babies trailing behind scurried around the patio. Their little black topknots bobbed as they gobbled up the seeds.

" Any other chores you want me to do?" she asked Eddie.

"Nah, you're done for the day." Eddie poured a cup of coffee and sat down at the table. "So," she began with a glint in her eye, "you thought I was a man, right?"

"Yep," Kitt confessed, "but I should have known. Even though you were dressed like a cowboy when I met you yesterday, you were soft-spoken for a man and seemed to have a gentle nature. Your home should have tipped me off; it has a woman's touch, tidy and well decorated. I did wonder if you were married and had neglected to mention your wife. Obviously, I was so preoccupied with my situation, I really wasn't thinking very clearly. But you know what?"

"What?"

"I'm more comfortable knowing you are a woman."

"I knew you'd be relieved, but I was having so much fun with the charade I just couldn't tell you. Pete almost gave me away last night. He usually says 'Hello, Mama' when he hears me coming down the hall, but he must have sensed I was pulling a fast one on you."

Eddie got up and reached for an apron hanging on a hook by the stove. "We're having bacon and eggs for breakfast. How do you like your eggs?"

"Over easy, please."

"We'll eat in a couple of minutes, " Eddie said, cracking an egg into the already-hot pan.

"You've gone all out," Kitt soon said, gazing down at the plate of bacon, eggs, and sourdough toast Eddie placed before her. She savored every bite.

Swallowing the last bit of bacon, Kitt said, "Thank you, that was delicious." She pushed her plate to the side, then looked intently at Eddie. "I don't mean to pry, Eddie, but on the way into town yesterday you mentioned you were headed out to your ranch. I'm curious to know how you got started ranching."

Eddie took the napkin off her lap and wiped her mouth. "My parents grew up on the East Coast, but my dad had always wanted to live in the West. When I was five years old, he persuaded my mother that they should move to Arizona and start a new life. They sold all their belongings and moved here because land was cheap. Dad bought a small herd of cattle, a few horses and hired a couple of men to work for him. By age ten I was able to help brand and castrate cattle. I was an only child, so he had no sons to help him run the ranch. Dad was proud of me and always called me his best hired hand."

A look of pride crossed Eddie's face. "All our hard work paid off. Dad used the money he made from the sale of cattle to expand the herd, and in a few years we had one of the largest cattle operations in Arizona."

The pride on her face turned to sadness. "In June of 1948, Dad was separating cattle when a bull charged and pinned him against the fence. The horn pierced his chest and he died instantly. Mother was despondent and was never the same after he died. For several years, she tried to manage the ranch but finally lost all interest. By default, I began to keep the books even though I was only sixteen years old. Thank heavens the hired men were committed to helping me keep the ranch operating."

Eddie stopped and took a deep breath. "One morning, I awoke to the sound of a shot. Mother had killed herself. I still remember the horror I felt when I ran into her bedroom and saw her lying on the floor with half her head blown off. One of my mother's sisters, Aunt Amanda, who was single and lived in New York, wanted me to come and stay with her, but I really didn't want to leave Arizona. The ranch was all that was left of the life I had known.

"Rather than insisting I come to New York," Eddie continued, "my dear Aunt Amanda moved to Arizona to be with me. It was a huge sacrifice on her part because she didn't like the Southwest. I never could have made it through those years without her. After I graduated from high school, Aunt Amanda felt I was mature enough to manage the ranch alone, so she returned home to New York."

Eddie took a swallow of coffee. "The anger I felt towards my mother for killing herself turned out to be a blessing in disguise; I promised myself I'd keep the ranch going, come hell or high water, and I did."

Eddie stood up and carried the dirty dishes over to the sink. "I started wearing men's clothes out of necessity. People around here are used to seeing me in men's clothes, and that's how they expect me to dress. I get gussied up when the need arises but I prefer wearing pants and boots. For the record, my name is Edwina but I prefer Eddie."

"Did you ever think about selling the ranch?" Kitt asked, getting up and walking toward the sink.

"About five years ago I considered it, but Bennie offered to take over the day-to-day operation. I decided not to sell. Bennie used to be my foreman but we fell in love and things changed. Never got married because we didn't see the need. When I told him I never wanted to have children, he respected my decision and didn't try to pressure me into changing my mind."

It's no wonder Eddie didn't want to have children, Kitt thought, *after witnessing the horrible deaths of her parents*. She reached out and touched Eddie's soapy hand. "I can't imagine what it would be like to try and cope with the suicide of a mother and keep a ranch operating at the same time. You are an incredibly strong woman."

Eddie walked over to the window in the living room. "On a lighter note, here's a sight I bet you don't see in Florence."

Kitt joined Eddie at the window and to her amazement she saw a herd of cattle heading down the main street of Empalme. A cowboy on a beautiful black and white Pinto prodded them on. A couple of cars had pulled to the side of the road to avoid colliding with the Herefords.

Kitt laughed at the odd sight. "Where are they going?" she asked.

"Cattle graze on open range around here. Sometimes the shortest route to get them back to a ranch is through town."

"Just when I think I've seen everything," Kitt said, shaking her head and walking over to the kitchen sink. "Let me finish the dishes."

"You wash and I'll wipe. After we get this mess cleaned up, we'll stop by Clyde's and check on your car. Then we can take a run out to the ranch. If you want to, that is."

"I'd love to see your ranch," Kitt responded eagerly.

"Put on a pair of jeans in case we decide to take a horseback ride."

The herd was gone and the main road clear when they left Eddie's house, got into the truck and headed out. The only evidence the cattle had left behind were some steaming cow pies marking the route they had taken through town.

Arriving at the gas station, Eddie pulled up to the pump and yelled to Clyde, who was standing just inside the door, "Fill her up."

Clyde walked over to the pickup. "What's all the hollering about?" he asked, smiling so broadly that his squinty eyes nearly disappeared from his face.

He must have taken his medication this morning, Kitt thought, surprised at his rather pleasant demeanor.

Clyde leaned through the window and looked at Kitt. "I should have your alternator by tomorrow afternoon. I'll get the engine cleaned up today." He looked over at Eddie. "Where you off to?"

"Thought I'd show Kitt around the ranch," Eddie replied.

"Trying to turn a city girl into a cowgirl, huh? She'll probably be branding cattle by tomorrow," Clyde teased.

Kitt laughed. "Actually, my husband would like it if I came home a cowgirl, but I'm afraid it'll take more than a day to make it happen."

"Since my car won't be ready until tomorrow," Kitt said as Eddie left the station and swung onto the road leading to the ranch, "how would you feel about putting me up for another night?"

"You're welcome to stay as long as you want," Eddie said.

About twenty minutes later, Eddie turned off the highway and onto a gravel road. The large wooden sign hanging between two tall poles read Rocky Rollins Ranch.

"My dad's name was John Rollins, but everyone called him Rocky," Eddie explained.

A large adobe house with red ceramic roof tiles came into sight. The windows and doors were framed with Spanish-style arches. It was the kind of house Cord and Kitt had always dreamed of owning.

Eddie pulled up in front of the house. They were met by three young Mexican children shouting, "*Mama, Mama, Eddie esta aqui!*"

Eddie stooped down and gave them all hugs. A beautiful Mexican woman appeared at the door. "*Hola, Eddie,*" she said with a bright smile. "*Como esta?*"

"*Bien, gracias,*" Eddie said, giving the short woman a hug. "Juanita, I want you to meet Kitt."

"I'm very pleased to meet you," Juanita said switching to English.

"*El gusto es mio,*" Kitt replied, as she shook Juanita's extended hand.

Kitt watched the children run back into the house. They were about the age of her grandchildren. She felt a momentary ache in her chest. Leaving her children and grandchildren in Minnesota had been the downside of moving to Arizona.

"Come in," Juanita said. "I made cookies this morning. Pablito, go tell Papa and Bennie we have company and to come for coffee."

The house was cool. The adobe walls provided natural air conditioning. Kitt stopped in the living room to admire the huge fireplace made of large stones. Eddie explained that her parents had found the colorful rocks while exploring their ranch and had used them to build the fireplace. Kitt was surprised to see a Charles Russell painting hanging over the mantel.

The kitchen, although small in comparison to the rest of the rooms in the house, had lots of cupboards and a pantry. Kitt took a deep breath. "It sure smells good in here." A plate of freshly baked chocolate chip cookies were sitting on top of the black iron stove in the corner.

A few minutes and a few cookies later, two rugged men of Mexican descent came into the kitchen and sat down at the large wooden table in the center of the room. The older man gave Eddie a peck on the cheek. Eddie introduced Bennie and Juanita's husband, Manuel, to Kitt.

Bennie had wrinkle lines around his dark brown eyes, sure signs of a sense of humor and a warm heart. Silver gray peppered his black hair. Although not tall, Bennie gave the impression it would be wise to avoid a confrontation with him. The muscles in his arms were well defined.

Manuel was very handsome. His eyes twinkled, and he had a wonderful laugh. Kitt immediately felt at ease with her new amigos.

Eddie pushed the plate of cookies towards her. "Want one more for the road?"

"I've already had three. I don't want to wear out my welcome."

"For crying out loud, Kitt. You won't wear out your welcome just because you have four cookies. Juanita will be insulted if you don't take another one."

"Oh, all right, one more for the road and my thighs."

"Manuel," Eddie said, "would you saddle a couple of horses, please? I'll ride Thunderbolt and Kitt can have Chico."

Kitt's anxiety began to rise as she thought about getting on a horse. She hadn't ridden in years.

As if reading her mind, Eddie smiled, "Don't worry. Chico is seventeen and likes to take it easy. He won't give you any trouble." She turned to Bennie. "Want to come along?"

"Wish I could, but I have too many things I need to get done today." Bennie gave Eddie's neck a squeeze as he walked behind her chair. "Have a nice ride and try not to come back with any strays this time." He gave her an affectionate smile.

By the time the two women got to the corral, the horses were saddled and waiting.

"Better put these on," Manuel said, handing each of the women a pair of chaps. Slipping them on, Eddie confidently mounted Thunderbolt. Kitt stepped into her chaps, looked at Chico and reached for the reins. Manuel, sensing Kitt's hesitancy, walked over to her and cupped his hands. "Step in my hands. I'll give you a boost up."

"Thanks, Manuel."

Once up, she reached forward and patted the side of Chico's beautiful head. "Be gentle with me. I'm your friend."

Eddie smiled at Kitt. "You're doing fine. Give him a gentle kick in the ribs with your heels." After making sure Kitt was underway, she said, "We'll ride out to the south range and check the fence line." The horses moved into a trot.

What a great morning for a ride, Kitt thought, falling into a rhythm with Chico. The temperature was perfect.

Eddie looked over at her and said, "I'm thinking about spending the night at the ranch. You wouldn't mind having the house in town to yourself tonight, would you? You can take my pickup back to Empalme, and I'll have Bennie bring me in tomorrow."

"But what if the alternator goes out? Will you come and rescue me again?" Kitt asked with a mischievous look.

"Nope, you'll just have to walk to town," Eddie replied. "I have better things to do tonight than babysit you."

Both women laughed, then continued in silence, drinking up the beauty of the desert. Chico moved with an amazing natural instinct around the cactus and rocks. Kitt reached down and again patted Chico's neck tenderly. "You should have on chaps, too. It's pretty scratchy out here."

She guessed they had ridden about three miles when Eddie stopped her horse beside some mesquite trees and dismounted. Kitt did likewise. Eddie walked over to some empty water bottles and picked them up. *How odd*, thought Kitt. *Who would leave empty bottles out here?*

She watched as Eddie pulled several full bottles of water out of her saddlebag and placed them by a rock. Eddie said over her shoulder, "A few years ago, when I was out here looking for strays, I heard a baby crying, so I stopped to look around. I found a Mexican man, his wife and three children hidden in the chaparral. The man told me he had given a smuggler several thousand dollars to get them across the border. The smuggler dropped them off just this side of the border and told them they would have to walk the rest of the way. The family had gotten lost and had been without water for two days. The man's name was Manuel; his wife's name was Juanita. Ever since then I've been leaving water out for anyone who might need it."

Kitt stood silently for a moment and let Eddie's story sink in. She felt a knot in her stomach. "I've been following newspaper reports about how smugglers leave people in the desert," she said. "I hate to think of what might have happened to Manuel and his family if you hadn't found them."

"Thousands of illegal immigrants have died trying to get into the United States," Eddie said, "and hundreds have died trying to cross the border in this particular area, the Tucson Sector. Some have died on my land. The smugglers, or coyotes as they're called, usually take the people through the most dangerous part of the desert where there are fewer border patrols, then they leave the illegal immigrants to fend for themselves. The coyotes tell them that there are water tanks along the way, but they fail to mention that if, and I mean if, they happen to find a tank, it will more often than not be dry."

Eddie looked intently at Kitt. "You know, the border patrol doesn't approve of what I'm doing. I trust you will keep this confidential."

Kitt was moved that Eddie had trusted her enough to share the help she was giving illegal immigrants. "Law enforcement may not approve, but my guess is God does. Your secret will always be safe with me."

Eddie nodded. "There's an organization called Humane Borders, which is a faith-based group that has put up water stations in the areas where immigrants have been known to die. I'm trying to do my part by putting water out on my land."

"What about the government? Are they doing anything?" Kitt asked.

"The government is in a tough spot. They don't want to encourage people to enter the country illegally, but they don't want them to die out in the desert either. They've started putting up some towers with beacons and emergency call buttons so people in trouble can summon help. After they get the medical care they need, they are returned to Mexico."

"I often wonder," Eddie continued, "what I'd do if I drew a bead on a smuggler. Guess I won't know whether or not I would pull the trigger until I have one in my sights. God knows they've been responsible for the deaths of many desperate people in search of better ways of life."

Eddie wiped her brow. "You heard Bennie tell me he hoped I wouldn't find any strays. He meant people crossing the border illegally. Occasionally, I find people out here. I take them back to the ranch and give them food and water and send them on their way. I don't ask which direction they're going because I don't want to know. Manuel and his family were so vulnerable I decided to take a chance and hire them. They're hard workers and have become like family to me; but they're here illegally and I'm not sure what the future holds for them."

"What happens to the bodies of people you find on your land?"

"I call the County Sheriff's Office, and they come and get them. If there isn't any identification, which is usually the case, people are buried in a pauper's cemetery. The marker just says John Doe or Jane Doe, and a number is assigned to the unidentified person."

Eddie handed her a fresh bottle of water. "Take a couple of swigs. It's starting to get hot. See that windmill off in the distance?" she asked pointing to the west. "That's where one of my tanks is located. I want to ride over and make sure it's pumping water; after that, we'll start back. The cookies have worn off and I'm hungry again."

A few hours later, Juanita hailed the two women as they walked back from the corral. "Come and eat," she called.

Kitt was famished. She devoured the delicious meal of tacos, tamales, and refried beans in record time. As the conversation subsided a bit, she silently contemplated the past twenty-four hours. Yesterday's troubles had become today's gift.

"Thank you so much for all your kindness," she said. "I hate to leave, but I better get going."

The drive back to Empalme was uneventful. She parked the pickup in front of Eddie's house and went inside. Suddenly she felt very tired. As Kitt passed Pete's cage, she called out, "Hello, Pete."

"Hello, Mama," the bird squawked.

"Better not say that around Eddie; she might not like you calling me Mama. Call me Auntie, or something."

Walking into her bedroom, Kitt put her sunglasses on the small nightstand, fluffed up the pillow and lay down. When she woke up, two hours later, it was four o'clock in the afternoon. Not having any other plan of action, Kitt decided to walk over to the cantina and have a beer. Maybe she'd run into some of her new-found friends.

4

Kitt gave Clyde a wave as she passed the station. Even though he was busy with a customer, he squinted at her and returned the wave.

Sal seemed happy to see Kitt when she entered the cantina. "Come on in! It's deader than a doornail in here. What'll you have?"

"That Mexican beer went down pretty good yesterday afternoon. I'll take a Corona, please."

The only other patron in the bar was the good-looking, pale man with whom Kitt had locked eyes the day before. She was surprised to see him.

"I saved you a seat," he said with a warm smile.

She took a seat on the stool beside him.

"Let me introduce myself; I'm Dr. Charles McGuire," he said, reaching over to shake her hand.

"Medical doctor?" she asked. The man had a firm, confident handshake.

"I'm a psychiatrist. I'm sorry, but I didn't catch your name yesterday when you came in."

"Kitt Logan."

Sal placed a bottle of Corona in front of her.

"So, Dr. McGuire, what are you doing in Empalme?" Kitt asked.

"Please, call me Charles. Let's see, where do I start? A few weeks ago, I decided to take a leave of absence from my mental health clinic in Michigan so I could get started on a research project," he said, pleased with the story. "When I happened upon Empalme, I thought it would be a nice, quiet place to do my research."

"What is the topic of your research?" Kitt asked.

What is the topic of my research? "Well, I'll summarize it. I don't want to bore you with the details," he said, his mind racing. He took a swallow of his beer, coughed and said, "I'm researching the influence of home environment on a person's propensity to kill."

He asked Sal for another beer and changed the subject. "The people here are very different from the academic types I usually associate with. The hot topic of conversation in Empalme is if a rancher should be able to kill a coyote that has been eating his calves. So, what do you do for a living?"

Caught off guard at the question, Kitt hesitated. Eddie's advice about not disclosing her occupation flashed through her mind. Dr. McGuire was a psychiatrist and she guessed she felt comfortable telling him she was a warden, but then he might mention it to other people. She opted for discretion and said, "I'm an educator." In a way, Kitt was an educator; she and her staff attempted to convince inmates that it was not in their best interests to keep committing crimes.

Her companion seemed satisfied with her answer. She redirected the conversation back to him. "How's the research going? Are you seeing any patterns yet?"

He took a pack of Marlboros out of his shirt pocket and offered one to her.

"No, thanks."

Sean Byrnes was pleased with Kitt's interest in his "research." He lit his cigarette and answered, "I'm finding some interesting data regarding mothers who are too strict, particularly with boys, during their teenage years. It's really too early to state any absolutes but, in my preliminary findings, I'm starting to see a pattern."

He looked at his watch. "I'd love to keep talking to you, but Josie will have dinner ready soon. She didn't have to work today, so she's making us a special meal tonight."

"I met Josie last night when Eddie and I had dinner over at the café," Kitt said. "I'll bet she's a good cook."

"She's okay. I'm paying her room and board while I do my research; there's nowhere else to stay in Empalme."

"I know what you mean. I'm staying with Eddie while my car is getting repaired."

"I better get going. It was nice talking to you, Kitt."

"Same here. I'll see you around," she said, as he stood to leave. Kitt had enjoyed talking to him, too.

"Hey, Sal! We need some beer out here. A person could thirst to death." The call came from the card table outside the door of the cantina.

Sal rolled her eyes. "They're back and they're thirsty. Fortunately, they're good tippers."

Kitt took a long pull of her beer and put the empty bottle on the bar. "See you later, Sal. Now that it's cooled off, I think I'll take a walk."

Neither card player acknowledged her as she walked out and past their table.

She decided to go towards the small Catholic church built of rust-colored brick. Above the bell tower was a small, white cross. Kitt turned east and started up a narrow, gravel road leading away from town. The road dipped down into an arroyo. A sign at the bottom of the arroyo read, DO NOT ENTER IF FLOODED. *I'm safe today*, she thought, looking up at the cloudless, twilight sky.

She followed the dirt road until she came to a small graveyard. A twisted metal sign across the large gate read, EMPALME CEME-TERY. Instructions below the sign read, "For Burial Permission Contact the Empalme Cemetery Committee." No address or phone number was listed on the sign. A rusty, barbed wire fence enclosed the graveyard.

She pushed the gate open and walked down the dusty path toward the graves.

The oldest stone markers were hard to read, but some of the dates were still visible. One read 1810 - 1905. Another indicated the deceased had lived to be one hundred and two.

A few of the graves had wooden markers. The sun and wind had long since erased the writing. A cross piece of wood from one of the graves had fallen off the upright piece. Kitt picked it up and placed it crosswise on the ground in front of the remaining stake. "Rest in peace," she said.

Most of the graves had rocks piled on top of them. Kitt surmised the rocks were an attempt to discourage wild animals from digging up the bodies. Small plants and weeds grew between the rocks.

A child's grave caught her eye. It had two angels etched into an expensive granite headstone. A small, plastic pinwheel, which had been secured to the headstone by electrical tape, was turning slowly in the evening breeze.

Darkness was falling fast as Kitt started back towards the gate. Out of the corner of her eye, she noticed movement about twenty feet in front of her. At first she thought it was a dog, but after getting a better look, she realized it was a coyote scratching at the ground. It scurried off out of sight when it saw her.

After making sure the coyote was gone, Kitt walked over to where it had been digging. She saw that she was in the oldest section of the cemetery. Rocks, which must have been placed on top of a now-disturbed grave many years ago, had obviously been rearranged recently. She stooped down to take a closer look.

In the dim twilight Kitt saw something pale among the rocks. She was shocked to recognize the remains of a human hand. Kitt struggled to push aside her panic. She moved a couple of rocks, uncovering an arm. The odor of death curled up through her nostrils. A silent scream choked her throat and bile began to rise from her stomach. She fought the urge to vomit.

Kitt stood up and took a couple of minutes to regain her composure. She had to get to a phone.

She turned, ran out of the cemetery and walked quickly back to the cantina. The bar was filled with customers. "Sal, I need to use your phone," she said out of breath.

Kitt dialed 911. The operator answered.

"My name is Katherine Logan. I am calling from Carlita's Cantina in Empalme, Arizona. There's a partially buried body under a pile of rocks in the cemetery. Can you put me through to the sheriff's office?"

"Please hold. I'll connect you."

The sheriff's dispatcher answered the phone. Kitt repeated what she had told the 911 operator and told him she would go back to the cemetery and wait for the sheriff to arrive.

Jeb, who was seated at the bar, overheard the call and jumped off his bar stool when Kitt put down the phone. Grabbing her arm, he said, "Sit down for a minute." Jeb guided her gently toward a nearby chair. "Tell us what's going on."

Sal was beside her with a glass of water.

She took a swallow but remained standing as she told Jeb and the others what had happened.

"I need to get back up there," she said, putting the glass down.

She glanced towards the door as Charles and Josie entered the cantina.

"What's happening?" Josie asked.

"Kitt was walking around the cemetery and discovered a body," Sal answered.

Sean froze. *Had Kitt found the body?* His first inclination was to run, but then he remembered who he was now. Sean Byrnes no longer existed. He was now the respected psychiatrist, Dr. Charles McGuire.

"How interesting, a dead body in the cemetery," he quipped. Seeing the shock on peoples' faces he added, "Excuse the joke, but at times like this, it is important to keep one's sense of humor. Are you all right, Kitt? You look a little pale."

"I'm fine, but I need to get back up to the cemetery to make sure nothing is disturbed before the sheriff gets there." As a warden, Kitt knew about the importance of protecting potential crime scenes. She knew that when either a body or surrounding area is disturbed, important information that would be needed to determine whether the person had been murdered, can be lost, as could clues leading to a perpetrator.

"I'd be glad to come along with you," Sean offered. He was curious to see how things would play out after the sheriff got there.

"Thanks, Charles. I'd appreciate having some help." She felt relief that she didn't need to go back there alone.

"I'll give you guys a lift," Jeb said.

The three walked over to Jeb's pickup. It was a tight squeeze into the front seat. Kitt noticed the gun rack behind the driver's seat; it contained a high-powered rifle.

She told Jeb to park on a side street near the cemetery. The three walked over to the front gate and waited for the officials to arrive.

A sheriff's car pulled up just outside the gate where the three had posted their watch. A middle-aged Mexican man stepped out of the squad car. He and Kitt exchanged knowing looks.

"Sheriff Martinez," Kitt said. She was surprised to see him. His office was in Florence, not far from the prison complex. "You must have been in the area to have gotten here so fast."

"I was in Arizona City when the call came through. It's good to see you again, Warden Logan, but not necessarily under these circumstances."

Sean, who had been gazing over towards the grave where the body lay, swung his head around and stared at Kitt. She was a warden.

"I'm glad you're here, Sheriff Martinez." The sheriff listened intently while Kitt told him why she was in Empalme and how she had come to find the body.

After Kitt finished she added, "We've been watching to make sure no one disturbs the gravesite."

"I'll need you to show me where the grave is," he said. "Who are these two men?"

"Sorry; I should have introduced you earlier. This is Dr. Charles McGuire and Jeb – what is your last name, Jeb?"

"Clanton, as in Ike Clanton," Jeb stammered, "of the Gunfight at the O. K. Corral. He was my father's uncle."

"Nice to meet you both," the sheriff said, nodding at the two men. "You stay outside the gate while Warden Logan takes me in. Make sure no one comes in except the investigators."

As Kitt and Martinez walked toward the grave at the end of the narrow dirt path, they heard growling. Three coyotes had gathered at the site and were fighting. The sheriff pulled his pistol out of the holster and fired a shot in the air. The coyotes scattered.

"I assume that's where you found the body," he said.

"Yes, it is."

"You can go back outside the gate now. Be sure you go back out the same way we came in. I'm going over to take a closer look."

She walked back and rejoined Jeb and Charles.

"So it's Warden Logan, is it?" Sean asked with a smirk.

She nodded. "I'm the warden at the prison complex in Florence, but I don't like to advertise it. Never know when I might run into a disgruntled former inmate," she added with a nervous laugh.

"I understand totally," he replied. "Many times I don't tell people I'm a psychiatrist because they'll want me to give them therapy on the spot."

Sheriff Martinez approached and passed them as he walked back to his squad car and picked up his cell phone. "It's a possible code eleven," they heard him say. "Start the notifications. I want the bureau chief of field operations down here as soon as possible."

He walked over to the three stationed outside the gate. "You two can leave," he said to the men, "but you'll need to stay, Warden, so I can interview you after the investigators arrive. In the meantime, let's try to keep the wild animals away from the grave. We'll follow the fence line over to the east side of the cemetery where we can watch for them."

Kitt watched Jeb and Charles get into the pickup and drive off.

"Do you have any idea what happened here?" Kitt asked, turning back to the sheriff.

"Not at this point. The body could be an undocumented alien who came across the border and died out on the desert. Sometimes we get anonymous calls from illegal aliens after they reach Phoenix or Tucson, saying they left a family member buried in a certain location, but we haven't received a call about a body being out here."

"What happens next?" Kitt asked.

"I've mobilized the sheriff's auxiliary volunteers. They'll set up a command center on the site. The detectives should be here any minute."

As if on cue, two cars and a van pulled up. "Wait here. I need to talk to them for a couple of minutes, and then I'll take your statement."

Several officers got out of the cars and began establishing a complete perimeter. Two more got out of the van and started unloading lights and a generator.

"Have you kept the party who found the body away from the site?" the crime scene detective asked the sheriff.

"She went in with me to show me where the body is located. That's her over there," he said, pointing at Kitt who was still standing by the fence. "She's the warden at Florence."

"A female warden; interesting," the detective said, glancing her way. "After the lights are operational, I'll get some pictures from the outside and then we'll go in."

"Okay. This would be a good time for me to take the warden's statement. Make sure you locate and talk to the caretaker to find out when he was last over in this area of the cemetery."

"I'll get to it as soon as I can," the investigator replied, sounding a bit miffed that Martinez felt the need to remind him to do the obvious.

Sheriff Martinez walked over to Kitt.

"It would be more comfortable to do the interview sitting down somewhere," she said. "I'm sure Sal has closed the cantina by now so we can't go there, and I'll bet the café is closed by this time, too. I'm staying with a woman named Eddie . . ."

"Eddie Rollins?" he interrupted.

"Yes. She's the one who helped me when I was stranded outside of town. We can go over to her house to do this. I'm surprised you know her."

"Most people of Mexican descent know and love Eddie. If there were more Eddies in this world, it would be a much better place. I'm not surprised she stopped to help you. Eddie has played Good Samaritan to more people than you can ever imagine."

"I think I know what you're getting at," Kitt said.

They got into Martinez's car and soon pulled up in front of the house. Kitt continued, "Eddie and I have become good friends in a short time. She took me out to her ranch this morning and I met Manuel and his family."

"Let's just leave it at that," Sheriff Martinez said cutting her off. "Some things are better left unsaid." Getting out of the car, Kitt led Martinez to the front door and let them both in.

"Agreed," Kitt said, wishing she hadn't mentioned Manuel.

"I don't think Eddie will mind if I make a pot of coffee and scrounge us up a snack," Kitt offered.

"Sounds good," he said, sinking down into the leather couch.

Kitt returned shortly with a tray of food. "I found some crackers, some cheese and a couple of apples. The coffee will be ready in a few minutes."

Martinez took out his tape recorder and began asking questions. An hour later, he thanked her for the hospitality and returned to the cemetery.

Kitt turned off the living room lights, said goodnight to Pete and then collapsed on her bed, too tired to get into her nightshirt or brush her teeth.

She was exhausted, but sleep wouldn't come. In the distance she could hear the lonesome howls of coyotes. She took the Smith and Wesson out of her purse and slipped it under her pillow.

Sometime after three o'clock in the morning, Kitt finally fell asleep.

5

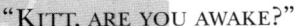

"Kɪᴛᴛ, ᴀʀᴇ ʏᴏᴜ ᴀᴡᴀᴋᴇ?"

The strange dream faded. Eddie was rapping on her bedroom door. Kitt immediately woke and sat up. "Come in, Eddie. I'm glad you're back. You'll never believe what happened last night."

"I already know," Eddie said, sitting down on the edge of the bed. "When Bennie brought me home this morning, we saw an emergency vehicle coming down the road from the cemetery. We drove up to see what was going on. Vinny Martinez was there and filled us in. Sounds like you had quite a night."

Eddie leaned forward and gently pushed hair out of Kitt's eyes. "I'm sorry I wasn't here with you last night. Are you okay?"

A smile curved Kitt's lips. "Other than not having much sleep, I'm doing fine."

"I'll get the coffee going and make us some breakfast while you get dressed." Eddie got up and walked out, leaving the door ajar.

Kitt got out of bed, walked to the bathroom and splashed water on her face. As she ran a brush through her hair, she noticed the gray strands. The last couple of days had probably added a few extra silver hairs.

"Breakfast's ready," Eddie called.

"Be right there!"

"Smells good in here," Kitt said, as she sat down at the table. "I haven't done my chores yet, but can I eat anyway?"

"You're off the hook this morning. I've already put out the seed. Do you want to talk about last night, or would you rather put it out of your mind?"

"There's no way I can forget about it so we might as well talk."
Eddie listened while Kitt told about how she had come to find the body. When she finished, Eddie said, "You've suffered quite a shock. There's a man living here, Dr. Charles McGuire, who is a psychiatrist. If you feel like really talking to someone, you might consider him."

"I met Charles. We were the only two in the cantina yesterday afternoon, so we had the opportunity to get acquainted. Your idea to debrief is a good one, but I think I'll wait until I get back to the prison to do it. We have a team of people trained specifically to help people who have had traumatic experiences." She paused, then said, "It isn't that I haven't seen a body before. It's just that last night, well . . . I was caught off guard."

She finished her coffee then said, "I think I'll go back up to the cemetery and see if Sheriff Martinez has any other questions. Do you feel like coming along?"

"Sure. The dishes can wait."

Sheriff Martinez waved at Kitt and Eddie as they climbed out of the pickup and approached the yellow crime scene tape. He was standing outside the sheeted area that enclosed the body.

"Thought you two might show up," he said, walking over to them. "How are you doing, Warden Logan?"

"Call me Kitt."

"Okay, if you'll call me Vinny instead of Sheriff. Now that we've taken care of the formalities, I'll ask again, how are you doing?"

"I'm getting a lot of tender, loving care," Kitt said, giving Eddie an appreciative smile.

"Doesn't surprise me." Vinny's smile revealed snow-white teeth, a stark contrast to his black mustache and the dark brown skin of his face.

"Is there anything you can tell us?" Kitt asked.

"We've completed a thorough investigation of the scene, but we'll have to wait until after the autopsy is done to confirm whether it is a homicide. The medical examiner arrived an hour ago. She's taken samples of insects and larvae from the body. The samples will be sent to the entomologist at the University of Arizona for a workup. After that, the entomologist will work with the medical examiner to determine how long the body has been here."

"Bugs can tell you how long the body has been here?" Eddie asked.

"In 98 percent of the cases, examination of insects around a body can determine the time of death."

"Unbelievable." Eddie shook her head.

"We know the victim is female," Vinny continued, "and, based on the clothes and shoes she was wearing, we can rule out the undocumented alien possibility. People coming across the border don't wear silk blouses and dress shoes. I'll notify the public information office when I get back to my office, and they'll do a press release. After that, you can expect to have helicopters from local television stations flying over, trying to get a look. Newspaper reporters will be here in droves, pestering the townsfolk for information."

"The ever-present media," Kitt sighed.

"I'm glad they haven't gotten wind of this yet," he said, nodding in agreement. "We have been able to do our jobs without distractions. Well, I better finish up so I can get back to my office and start looking through the missing persons lists."

The trio turned to watch as the body bag was loaded into a nearby emergency vehicle. The sheets, which had been put up to protect the privacy of the victim, were folded up and put back into the van.

"I'll see you later if you're still here," Vinny said. He turned and walked back over to a couple of the inspectors who were huddled near the grave where the body had been.

A small crowd of onlookers had gathered outside the cemetery. Charles and Josie were in the crowd, as were the two card players from the cantina. All were staring intently at the proceedings.

It would be days before the autopsy was completed and the cause of death determined. Kitt was certain the autopsy would confirm what she already knew; the body of the woman she had found had been murdered. What else could have happened? She felt herself slipping into the role of crime solver. "Eddie, what do you know about those two guys?" She nodded toward the two card players.

"Not much. They stay to themselves for the most part. I'd guess you'd call them drifters. I don't know where they get their money; as far as I know, they don't work. They've been living in

Empalme for a couple of months, but I really haven't paid much attention to them. Why?"

"Just curious. I'm betting they've had their fair share of encounters with the law. If this turns out to be foul play, Vinny will want to do background checks on them. Of course," she paused and looked directly into Eddie's eyes, "if this is a murder, I could be the prime suspect."

"You're kidding. Why would you say that?"

Kitt laughed at the shocked look on Eddie's face. "Why? Because I'm the one who found the body, that's why." She explained to Eddie that often a killer leads investigators to a body thinking he or she will not be considered a suspect. "What these kinds of killers don't know is that investigators always check them out first. Crime solvers also take a good look at the victim's family members and close friends. More often than not, the killer is a close acquaintance or someone in the family."

"Well, if you want me to put in a good word for you with Vinny, I'll do it," Eddie said with a snort.

"No need. If this is a murder, I have a great alibi. I was most likely inside a prison when it was committed."

"I'll keep that in mind," Vinny said, coming up behind them. "Just wanted to say goodbye. I'm going back to my office."

"You're welcome to stop by the house for some breakfast before you start back," Eddie offered.

"Thanks. I appreciate the offer, but I'd best be going. How about a rain check?"

"You got it. Next time you're down this way, arrange your schedule so we can take a run out to the ranch. It's been awhile since you've spent time with Manuel and the family."

"I'll work it out one of these days." He turned to Kitt. "I'll stay in touch with you, Kitt. If you think of anything else, give me a call."

"I certainly will."

"We might as well leave, too, Eddie," Kitt said. "There's really nothing we can do here."

"Let's go check on your car," Eddie suggested. "Clyde probably has it all ready to go."

They found Clyde under the hood of Kitt's car.

"Hello, ladies," came the muffled greeting. "The part came in early so I was able to get at it right away this morning. You'll get thousands of miles off this alternator, Kitt."

He stood up and stretched his back. "I'll crank her over for you," he said, getting into the car. It started immediately. "She's purring like a kitten," he said, with a look of pride spreading across his face.

"Just think," he said, stepping out of the car and handing Kitt her car keys, "if we hadn't had to wait for the alternator, that body you found last night would have laid up there a lot longer before anyone found it, that or been chewed up by coyotes."

"I guess you're right, Clyde," she said, wondering for a split second if he would have preferred that scenario.

She settled up with him and followed Eddie home.

Kitt took one last look around the bedroom to make sure she was not leaving anything behind. Walking back into the living room she said, "I'm glad my car is fixed, but I'm going to miss you, Eddie. I don't know what I would have done without you."

"It's not like we'll be thousands of miles apart. Just come back soon, and bring Cord with you. I'm anxious to meet him."

"He'd love it here. By the way, here's my home address and phone number." She took a pad out of her bag and wrote the information. "If you're ever in Florence and want a hot meal and a bed, you have an open invitation, and I don't mean at the prison," Kitt added. She gave Eddie a hug and said, "Take care of yourself."

Eddie walked out to the car with Kitt. "I'll be watching people here more closely from now on. I don't like to think we might have a murderer in our midst."

"Listen, Eddie, even if this turns out to be murder, the victim could have been killed somewhere else and left here. Maybe the perpetrator came through Empalme and decided it was a good place to dump the body and then kept on going. The important thing is to stay vigilant. If you notice any strange behavior, tell Vinny." She gave Eddie's arm a reassuring squeeze, put her bag in the car and slipped in after it.

Once on the road, the landscape flattened out. The drive to Florence would take about three hours. She wanted to get home before Cord so he wouldn't worry.

Kitt was not anxious to tell him about the bizarre things that happened on her return trip from Mexico. She knew exactly what his reaction would be. After he calmed down and realized she was okay, he'd go into his I-told-you-not-to-drive lecture.

The house looked welcoming as Kitt pulled into the driveway. "There's no place like home, there's no place like home," she said aloud as she stepped out of the car and clicked the heels of her sandals together. Too bad no one was around to appreciate her humor. Cord's pickup wasn't in the garage.

After a long soak in the whirlpool, Kitt felt the stress of the past few days leaving her body. She put on a robe and went out to the kitchen. After surveying the empty refrigerator, she took a gallon of maple nut ice cream out of the freezer, rummaged for a spoon and began eating directly out of the container.

A few minutes later she heard the rumble of some very familiar pipes. Kitt rushed to the window just as Cord pulled into the driveway. She ran out the door and into his outstretched arms.

"What will the neighbors think, seeing you out here in your bathrobe?" he said, gently kissing her. "Might start some nasty rumors. Let's go inside."

Stepping into the kitchen, Cord put his suitcase down and took her in his arms. Kitt looked up into his sea-green eyes. "My handsome silver fox," she said, running her hand through his silver-gray hair. His thick white mustache tickled her upper lip.

"Since you're so scantily clad, I think I'll get that way, too."

While Cord showered, Kitt put on some soft music, closed the bedroom curtains and lit a scented candle.

Their lovemaking was gentle and caring, a blending of bodies and spirits. Kitt seemed to fit perfectly into Cord's muscular arms as they lay together afterwards, savoring their love, and dropping off to sleep.

Waking about an hour later, Kitt gently nudged Cord. "I'm anxious to hear about your trip. How about you open a bottle of merlot, and I'll scrounge something up for dinner."

A few minutes later she dropped down beside Cord on the living room couch and picked up her glass of wine. "I found a container of that wild rice casserole we had a couple of weeks ago in the freezer. It's thawing out in the microwave. So, how was Chicago?"

"I had a good time. The Chicago Hilton was spectacular but very pricey. The first night I ordered a glass of wine with dinner and it cost me seven dollars and fifty cents. The next day some of us decided to go to the liquor store and buy our own bottles. For the rest of the week we met in my room for drinks before the evening activities."

"Did you hear any good speakers?"

"They were so-so. Several members of Congress addressed the convention and promised to continue the good fight for the rights of working people. They said it's a hard sell in D.C. these days because there's not much sympathy from the administration for working stiffs."

"Doesn't surprise me," Kitt replied. "How was the banquet?"

"It was one of the best. Guess who provided the music for the dance?" Without waiting for a response he said, "The Platters. I didn't know they still performed. One of them was an original member. He has to be seventy if he's a day. I kept wishing you could have been there to hear them and dance with me. That's pretty much it, I guess. Now it's your turn."

Kitt wondered where to begin. "Louise is doing great. We had a lot of fun and caught up on what's going on in each other's lives. She invited us to stay with them when we go to Minnesota for my warden's conference, but I told her we had already booked a room at the St. Paul Hotel."

She took a sip of wine, then told him about her return trip to Florence. Cord listened without interrupting. When Kitt finished, Cord shook his head and exhaled loudly through his mouth. "You know I didn't want you to drive down there alone, but you were hell-bent on doing it and wouldn't listen. Are you okay?"

Kitt felt like telling him she didn't need to be lectured, but held her tongue; she knew Cord was just worried about her. "I'm okay, but I had a nightmare last night. Makes me think I'm more bothered than I'm willing to admit. In my dream, a hand reached up from a grave, just like the one in Empalme, grabbed me by the neck and wouldn't let go." She went on, "Eddie suggested I debrief with a professional, and I think I will. When I go back to work tomorrow, I'll ask someone from the stress debriefing team to spend some time with me."

She looked at the clock on the mantel. "Speaking of work, I'd better give Dale a call before we eat. I should let him know I'll be back tomorrow."

Reaching for the phone, she lifted the receiver and dialed the number. Kitt was glad to find that the deputy warden was still in his office. "Warden Logan, glad you're back. Hope you had a good vacation."

"It was great – until the trip back. I'll tell you about it another time."

"Well, everything I have can wait but I would like to see you first thing tomorrow morning if that works for you."

"Tell Mary to schedule us for eight o'clock."

"Okay."

Kitt hung up the phone. Her thoughts turned to Eddie. "I want to go back to Empalme and take you with me so you can meet Eddie and all the others," she told Cord. "You'll probably think some of the people are a little odd, but once you get to know them, you'll like them."

"Sounds good. I'd like to thank Eddie personally for helping you." He leaned back into the couch and folded his arms. "Just promise me you won't go looking for any more bodies."

6

WHAT CRISIS AWAITS ME BACK AT THE OFFICE? Kitt wondered as she backed out of the driveway and headed toward the prison complex. She would have about twenty minutes to settle in before her eight o'clock meeting with Dale Whipple.

Once Kitt arrived, Kitt's secretary, Mary, was already at her desk. Mary's long, platinum hair was pulled back from her tanned face and secured at the base of her neck by a beaded Apache barrette. She was tall, striking in appearance and looked much younger than her fifty years. People in passing, especially the men, always gave Mary a second look. Besides being extraordinarily attractive, she was smart and efficient.

The deputy warden was standing by Mary's desk visiting when Kitt walked in. "Good morning," Kitt said.

"Good morning," the two responded simultaneously.

"Dale, you're early. This must be important." *Either that or you want some time with Mary*, Kitt thought. She noticed that Dale often found excuses to be around Mary.

"It is important. We have a situation which involves an officer and an inmate."

"Come on in. I'll put on a pot of coffee."

"I already made one," Mary said. "It should be brewed by now."

Mary went to fetch them clean cups. Kitt noticed how Dale's eyes followed Mary out of the room.

Dale thanked Mary and blushed when she handed him the fresh cup of coffee. Kitt poured her own and took a seat across from Dale. "So, what's up?" she asked.

Dale adjusted his wire-rimmed glasses and began. "We had to lock out one of our officers. He's a new hire, and as it turns out, a bit ill at ease around inmates. It didn't take long for one of our inmates to figure out Officer Long was an easy mark. The inmate told Long that if he didn't bring in fifty dollars for the inmate, he would tell his contacts on the outside to hurt the officer's family. His fear of the inmate overrode good judgment; instead of immediately telling his supervisor, he gave the inmate the money. Internal Affairs will have their report ready for you later today."

Kitt walked over to the window. Her shoulders slumped in disappointment. "Inmates are such geniuses at finding weaknesses in people. If only they could use their talents in a positive way." She turned and walked back to her seat. Dale was absent-mindedly picking some lint off his trousers, probably asking himself the same question.

"Let's schedule another round of training for avoiding set-ups," she said, penciling in an additional item on her agenda for the morning meeting. "Is there anything else I should know about?"

"Nothing very important. A couple of inmates got into a fight Saturday night. They were both drunk. The officers found a stash of hooch in one of the guys' cells that stunk to high heaven. I don't know how anyone can drink that stuff. I'm surprised they don't poison themselves."

"What did they use to make it?" she asked.

"The usual. They got yeast from slices of bread and started hoarding sugar packets so they could get the stuff fermented. This batch was orange-flavored. Apparently, several inmates had been stashing bread, oranges and sugar inside their pockets from the food line while another inmate distracted the nearby officers. After they accumulated all the ingredients, they threw the conglomeration together and brewed it in a big, plastic ice cream container that one of the inmates had in his cell. They got the hooch brewed between shakedowns. It was a great party until two of them started fighting and got busted."

"It's amazing how brilliant they are when it comes to getting into trouble. Well, thanks, Dale. If you don't have anything else, I'll catch up with you later."

Kitt followed Dale out of her office, sat down in the chair beside Mary's desk and told her about being stranded in Empalme. Mary couldn't believe the run of bad luck. "I had no idea you went through all that. You were supposed to come back all relaxed."

"It was a trip I won't soon forget. Anyway, what do I have on my schedule?"

Mary looked at the schedule. "You're clear this morning."

Since nothing needed her immediate attention, Kitt decided to take a walk through one of the cell halls. Line staff always appreciated it when she came through, since it gave them the opportunity to speak to her.

As usual, when the inmates saw the warden, they started yelling to get her attention.

"Warden Logan, can you come over here for a minute?" came a plea from one nearby cell. "I don't feel so good. I need to see the doctor, and they won't let me go. No one gives a damn if I die in here."

"He's a hypochondriac. He'd go see the doctor ten times a day if we'd let him," the officer near Kitt explained. "He says he's too sick to work, so we locked him down just in case he's contagious. No phone calls, and he's getting his meals in his cell. My guess is he'll be feeling back to normal by this afternoon."

Another called to Kitt. "Warden, I sent you a very important kite, and you haven't answered it yet."

The inmates were always sending her requests, or kites as they were called in prison. She walked over to his cell. "I get a lot of kites. You'll just have to wait until I get to yours."

"Here's the deal, Warden," the inmate persisted. "I've fallen in love with a lady who wrote to me for a year. Now she comes to see me every Sunday. We wanna get married while I'm still inside. She knows I'm innocent and that I didn't murder nobody."

"How long have you got left on your sentence?"

"Well, I got life but I'm appealing my sentence. Like I said, I didn't murder nobody."

"Hmm," she said nodding. "We'll review your kite and get back to you."

"Thanks, Warden," he called, as she walked away. "I knew you'd understand, being a lady and all."

Kitt returned to her office and dashed off a quick thank you note to Eddie. She slipped it into the outgoing bin on Mary's desk and left a note saying she would be in the chaplain's office.

A few minutes later Kitt arrived at the chapel. "Good morning," she said, giving a rap on the door that stood ajar. "Thought I'd stop by and get an update on the religious diversity symposium you're planning."

"Have a chair. I'm glad you're here. I want to run some things by you. Would you like a cup of coffee?"

"No, thanks. I've had my daily allowance." She looked down as her pager began to vibrate. It was Mary's number. "May I use your phone? My secretary is paging me."

"Sure."

Mary answered on the first ring. "Dr. Reynolds called and asked if you were in. He'd like to see you in health services at your earliest convenience."

"Did he say what it's about?"

"No, but it sounded urgent."

"Okay, thanks." She turned back to the chaplain. "I'm sorry but I need to go over to Health Services. I'll have to get back to you later."

Kitt headed down the hall towards the Health Services unit.

She found Doctor Reynolds seated at his desk. An inmate was leaning against the wall opposite him. The middle-aged prisoner's thin blond hair was swept from the left side across the top of his head in an effort to hide a bald spot. His complexion was grayish, and acne scars pitted his face. His pants were belted below his large belly.

"What is it?" Kitt asked, glancing from the inmate to the doctor.

"I'll let Mr. Smith explain the problem," the doctor replied, with more than a hint of exasperation in his voice.

Kitt took a seat and pointed to a chair near the inmate. "Sit down, Mr. Smith," she said, "and tell me what's going on."

"I don't think it would be a good idea for me to sit down, Warden," the inmate replied sheepishly.

"He's right about that," the doctor concurred, avoiding eye contact with Kitt.

She looked back at the inmate. "Well?"

Shaking his head in a bewildered manner, Mr. Smith began his explanation. "You'll never guess what happened."

"Try me."

"The thing is, my cell is haunted. I was lying on my bed reading when suddenly the light bulb in my lamp flew out of the lamp and up my keister."

"Your what?" Kitt asked, trying to hide her astonishment.

"You know, my ass. See, it's up there and it won't come out and . . ."

"Never mind," she interrupted. "I get the drift. So, now what, Doctor Reynolds?"

"He'll need to be transported to the hospital in Phoenix right away. If the light bulb bursts, Mr. Smith is in big trouble."

"I'll make the call to Captain Mahoney right now," Kitt said, reaching for the phone. She dreaded having to tell the captain about Smith. Mahoney had no tolerance for the idiotic things some of the inmates did. He would most likely advise her to let the light bulb work its way out naturally.

After listening to the captain bellow about the Smith situation, Kitt hung up the phone and reported that transport officers were on the way.

"Mr. Smith needs psychiatric help," Dr. Reynolds said after the officers escorted the inmate out of the room. "It's been over a month since Dr. Shelton was killed in the car accident. I'm a medical doctor. I don't have the time or skills to deal with the psychiatric problems of inmates."

"I know you don't, but I need you to help out in crisis situations until Dr. Mease gets on board. You know I moved as quickly as I could to hire him, but he had to give notice he was leaving his job in New Mexico." Kitt knew she sounded a bit defensive. She didn't mean to. Reynolds had a valid concern.

"You're right about Smith and a lot of other inmates needing psychiatric help," she continued. "Believe me, I've tried to get temporary help, but I can't find a psychiatrist who wants a thirty-day assignment. The only thing I can do is keep trying," she said, more to herself than to Dr. Reynolds.

Kitt walked back to her office, deep in thought. She had tried to find someone to fill in after Dr. Shelton was killed, but no one had been interested in a temporary appointment. Most mental health professionals who were looking for work wanted full-time, permanent positions. Where would she be able to find a psychiatrist who would be willing to fill in for a month?

Suddenly, it struck her. Dr. Charles McGuire, the psychiatrist she had met in Empalme. He was working on his research but maybe, just maybe, he would consider taking a temporary assignment. It couldn't hurt to ask, Kitt decided.

7

"JUST WHEN I THINK I'VE HEARD IT ALL," Mary said, after Kitt told her the bizarre story of Mr. Smith and the light bulb.

"This latest incident drives home how critical it is that we get a psychiatrist to come in on a temporary basis. It's been over a month since Dr. Shelton was killed in the car accident, and it'll be another month before Dr. Mease is on board. While I was walking back to my office I came up with a possibility, but it's a long shot."

"What kind of long shot?"

"I haven't had a chance to tell you everything about being stranded in Empalme. While I was there, I met a psychiatrist named Dr. Charles McGuire. He's on a leave of absence from his mental health clinic in Saginaw, Michigan. I'm going to give him a call and see if he'd consider taking a temporary assignment."

"Sounds like a good idea. Do you want me to get him on the line for you?"

"I don't have his phone number, but I can get it from the woman I stayed with in Empalme." Kitt went into her office and thumbed through her address book until she found Eddie's number, and quickly dialed the number.

Eddie answered on the first ring. "Hi Eddie, it's Kitt. You either have extra sensory perception or you were expecting a call."

"I was standing right by the phone when it rang. Hey, it's good to hear from you. How's life in the fast lane?"

"I'd rather be at your ranch."

"Rough day?"

"Just business as usual. The reason I'm calling is that I need to reach your resident psychiatrist, Charles McGuire, and I don't have Josie's phone number. I couldn't remember her last name, or I would have called information."

"I just got off the phone with Josie. I think Charles is there now, so this would be a good time to call. Can I ask what this is about, or is it none of my business?"

"I'll tell you but keep it under wraps. Our prison psychiatrist was recently killed in a car accident, and the man I've hired to replace him had to give thirty days notice so he can't start until the middle of next month. The lid's about to blow in my mental health unit, and I'm desperate. I need to find a psychiatrist willing to take a temporary job. I don't have a clue if Charles would be interested, but I guess the worst that can happen is he'll say no."

"It sure can't hurt to give him a try. On another subject, when are you and Cord coming down?"

"Soon, I hope. When I told him you invited us to spend some time at your ranch, he got excited. He'd love to get back on a horse again. Listen, I hate to cut this short, but I better try to catch Charles. Wish me luck."

"Good luck. Give me a call and let me know when you're coming."

"Will do."

Hanging up immediately, Kitt dialed Josie's number.

"Hello," Josie answered.

"Hi, Josie, it's Kitt Logan."

After a brief pause, Josie said, "Oh."

"How's everything going?"

"Okay." Josie replied cautiously.

"Is Charles around?"

"Sure. He's right here."

Kitt heard muffled voices as Josie handed the phone over to Charles. "Who is it?" Charles asked. Kitt heard Josie say, "It's the warden we met last week."

A moment later he was on the phone. "Kitt. I wasn't expecting a call from you."

"Not surprising. You probably thought you'd never hear from me again."

"How did you get my number?" he asked.

"From Eddie. Listen, I'll cut to the chase, Charles. The reason I'm calling is I need a psychiatrist to fill in on a temporary basis in my mental health unit." She explained her situation to him, then said, "I'm calling to ask if you would consider taking a temporary position."

Charles didn't say anything for a couple of moments. *At least he hasn't rejected the idea immediately, which is a good sign*, she thought. When he remained silent, Kitt added, "If you are uneasy about the thought of working with inmates, I certainly understand."

Sean Byrne's mind was racing. *What a trip*, he thought, *a former prisoner being asked to go to work in a prison. As a psychiatrist, no less. Dr. McGuire, prison psychiatrist.* It was all he could do to keep from laughing. Sean knew Kitt wouldn't have called him unless she was desperate, so he decided to keep her in suspense for a while.

"As you might guess," he began, "I'll need some time to think over the idea. As far as working in a prison goes, it is something I'm very comfortable doing. Before I left Michigan, I was on contract with the Saginaw Correctional Facility."

"You were? I had no idea."

Charles took a slow breath. "To tell you the truth, I'm at a stopping point in my research." He paused momentarily to drag out the suspense, then said in the most professional voice he could muster, "I am willing to consider your offer."

Kitt couldn't believe her ears. "Would you be able to come to Florence? You could get a quick look at the prison complex, and we could discuss the temporary position in more detail."

"I could arrange to come tomorrow around noon."

"Good. I'll buy lunch, so bring your appetite."

Kitt gave him directions and told him to go to the reception desk when he arrived at the prison. "Someone will be there to escort you to my office."

Sean hung up the phone. An escort to the warden's office; how ironic. He remembered when, as a prisoner, he had been escorted to segregation for threatening a guard. Tomorrow, an officer would be taking him to the warden's office where he would agree to take a job as a prison psychiatrist. He threw back his head and laughed until his side hurt.

"What's so funny?" Josie asked.

"Oh, it's something Kitt said. She has a great sense of humor. By the way, I'm going to Florence tomorrow to talk to her about a job. She asked me to help her out until the new psychiatrist she hired starts next month."

"Are you going to accept the job?"

"Sure."

"What about your research?" Josie asked.

"It can wait," he snapped.

"I'm just thinking if you take the job you'll have to live in Florence, won't you?"

"Do you think I'd want to spend six hours commuting every day? You know, Josie, I get the feeling you don't want me to take this job."

"It's just that I'll miss you, Charles," she said, her eyes filling with tears. "In fact, I'm worried you might not come back to Empalme."

Soon after Sean moved in with Josie, he could see that she was smitten with him. He had led Josie to believe the feeling was mutual. Sensing a romantic relationship in the making, Josie had not asked him to pay board and room. Now Sean was paying the price. He walked over to her and gave her a peck on the cheek. "Come on, Josie. Stop crying. If I decide to take the job, I'll only be gone thirty days. Maybe I can work it out so I can come back on weekends." He looked at his watch. "You better get going or you'll be late for work."

Josie blew her nose and smiled. "You're right. I'm sorry I get so emotional."

Yeah, thought Sean. He shot her a look as she grabbed her bag and walked out the front door.

Filled with relief, Kitt went out to tell Mary the good news. "I've been on the phone with Charles McGuire. It sounds like he may take the temporary position. He's coming here tomorrow to discuss the details. Will you get Dr. McGuire cleared with security and tell them to have an escort ready to bring him back to my office as soon as he gets here? My meeting with him takes precedence over everything else on my calendar tomorrow afternoon. I don't know how long he'll want to spend talking about the job."

Mary had been taking notes. "I'll take care of everything," she said. "What time do you expect him to be here?"

"About noon."

"Nice work, Kitt."

"It's not set in concrete yet, but here's hoping," Kitt said, crossing her fingers.

8

THE FOLLOWING DAY MARY STUCK her head in Kitt's office just before noon. "Dr. McGuire is here."

"Good." Kitt stood up and walked out to meet him.

Charles was dressed in slacks and a polo shirt. "Warden Logan, it is so good to see you again," he said, walking over to shake her outstretched hand. He flashed a charming smile.

"Welcome, Dr. McGuire." Kitt returned his smile. "Mary," she said turning back to her secretary, "I'd like you to meet Dr. Charles McGuire."

Mary blushed slightly as she stood up and shook the handsome psychiatrist's hand.

"How's Josie?" Kitt asked.

"Last night she got a call from her sister, who lives on the East Coast. Her mother is very ill, and Josie flew home so she could be with her. Fortunately she was able to catch a flight out of Phoenix this morning."

"I'm sorry to hear about Josie's mother. Come on in," she said, nodding toward her office.

"Nice office," he said as he walked over to the window and looked out at the razor ribbon fence surrounding the prison yard. Sean remembered the inmate in Michigan who tried to escape through a razor ribbon and, as a result, spent a long time in the hospital. He felt no sympathy for the man; anyone stupid enough to try and escape through razor ribbon deserved to be hurt.

"I see you like plants," he said, looking down at the two large plants positioned on either side of the window.

"I don't have a green thumb, but Mary keeps an eye on my plants for me."

He walked over to the huge bookshelf. "Have you read all these books?"

"Not really. Most of them are reference books. I only use them when I need some specific information. These are the state statutes," she said, running her hand across one shelf of books.

Noticing the pictures on Kitt's large desk, Sean said, "Your family?"

Kitt smiled and said they were. "Let's sit over there," she said.

Byrnes sat down on a chair beside the coffee table. He still couldn't get over the fact that he was in a warden's office being offered a job. A smile crossed his lips. He certainly didn't need to worry about having the proper credentials to work as a prison psychiatrist. The résumé in his briefcase would answer any questions Kitt might have about his ability to perform the job.

"I've thought about you a lot lately," he said empathically. "It must have been a terrible shock to find the body in the cemetery. Tell me, how are you doing?"

"I'm doing fine," Kitt said.

"Good. You seem like a strong woman but just thought I'd check. We psychiatrists tend to worry a little too much about people and their emotional well-being. Nature of the beast, I guess."

Kitt was anxious to get to the business at hand. "Have you had time to think about my offer?"

"As I told you on the phone, I'm at a stopping point with my research. I can't go forward until I get some new case files to review. I thought about returning to my practice up north, but there's no reason to rush back. And, to be candid," he said with a chuckle, "it would be hard to go back to the frigid Michigan temperatures."

He opened Dr. McGuire's briefcase. "I brought you a copy of my résumé in case you'd like to see it."

Kitt quickly scanned it. "This is impressive."

"Notice my prison experience," he said, pointing to the middle of the page. "I found working with inmates to be very rewarding, not in terms of salary but by being able to make a difference in the lives of prisoners who are mentally ill." *That line of bull ought to impress her,* Sean thought.

Kitt knew she was making a spur-of-the-moment decision, but

decided she had no other choice. Dr. McGuire's education and experience certainly met the job requirements. There was something about Charles she found a bit unsettling, but then, all psychiatrists seemed a bit odd to her.

After giving him a detailed a description of the job, she asked, "Do you feel like you have enough information to make a decision?"

"Yes," Dr. McGuire said, nodding slowly. "You were very thorough in your explanation of the job responsibilities." He rubbed his forehead as if deep in thought, then said, "I will accept your offer."

"Good. I'd like to get you on board as soon as possible. We'll have to do a criminal history check but from the looks of your résumé, it won't take long. Background checks for temporary hires aren't as comprehensive as the checks are for permanent position hires."

Byrnes stiffened, then relaxed. The background check would be on McGuire, not him. The real psychiatrist would come up smelling like a rose, even though he was pushing up daisies. Sean fought back a smirk.

What if Kitt wanted to do reference checks? He began tapping the heel of his left foot lightly on the floor. He had to say something to make sure she didn't start calling people listed as references on the résumé.

"Do you need to contact anyone for references?" he asked. "If my partners get wind of this, they might try to persuade me to return to the clinic since my research is on hold."

"We don't tend to do reference checks on people taking temporary assignments. The only thing the law requires is the criminal history check." Kitt made a copy of the résumé and handed the original back to Sean. "I don't know about you, but I'm starved. Let's go get something to eat."

Sean took back the résumé and put it in his briefcase.

After lunch, Kitt dropped Charles off beside his car and said, "Be sure to say hello to everyone in Empalme for me and tell Josie I'll keep her mother in my prayers."

"I'll stop by the cantina tonight when I get back. I've got to fill everyone in about what's going on with Josie's mother. She got the call about her mother late last night. We left for the airport early this morning, so she didn't get a chance to tell anyone she was leaving."

During lunch, Kitt had told him he'd be getting a call from the human resources director. "I'll expect a call on Monday," Sean said as he got out of the car.

When Kitt returned to her office, Mary said, "I hope you don't mind my asking, but is Dr. McGuire married? I haven't seen anyone that good-looking in a long time. Is he taking the job?"

"Whoa, one question at a time. Yes, he is taking the job, and I agree he is very good-looking. He hasn't said anything to me about having a wife, so I doubt he's married; could be divorced, I suppose. He's been renting a room from a woman named Josie in Empalme. I'm guessing there is some kind of relationship there, but I don't have any idea how serious it is. The bartender in the cantina mentioned Josie had taken a shine to Charles, but I'm not sure he feels the same way towards her."

"And now, if I've answered all your questions about Dr. McGuire," Kitt teased, "I think I'll bail out. Do you need me for anything else before I go?"

"I need your signature on some letters. They're on your desk. If anything important comes up, I'll page you."

"Don't let me forget to notify human resources about McGuire first thing Monday morning."

Mary followed Kitt into her office and watched as the warden signed the letters.

"Do you have any exciting plans for this weekend, Mary?"

"Nope. I'm looking forward to a quiet weekend. I'll probably rent a couple of movies. That'll be enough excitement for me."

"I know what you mean. Have a good one, Mary."

"You, too."

Kitt let out a deep sigh as she unlocked her car and slid behind the wheel. It had been a stressful week, but now that Charles had agreed to fill in, her stress was rapidly dissipating.

When she pulled into the driveway, Cord was in the garage working on his motorcycle. He had his boots on so she knew he'd been out on his bike.

He looked up and grinned. "Hi, Red."

"Did you have a good ride?"

"I always have a good ride. Are you ever going to get on your bike again?"

Kitt glanced affectionately at her red Yamaha Royal Star Venture, which was identical to Cord's. "Of course I'm going to ride again but, sadly, I had to work today. Someone needs to bring home the bacon."

"Forget it. No sermon necessary," Cord said, feigning anger. He gave her a hug. "The dealer called to say the parts I ordered are in. Do you want to take a run up to Phoenix with me?"

"Sure. What did you order?"

"Roll bars. I ordered some for your bike, too. Consider it an early birthday present."

"You sweetie pie," she said, giving him a kiss. "Thank you!"

"You're welcome. Do you want to do an overnight? It's been a long time since we had a night out on the town. I wouldn't mind seeing a movie."

"Sounds like fun," Kitt said. "I'll go change clothes and pack a bag."

On her way into the house, she glanced through the window of Cord's pickup as she passed by. His overnight bag was sitting on the back seat.

"You sure take me for granted, Cordell Logan," she said, tapping her foot on the concrete driveway.

He slapped her on the butt. "Knock off the dramatics and get moving!"

9

"I COULD REALLY GET INTO THE RETIREMENT MODE if I let myself," Kitt said, looking across the table at Cord. The weekend had passed quickly and Monday was already upon them.

"Hey, I understand. I felt the same way when I got close to retirement."

Kitt cleared the dirty dishes off the table and put them in the sink. "I gotta get going. What's on your calendar for today?"

"I'm going to put the roll bars on our bikes. Maybe, if you get home early enough, we can go for a spin." Looking affectionately into her brown eyes, he added, "If you want, I'll go over your pension estimates with you. Maybe, between the two of us, we can find a way to get you retired next year."

"I'll bring my retirement file home tonight." She picked up her purse and took out her car keys. "I love you, Cordell Logan."

"I love you, too, Warden Logan. Now get out of my way so I can get started on my housework."

Mary was on the phone when Kitt arrived at her office. "Good morning," Mary said, putting the phone down.

"Good morning, Mary. How was your weekend?"

"It was okay, after I got my swamp cooler fixed. It was out when I got home Friday, and I couldn't get anyone to fix it until late Saturday afternoon. How was your weekend?"

"Good. We went to Phoenix Friday night to pick up some parts for our bikes. We had dinner at a wonderful Italian restaurant and then went to a movie. It was the first date we'd had in ages. So, what do I have going on today?"

"Not much. You asked me to remind you to call Human Resources about the temporary position for Dr. McGuire," Mary responded. "I hope you'll make it a priority."

Kitt laughed. "I get the feeling you're quite taken with Dr. McGuire. I'll take care of it in the meeting this morning. Would you please call Dr. Reynolds and tell him I want him in the meeting if he can arrange his schedule? He'll be glad to hear we've found someone to fill in until Dr. Mease gets here."

A few minutes later, Mary stuck her head in Kitt's office. "Sheriff Martinez is here to see you. He doesn't have an appointment. Do you have time for him?"

"Sure. Send him in."

"Hello, Vinny," she said as the sheriff came into her office. "It's good to see you again."

"I was in the area so I decided to stop by."

"I'm glad you did. How's the investigation going?"

"In a word, slowly. We haven't identified the victim yet, but the medical examiner found bruising around her neck and has determined she was strangled. The entomologist said the victim had been dead for about ten days when you found her. Investigators were able to lift some tire tracks on the dirt road inside the cemetery, thanks to the dry spell we've had lately. The tracks didn't match the tires on the groundskeeper's car. Since no one has been buried up there for over a month, we believe the tracks were made by the perpetrator's car. We found a couple cigarette butts near the grave, which might help us put a suspect at the site—after we have a suspect, that is. This information I am giving you is confidential, which I'm sure you know."

"It's in my vault," Kitt assured him.

"Because the body was dumped in Empalme, there's the possibility that the perpetrator lives there. Did you happen to notice any suspicious-looking characters while you were there? Eddie mentioned that you asked her about a couple of guys that hang around the cantina."

"I noticed a couple of tough guys, probably bikers. One had a Hell's Angels tattoo. I wouldn't be surprised if they've done time."

"Right. That's who I thought you meant. I'm in the process of running background checks on them. Anyone else?"

Kitt paused. "Not really. Of course, I didn't get to know very many people while I was there."

"Well, let me know if anyone else comes to mind." He glanced at his watch. "I better get going. I'm driving down to Empalme to snoop around a little. Thanks for your time, Kitt."

"Feel free to stop by anytime."

Kitt grabbed the administrative staff meeting file and walked across the hall to the warden's conference room. Her staff was assembled and seemed to be in good spirits, considering it was Monday morning.

"Good morning," Kitt said, as she poured a cup of coffee and sat down at the head of the table.

"Good morning, Warden," the various staff members replied in unison.

Kitt laughed and sat down at the head of the table. She opened the file she had carried into the room.

After studying it for a moment she looked up. "Most of you have heard about the officer we lost because of an inmate set-up. Instead of having a job, he'll now be doing time. We invest a lot of time and money on recruitment and training, so when we lose staff, it is a waste of our limited resources." Kitt looked over at the director of staff training. "How long has it been since we've held avoiding set-ups training?" she asked.

"It's been a year or more," he said.

"Let's get a refresher course going as soon as we can. Speaking of training," Kitt said, "I've asked the chaplain to develop some training on religious diversity. It's going to be mandatory for all staff, and I expect all of you to attend the training. Captain, you'll need to work out a schedule for your officers so they can attend."

Captain Mahoney leaned his six-foot-three-inch, two-hundred-and-sixty-pound body back in the chair, folded his arms and cleared his throat. Kitt knew what his response would be. She'd heard it every time mandatory training was discussed.

"This is going to be a scheduling nightmare," he began in his gravelly voice. "In order to get all the officers trained, you're going to need at least three separate sessions. One will have to be before third shift comes on. I'm not going to force officers to sit through a two-hour training class right after they come off the midnight shift. The only other option would be for me to lock down the prison, and that's out of the question. The only time I'm going to lock this place down is if we're doing a drug and weapon shakedown or if one of our snitches tells us there's going to be a disturbance. That being said, you'll need to pay a lot of overtime. I hope you have the money."

"Captain, I'm not asking you to lock down the prison, but in the event I should tell you to do it, I presume it would get done." Kitt leaned forward toward him. "And for the record, I'm the person who has to worry about having money in the budget to pay overtime, not you."

Some of the staff began shuffling the papers in front of them. During this exchange, no one wanted to make eye contact with either the warden or the captain.

Kitt took an audible deep breath. "Captain Mahoney, I want you and the chaplain to meet in the next couple of days to work out the scheduling. I'll expect a progress report on my desk by the end of the week."

Captain Mahoney's face flushed. He started to say something, then thought better of it. He unfolded his arms, picked up a pen and started tapping the table.

I'll be damned if I'll let him intimidate me like he does everyone else, Kitt thought as she looked down at her agenda. Most of her staff didn't particularly like Captain Mahoney, but everyone, including Kitt, respected his ability to keep the prison running smoothly. There had not been a major incident at the prison since he had become the captain five years ago.

Kitt looked up as Dr. Reynolds walked through the door. "Perfect timing," she said, as he pulled a chair up to the table. "I was just moving to the next item on my agenda, an item which should interest you."

Dr. Reynolds looked at her with anticipation.

"I contacted a psychiatrist I met while I was in Empalme. He's on a leave of absence from his mental health clinic up north and is living there. I was able to persuade him to take a thirty-day, temporary position with us. Assuming his background check comes back clean, he'll be here later this week."

"That is good news," responded Dr. Reynolds. "What's his name?"

"Dr. Charles McGuire. Have you heard of him?"

"I think so. I believe he was a presenter at the American Correctional Association convention a few years ago. I wasn't able to attend his session but I heard good things about him from a psychiatrist friend of mine who was at the session."

"Has he had any experience working in a prison?" Captain Mahoney growled. "I don't want someone in here who's going to jeopardize the safety of my prison."

"I don't want anyone putting staff or inmates at risk either, Captain Mahoney," Kitt replied in an overly calm, steady voice. Again, staff dropped their heads and busied themselves with studying the meeting's agenda.

"For your information, Captain," she continued, "Dr. McGuire was working on contract with the Saginaw Correctional Facility in Michigan before he went on his leave of absence. Any more questions, anyone?" She looked directly at Mahoney.

The room was silent.

She looked at her Human Resource director. "Would you please make a note on Dr. McGuire's criminal history request asking that it be processed immediately? Mark the request urgent. As soon as you get the results, let Mary know and then call Dr. McGuire so he can plan accordingly. You can get his phone number from Mary."

After taking a quick look at the agenda to make sure she'd covered everything, Kitt looked up. "That's all I have. Does anyone have anything else?"

Heads shook as everyone quickly gathered up the papers in front of them. None were interested in witnessing another exchange between the warden and the captain.

Kitt was angry for some time after the meeting. Maybe Captain Mahoney enjoyed the constant sparring that went on between them, but she didn't. In her opinion, the captain was bordering on insubordination. One of these days she'd have to address the issue with him in a private meeting. Her retirement was looking better all the time.

Kitt's desk was a sea of paperwork. Letters needed to be signed, reports read and inmate kites answered; the list went on and on. She picked up a pen and started through the pile.

Mary tapped lightly on the door. "Dr. McGuire's criminal history check came back this afternoon. As expected, he passed with flying colors."

"Good. I'm glad they were able to get it done today."

"Everything is in motion for Dr. McGuire to start on Wednesday. Do you want me to schedule time for you to meet with him that morning? Your calendar is clear until eleven o'clock."

"See if he can be here at nine-thirty. I'd like to give him a mini tour before I take him over to the mental health wing to meet the staff. Oh, and ask Dr. Reynolds if he can meet us there about ten thirty. We need to decide on a course of action for Mr. Smith, the inmate who stuck the light bulb. . ." she quit mid-sentence. "You know the one."

10

"Is Dr. McGuire here yet?" Kitt asked, out of breath from taking the front steps two at a time. Her breakfast meeting had gone longer than anticipated.

"Not yet," Mary replied.

"Good," she said, taking a seat in the chair beside Mary's desk. Mary, as usual, was smartly dressed. She had on a turquoise shirt-waist dress. Silver Hopi earrings dangled from her ear lobes.

"When I called Dr. McGuire on Monday to set things up, he asked if I knew anywhere he could rent an apartment for a month. I told him I'd check around, but I haven't been able to find anything. Since I'm an empty nester, I have more space than I need. Do you think I should offer to rent him a room?"

"Sounds like a good idea." Kitt stood up. "You'd be solving his problem and making some extra money for yourself. Talk to him about it when he gets here and then send him in to see me."

Not long after, Kitt heard Charles and Mary talking in the outer office. When Mary asked him if he wanted to rent a room from her, he jumped at the offer.

Charles looked handsome in his navy blue suit, white shirt and paisley tie. He was carrying his expensive leather briefcase.

"I blocked off some time this morning so I can give you a quick tour of the prison before I take you over to meet the staff in the mental health wing. You can leave your briefcase here if you want to."

"Thanks, but I'll take it with me. It isn't that heavy."

She locked her office door, and the two started down the hall.

"I'm really looking forward to working with you, Kitt. Can you believe it? We've only known each other a couple of weeks and now we're working together. It was meant to be, I guess."

"Well, I'm relieved to have a psychiatrist back on staff, that's for sure. Thanks again for agreeing to help us out. By the way, I will always call you Dr. McGuire when we're at work and other staff are around. We're pretty formal with our job titles; it's Warden, Captain, Chaplain, Doctor, Lieutenant and Sergeant. Officers below the sergeant rank are referred to as Officer so-and-so. Inmates are Mr., followed by their last name. Clerical personnel prefer to be called by their first names, as does the nursing staff."

"Sounds familiar. That's how we operated at Saginaw. I presume staff and inmates are required to wear their identification badges at all times?"

"That's right. Speaking of ID badges, here's where you get yours." Kitt led him into a large office.

"Good morning, Lieutenant," she said to a tall, handsome, blond-haired man. "I'd like you to meet Dr. McGuire. He'll be supervising the mental health wing until Dr. Mease gets here. Will you please make Dr. McGuire an ID?"

"Sure will. Nice to meet you, Dr. McGuire. Follow me."

The lieutenant and Charles disappeared into a small room. Kitt walked over to the secretary. "How's it going?" she asked.

"Busy, as usual," the friendly woman answered. "We have six or seven investigations going. The good news is we never get bored around here."

"If you need any help getting interview tapes transcribed, let Mary know. She can usually find someone who can help out," Kitt said.

"Thanks, Warden. I appreciate your offer."

A few minutes later, Charles returned, his ID badge in hand. "Thanks, Lieutenant. Where to now, Warden?"

"Next stop is Captain Mahoney's office. Don't be surprised if he gives you the third degree. The captain is not what you'd call a touchy feely sort of guy. He's more inclined to tear your head off. That said, he's as good a captain as you'll find anywhere in terms of security issues. All things considered, I'd rather have a captain focusing on the safety of staff and inmates than one trying to be a crowd pleaser."

Kitt needed to remind herself how much she relied on

Mahoney to keep things running smoothly inside the prison. "He'll tell you to read our policies and procedures manual. Remind me to get a copy for you when I go back to my office. You can pick it up on your way out this afternoon."

"Here we are." She hesitated, then rapped loudly on the closed door.

"Come in," Mahoney bellowed.

"Hope we're not interrupting you."

The captain stood up. "No problem. I'm always being interrupted. I presume this is Dr. McGuire."

"And you must be Captain Mahoney," Charles responded, looking up at the large, red haired man with no neck. The captain's head appeared to sit directly on top of his shoulders. He reminded Sean of a cartoon character.

"That's what it says on my door," came the captain's rude response.

Sean felt the urge to punch the guy. Instead, he pasted on a smile and said, "It's nice to meet you, Captain. Warden Logan has spoken very highly of you. I know from my past experience working in a prison how critical your job is. Everyone depends on you to keep things running smoothly. Our lives are in your hands, so to speak. That's a huge responsibility."

Captain Mahoney's already large head appeared to swell ever so slightly. "I'm glad you understand my job."

"Warden Logan is going to give me a copy of the policies and procedures manual this afternoon. I'm anxious to start reading it so I can better understand how your prison operates. I want to do everything I can to help make your job easier."

Kitt observed the captain's normally sour disposition dissipate. Charles apparently had the uncanny ability to placate Mahoney. Not many people were able to play him like that.

The burly captain lowered his red eyebrows and squinted his eyes. "The mental health wing is very volatile right now, but there will be an emergency squad a couple of minutes away at all times. If there's any hint of trouble, anything that looks at all suspicious, call security right away. I'd rather have you err on the side of caution than wait and let things get out of control. One more safety valve I want you to remember," he added. "If you ever find yourself in trouble and unable to call security, try to position yourself by a phone, then knock the receiver off the hook. An alarm goes off in the security office anytime a receiver is off the hook for more than thirty seconds and there's no connection. The squad will be sent to your area immediately."

"Thank you, Captain Mahoney. That's a very helpful piece of information. There's no question in my mind that this prison is in excellent hands."

"We've taken enough of your time, Captain Mahoney," Kitt said, "We need to get over to the mental health wing. Dr. McGuire is anxious to get settled in his office."

"Let me know if I can be of any assistance to you," the captain said, "and, by the way, welcome aboard."

"You won him over, Charles," Kitt said after they were out of hearing distance.

"That was my plan," he said with a wink. "On another subject, does the prison have an electric chair?"

"No, we don't. Most of the time we use lethal injection. We do have a gas chamber that gets used occasionally. Inmates who were sentenced to death before 1992 have their choice of death by gas or by lethal injection. Prisoners who received the death penalty after 1992 have no choice. I don't have time to take you over to death row now, but we'll work it in another time if you'd like to see that part of the facility."

"There's no rush. I was just curious."

"You're wearing your identification badge?" she asked, glancing at his lapel. They had arrived at the security bubble. Kitt led him through the metal detector. They waited while the steel door in front of them groaned open.

The female officer inside the bulletproof glass smiled. "Good morning, Warden."

"Good morning. I have Dr. McGuire with me. You'll be seeing him regularly. He's going to be supervising the mental health wing until Dr. Mease gets here."

"Welcome, Dr. McGuire," the officer replied with a big smile.

"My pleasure," he responded.

"The officer inside the next door will search your briefcase," Kitt explained.

"Is that the normal procedure, or are they singling me out because I look suspicious?" he asked with a teasing smile.

"Regular procedure. Purses, lunch buckets, briefcases; everything anyone carries inside gets searched."

"I know. I was just kidding."

The steel door behind them slammed shut with a resounding clang. Another door slowly opened. Two officers stood by a table near the door.

"You'll need to get your hand stamped with iridescent ink or they won't let you back out." Kitt extended her hand toward one of the officers.

"I'd say that's pretty important. Stamp away," he directed the officer.

The second officer looked inside his briefcase. Sean had been smart enough to leave the Bowie knife in his car. After the officer was satisfied everything was in order, the door opened.

Sean Byrnes was back inside a prison. To the right was a holding cell. He had been in a holding cell while he was being processed into prison and again when he was being released.

Sean guessed that the prisoner inside the cell was waiting for his release papers to be signed. As they started past the cell, the prisoner called out, "Hope you don't miss me too much, Warden Logan. I'm getting out this morning."

She walked over to him and shook hands. "I don't want to see you back here, okay? Good luck to you."

"Thanks, Warden," the inmate replied. "You won't see me back here, ever."

"Sadly," she murmured as they walked off, "odds are he *will* be back. Our recidivism rate is high. Guess that's not news to you, is it?"

"Nope. It's the same story everywhere. Very few prisoners who are released are able to make it on the outside." *I, of course, am the exception to the rule.*

To the left was a large cell hall. "When possible, we assign the younger prisoners a cell in here," Kitt said, pausing by the door to the cell hall. She directed his attention to the cell hall on the other side of the large hallway, "Older inmates are housed over there. It's quieter. Not as many disturbances."

Kitt noticed that Charles didn't seem to be intimidated by the inmates passing them in the hallway. When they stared at him, he smiled and greeted them.

"That's the segregation unit over there. Want to take a look inside?"

"Sure," he said agreeably.

She walked over to an intercom on the side of the wall by the door and pushed the button. "It's Warden Logan. I'm going to give Dr. McGuire a quick tour through segregation."

A tall, black lieutenant opened the door.

Inside the cell nearest the lieutenant's desk was a naked inmate in restraints. Blood was dripping from his nose, and his face was swollen.

"What's going on, Lieutenant?" Kitt asked.

"Mr. Hoffman was moved to protective custody yesterday because he is suicidal. This morning he tried to hang himself, so we took his clothes away. About ten minutes ago, he started banging his head against the wall. We got to him as fast as we could, but he bloodied himself up before we could get him in restraints. We'll get him dressed as soon as the squad gets here and take him over to the mental health unit. In the meantime, we're keeping him under constant observation."

"Sounds like you have everything under control. Speaking of the mental health wing, this is Dr. McGuire. He's going to be supervising the wing until the middle of next month."

Charles and the lieutenant shook hands.

"Nice to meet you, Dr. McGuire. Hope you can give Mr. Hoffman some help."

"I'll see what I can do for him," Sean replied pleasantly.

"Sorry about the excitement on your first day," Kitt said, as they left segregation and started towards the mental health unit. "I don't want to scare you off."

"Not to worry. I've seen a lot worse."

Kitt nodded to the security officer stationed at the door of the mental health wing. She introduced Charles to the officer in the bubble. The door opened and they were inside the unit.

A stone-faced lieutenant of American Indian descent was leaning against the wall. He stared as they entered the unit. The dark, penetrating eyes made Sean uneasy; it felt like the man could see right through him. Without breaking eye contact, the officer pushed back from the wall and walked over to them. "Morning, Warden Logan," he said.

"Good morning, Lieutenant Taza," Kitt said warmly. She introduced the two men, then looked back at Charles. "Lieutenant Taza supervises the security staff in this area."

The lieutenant stared at Sean for a moment then, without a smile, simply nodded.

An attractive woman with black hair rounded the corner. She looked at the three gathered in the hallway and walked over to join them. *She has a striking resemblance to that dead movie star – what's her name? – Natalie Wood,* Sean thought.

"Good morning," the nurse said, looking up at the newly hired psychiatrist. The skin around her large brown eyes crinkled into crow's feet when she smiled. "The rumor mill alerted me that you were on you way over."

Kitt could see signs of stress on her face. "Good morning, Nancy. This is Dr. Charles McGuire, your new supervisor," she turned to Charles, "and this is Nancy Mirabal. She's had to manage the wing while we've been without a psychiatrist, and she's done one heck of a job."

"Thanks." Nancy's brown eyes twinkled in response to Kitt's compliment. She looked up at her new supervisor, "You have no idea how relieved I am to have you here. Oh, before I forget; Dr. Reynolds asked me to tell you that he was sorry he couldn't be here this morning. He had an appointment he couldn't cancel."

Kitt explained to Charles that Dr. Reynolds was the prison's medical doctor and that he had been helping out in the mental health unit when he wasn't seeing to the physical health problems of inmates.

Nancy looked at her handsome new supervisor apologetically. "I know this is your first day on the job, but we have an urgent matter. One of our inmates, Mr. Smith, has some serious issues. I put his file on your desk."

Kitt sighed. "Oh, yes, Mr. Smith. He does have some issues that need to be addressed as soon as possible."

"Then, Mr. Smith will be my priority," he assured the two women.

"Dr. Reynolds wants to meet with you to discuss the Smith case tomorrow morning, if that works for you, Dr. McGuire," Nancy said.

"I shouldn't have anything scheduled yet; go ahead and arrange the meeting."

Kitt looked at the clock on the wall. "I need to get back to my office for a meeting. Stop by my office on your way out this afternoon, Dr. McGuire. I'll have the policy and procedures manual ready for you to pick up."

"Will do, Warden," he replied.

Lieutenant Taza had been standing silently watching the proceedings. "If you don't need anything from me, I'll go back to my office," he said.

"Thank you, Lieutenant." Sean was glad to have him leave. Those dark, piercing eyes were starting to get on his nerves.

"Well," he said, turning back to Nancy, "I'm all yours."

"How about we start with a tour?"

"Lead the way."

The inmates in the unit had been peering out through the bars of their cells, straining to hear the conversation. Sean greeted them as he passed by.

"Hey, Doc. I need to get some time with you," one prisoner pleaded.

"As soon as I get settled in," Sean said with a smile.

"Me, too," came another voice. "Be sure to remind him to see me, Nurse Mirabal." The inmate's voice trailed off as they walked past the cell and on down the hallway.

"The people housed in this wing are too mentally ill to be in the general prison population," Nancy said. "You'll be seeing them regularly. There are other inmates in the general population who should be here, but we only have one hundred cells and can't accommodate everyone. We use a screening process to help us prioritize who comes to the mental health wing.

"Besides seeing inmates housed here," she continued, "you'll get requests from inmates in the general population. I'll help you sort through those requests, if you want."

"That would be helpful," Charles said. "When I worked at the Saginaw facility, inmates requested to see me just so they could get out of their work assignments."

Nancy nodded. "I'll do my best to sort things out ahead of time for you. Our screening system isn't foolproof, but it's the best we can come up with. You, of course, have the final say in everything."

"What's up with Lieutenant Taza? He kept staring at me all the while he was in the room with us."

"You'll get used to him. He's an excellent officer, and we're fortunate to have him on our staff. It's hard to recruit American Indians to work in prison, since incarceration tends to be counter to their cultural beliefs. Lieutenant Taza has worked here for over fifteen years. He's committed to a career in corrections because he realizes how important it is for American Indian prisoners to have staff they can relate to while they're incarcerated. Taza's helped to de-escalate several situations that could easily have gotten out of control."

"I'm sure he's a good officer. It's just that I have the feeling he doesn't like me."

"He doesn't have any reason not to like you; you just met for the first time today. Lieutenant Taza is an observer. He seems to have a sixth sense at times; he anticipates what's going to happen. That's one of the things that make him so good at his job."

Has a sixth sense? Sean wondered. He didn't believe in things like extrasensory perception. Yet Taza's eyes seemed to bore right through him.

The yellow concrete walls of the mental health wing had been freshly painted, but they didn't help the dreary surroundings. Nancy led him over to a small commons area where several inmates were seated on a couch watching television.

"Some of the inmates housed in this wing are able to be out of their cells during the day," she explained. "Those who have serious chronic mental health problems or present a risk either to themselves, or to others, are in their cells twenty-three hours a day. They get one hour a day in the yard for exercise. Anytime inmates leave their cells to go to the yard, or to any other location outside the unit, they are escorted by security officers."

The inmates who were watching television turned their attention away from *The Price Is Right* to watch as the two passed by.

"Here is your office," Nancy said, unlocking the door. "Mine is just down the hall."

Sean looked around at the drab office. Nancy must have been reading his thoughts. "A couple of pictures and an artificial plant will help," she suggested. "Real plants don't do well down here. Not enough sunlight. I'll let you settle in before I bring in the prescription refills for your review and signature," she said, handing a piece of paper to him. "Here's my extension. Give me a call when you're ready."

Sean put the briefcase on top of the green metal desk and sat down in the black leather chair. He pulled out each drawer and inspected the contents that had been left by his predecessor. Nothing of value.

The bookcase against the wall was filled with reference books. Sean walked over and pulled out *Serial Murderers and Their Victims*, by Eric W. Hickey. He sat back down at his desk and opened the book to the chapter that profiled Theodore Bundy. After scanning a couple paragraphs, he grew tired of reading and spun around in his chair a few times. He got up, put the book back on the shelf and picked up the Smith file that Nancy had placed on his desk. When he came to the part about the light bulb, he laughed. How stupid could someone be? He closed the file and dialed Nancy's extension.

Moments later, Nancy arrived with a stack of papers in her hand. "These are the prescription refills." She handed them to Charles.

"I'll need your opinion about refilling these prescriptions. You know these inmates and I don't," he said, accepting the pile of papers. "In fact, I'll need to rely on you a lot for the first few days. Even though I have experience working in a prison, not all prisons operate the same way and I'll need time to get to know our patients."

"I'll help you all I can, Dr. McGuire. Right now, the prescription refills are the most urgent matter. I don't have the authority to sign these refills, or I would have done it already."

"Is it your opinion they should all be refilled?"

"Yes, I've gone through them."

Sean pulled open a drawer and took out a pen. With a start, he realized he didn't have a clue what the real Dr. McGuire's signature looked like. Then he remembered that no one in this prison had seen the real signature either. Assuming an air of confidence, he began to scribble a signature on the stack of prescriptions refills.

Having the power to sign prescriptions felt good, and he wanted to consider the potential pay-off of writing up other prescriptions. There were people who would be willing to pay him a lot of money for prescribed drugs. It could be a very lucrative business; but first he'd have to learn a lot more about medications. In the meantime, he would have to rely on Nancy.

He handed the signed stack back to Nancy. "What's next on the agenda?"

"Would you like to begin reviewing some case files?"

Sean nodded.

"Mr. Smith's file is there," she said, pointing to the file on top of his desk. "I'll bring you the files of inmates with the most acute mental illness issues. They'll be the ones you'll want to see first."

"That sounds good. I've already started reading the Smith file but didn't get all the way through it." He glanced at the expensive Rolex watch on his wrist. It was already eleven thirty. "I'm getting hungry. Let's take a lunch break. I'll finish reading Mr. Smith's file after we eat. By the way, where is lunch?"

Nancy, in her excitement about having a supervisor in the unit again, was surprised the morning had gone by so quickly. "I have an extra lunch ticket you can have. I'll treat you to lunch since it's your first day."

Sean followed Nancy down the hall to her office. She took off her white jacket and hung it on a hook behind the door. Nancy's blue and white floral blouse was tucked neatly into her white pants. The jacket had hidden her voluptuous figure. She reached into her desk and took out two lunch tickets. She handed one to him.

"You can buy lunch tickets from the secretary in the Human Resources office. Some people pack lunches and bring them to work, but I don't. It's a hassle since security digs through everything to check for contraband."

She looked up at Charles and smiled. "Let's go eat."

He took the lunch tickets and motioned for Nancy to move through the open doorway. "Beauty before age," he said.

The dining room was swarming with inmates. *Why don't prisons have special accommodations for staff?* Sean wondered. *We should at least be able to get in line ahead of the prisoners.*

The smell of a prison cafeteria nauseated him. Sean had been forced to eat prison food for years, but now that he was a prison psychiatrist, he shouldn't have to eat the same food inmates ate.

Nancy led him through the cafeteria line and over to a table in a small room where a group of staff were eating. As expected, the prisoners stopped eating long enough to give Sean a sullen stare.

Yes, boys, there's a new sheriff in town, he thought, as he confidently returned their hard looks.

11

SEAN PULLED HIS OFFICE DOOR SHUT and walked down the hall to find Nancy. She was in her office.

"I'm calling it a day, Nancy. The warden asked me to stop by her office this afternoon, so I'm going to try and catch her before she leaves."

"Have a nice evening," Nancy replied with a bright smile.

"You, too." He gave her a wink. "See you tomorrow."

Mary was still at her desk when he rounded the corner to Kitt's office. "Dr. McGuire," she said, looking up from her computer screen, "I see you survived your first day on the job."

"Everything went well, but it will take me some time to get acclimated to my new surroundings."

"You'll do just fine. Warden Logan told me you made a good impression on Captain Mahoney. That's fifty percent of the battle."

"Speaking of the warden, she told me to stop by and see her."

"She had to leave for a meeting and won't be back in her office today, but she wants to have coffee with you at eight o'clock tomorrow morning. At eight thirty she'll take you into the morning meeting so she can introduce you to administrative staff."

"I'll be here," he replied. "Did she get me a copy of the policy and procedures manual?" For appearances sake, he would take the manual even though it would be a cold day in hell before he'd ever read it.

"Oh, thanks for reminding me. The manual is over there on the table."

"Looks like an easy read," he said, lifting the large book.

Mary took her purse out of her desk drawer. "If you're ready to leave, you can follow me home."

Together they passed through the prison's series of security doors and out into the glare of the late afternoon. The hot, windy afternoon air felt like a blast furnace. Sean awkwardly pulled off his suit jacket and laid it over the manual he was carrying.

"Where are you parked, Dr. McGuire?"

"In the visitor's parking lot."

"Tomorrow you can park in this lot. It's reserved for staff. That reminds me, I got you a parking sticker." Mary reached into her purse and handed it to him. "Put this in the lower corner of your windshield so security won't tow your car." She stopped by a white Ford Taurus. "I'll give you a lift over to your car."

Mary dropped him off beside a Buick Regal. He threw the briefcase, manual and jacket into the back seat of the car and slid behind the wheel. "Lead the way," he yelled to Mary.

The drive to Mary's house took less than ten minutes. Her house was an adobe rambler. Dark red trim surrounded the arched windows. The yard was peppered with many varieties of cactus, all in bloom. A couple of cactus wrens splashed around in the birdbath.

Mary unlocked the door. "Before I forget, here's your house key, Dr. McGuire."

"Thanks. By the way, call me Charles when we're not at work. I've got a feeling we're going to be very close friends."

Sean walked into the living room. Mary kept a neat house, just like his mother always had. A large red, black and white Navajo rug separated two chairs from the southwestern-style sofa. Indian pottery was displayed on the mantel above the fireplace. He opened the large sliding glass door and stepped out onto the patio.

"Would you like something to drink, Charles? I have ice tea, lemonade and beer." Mary said, sticking her head through the patio doorway."

He thought about asking her if she had anything stronger than beer but decided otherwise. "A beer sounds good."

Mary met him with a Corona when he turned to go back into the living room.

"You have a nice house," he said, casually surveying his new surroundings.

"When my kids were teenagers it seemed a little small, but now that they're gone I have more space than I need."

"That's lucky for me," he said.

"Your bedroom is over there, if you want to take a look. It used to be my son's room." She directed him down the hallway to a closed door.

"Where are your children?"

"After my son graduated from high school, he enlisted in the army. He's stationed in Afghanistan. He'll be home in about six months unless the army extends his duty. I try not to worry about him; Afghanistan is so unstable. The only good thing about his being there is that he's not in Iraq."

"I'm sure he'll be just fine. You say you have other children?"

"My daughter is married and lives in Tucson. She and her husband are expecting a child, so I'll be a grandmother in a few months."

"You don't look old enough to be a grandmother."

"Thanks, that's what you're supposed to say," Mary said beaming. "I turned fifty a couple of months ago."

"Where is your husband?" Sean wasn't the least bit interested in Mary's life, but he wanted to fully understand her situation. He knew he'd be able to use the information.

"My husband and I divorced fifteen years ago. He left Phoenix and moved to Santa Fe. The kids didn't see very much of him after that."

"That's too bad," he said, nodding in mock sympathy. "Why did you decide to work in a prison?"

"About nine years ago, I saw a job advertisement for warden's secretary in the paper. I applied for it and was hired. Wardens come and go, but I've been fortunate enough to stay. I've worked for three different wardens. There now, you know the story of my life."

"I'm interested in your life. We psychiatrists like to know what makes people tick. It's the nature of the job, I guess." He stopped talking momentarily to swallow a big gulp of beer. "The wardens have been fortunate to have someone like you working for them. I'm sure you're very good at your job; besides, your good looks and personality brighten up the work environment."

She blushed. "Thanks."

Sean could tell from Mary's reddened cheeks that it wouldn't be long before she would begin to fall for him. Business as usual, he thought.

He put his empty beer bottle down on the end table beside the couch. "I guess I should bring my things in from the car and get settled in my room."

"While you're doing that, I'll start dinner. Do you like fried chicken?"

"One of my favorite meals."

Mary watched as he took the car keys out of his pocket and walked out to the car to get his luggage. He had a confident stride.

The bedroom was smaller than Sean had expected, but it was definitely larger than a prison cell, and larger than his room at Josie's. He took off his suit and hung it neatly in the closet. Thanks to Dr. McGuire's American Express card, he had been able to buy clothes befitting a psychiatrist. His new shirts were wrinkled from being in the suitcase all day. He made a mental note to mention his wrinkled shirts to Mary. She'd probably volunteer to iron them for him.

Sean was anxious to buy a few more things. Between McGuire's credit cards and some other cash he had gotten his hands on, he could purchase all the things he wanted. He slipped on a red polo shirt and a pair of comfortable jeans. The smell of fried chicken started to come from the kitchen. His stomach growled in response.

"Soup's on," Mary's called.

"It smells a lot better than soup," he said, walking into the kitchen.

Sean looked down at the fried chicken, mashed potatoes and fresh green beans Mary had put on the table. He stood politely while she took off her apron, then he pulled Mary's chair out and gestured that she sit.

While Sean was growing up, his mother had harped at him about being a gentleman. She had watched his every move, always looking for something to criticize. He had resented her constantly telling him things a gentleman should do, but he had come to realize the lessons came in handy.

Before Mary picked up her fork she asked, "Do you mind if I say a prayer thanking God for this meal?"

"Not at all. Please, go ahead." His mother had always insisted on saying a blessing before eating, too. With a little luck, Mary's prayer would be short. Sean was starved.

During dinner, Mary talked about the people he would be working with. She gave him insights into their different personalities and some of their quirks. Even though he was confident about his ability to manipulate people, the information Mary was giving him could be helpful.

"My compliments to the cook," he said, looking down at his clean plate. Mary was a good cook, maybe even better than Josie. Time would tell.

"Would you like another piece of chicken, Charles?"

"No thanks. It was delicious, but I'm stuffed."

"If it's okay with you, we'll let our stomachs settle and have dessert later."

"All this and dessert, too?"

Mary laughed. She got up and carried the dirty dishes over to the sink. "The remote control is on the coffee table if you want to watch television while I clean up the kitchen."

Moving to the couch, Sean began flipping through the channels and then finally settled on the classic western movie *Shane*. The noise Mary was making in the kitchen was distracting. He wanted to tell her to keep it down, but he opted for turning up the sound instead.

After Mary finished in the kitchen, she joined him in the living room. "I love this movie," she said. "I've seen it many times."

He was concentrating on the movie and didn't answer.

After the movie was over, Mary asked, "Would you like dessert now?"

"Sure," Sean answered, realizing he was hungry again.

A few minutes later she handed him blueberry pie with ice cream. He ate his dessert, then abruptly announced he was going to bed.

Even though the bed was comfortable, Sean had trouble falling asleep. It wasn't because he was worried about his new job; being a psychiatrist was going to be easy. Maybe it was his new living arrangement. Josie had been a pushover. She quickly worshipped him and would do anything he told her to. That is, up until their last night together. He figured Mary to be more of a women's libber. She was a single mom and a career woman. She was definitely more independent than Josie had been. He might have to work a little harder to win her over.

Earlier in the evening, Mary had asked him about his family. He told her the same lie his mother had told him for years, that his father had been killed in the Korean War when he was a year old. The only other information he volunteered was that he had been an only child, he had grown up in Michigan and that his mother was dead.

Sean had always resented being an only child, given the way his mother watched his every move. She never showed him any affection and often whipped him with a belt until he had welts. He had learned early on to become a convincing liar to avoid his mother's wrath.

It was her fault he had started stealing. She refused to buy him the toys he wanted. One day his mother caught him playing with a toy truck and demanded to know where it had come from. He said one of his friends had given it to him. Knowing he had no friends, his mother called him a liar and slapped him across the face. Then, she forced him to suck on a bar of soap until he threw up.

The truth was, Sean had taken the truck from a neighbor's kid and threatened to beat up the boy if he told anyone. He soon realized he would have to hide the toys he took and only play with them when his mother wasn't around.

Some toys he shoplifted from stores. The clerks never suspected he was stealing because he was so polite to them. Then one day he was caught in the act. At the time, he was only eleven years old and so he wasn't charged. The police took him home and told his mother what had happened. She gave him a vicious whipping and sent him to bed without dinner.

When Sean was fourteen, he had killed and then dissected the neighbor's cat. The cat had hissed at him when he picked it up, so he punished the animal by swinging it around by its tail. In an effort to defend itself, the cat scratched Sean's arm, drawing blood. Furious, he took the cat behind the garage and wrung its neck. Afterwards he decided to cut it open and see what was inside.

Jimmy, the little neighbor kid whose family owned the cat, stumbled upon the grisly scene while Sean was massaging the cat's heart. He wanted to see if he could get it to beat again. Sean quickly placed his body between the cat and the boy. "Jimmy," he had said, "turn around and don't look. Your cat got run over by a car. I tried to get its heart started again but it didn't work. Your cat is dead. Go get the shovel out of my garage. We'll bury him back here behind the garage."

Jimmy began sobbing, but he ran to the garage to get the shovel. To shut him up, Sean said they would have a funeral for the cat. Sean washed his bloody hands with the garden hose, then began the service. It went well. Sean had attended a couple of funerals with his mother. He pretty much knew what to say, like, "Ashes to ashes and dust to dust." Sean concluded the funeral by telling Jimmy to say the Lord's Prayer with him.

After the service Sean said, "Let's go tell your mother what happened. You tell her the cat got run over by a car, and that I helped you bury him. I'll tell her about the funeral."

Jimmy's mother had been very impressed with the sensitive way Sean had handled the death of the cat. She was especially grateful he had been the one to scrape the cat off the pavement and bury it. When he told her about the funeral, Jimmy's mother hugged him then phoned his mother and told her what a thoughtful child Sean was.

Sean graduated from high school in spite of his truancy and minor troubles with the law. When he was a senior in high school, his mother had allowed him to take a driver's education class. After Sean finished the class, he had stolen a car so he could put his newly acquired skills to the test. A couple hours later he left the car on a quiet street near his home. They never caught him.

While Sean was growing up, his mother worked as a secretary at Saginaw Valley State University. For eighteen years she put fifty dollars from each paycheck into a savings account for his college education. He'd tried in vain to persuade her to give him the money so he could buy a car when he graduated from high school. Sean told her he wasn't ready for college. He said it would be better for him to work for a year or two before enrolling in college but, as usual, she wouldn't listen to him.

To get his mother off his back, Sean finally agreed to apply for admittance to Saginaw State. He was accepted in spite of his low grade point average. The dean of the college most likely admitted him as a favor to his mother, a thank you for her years of dedicated service to the institution.

It wasn't long into his freshman year before Sean decided his professors were ignorant and unreasonable. He dropped out and asked his mother for the money that remained in his college education account. His mother again refused to give it to him. She said that if he wasn't going back to college, he had to get a job and start paying her rent.

The job at the movie theater had been fun for a while. He'd been able to see all the new movies, but the pay wasn't enough and he soon quit.

He waited tables in a nice restaurant for a few months. The tips were very good and the patrons seemed to like him. The down side of the job was he had to work with the cooks. They always criticized the way he wrote up the orders. One day, the owner of the restaurant realized Sean was not charging some of his best tipping customers for their drinks. Sean then lost his job.

Sean's favorite job had been when he was a lifeguard at the municipal swimming pool. He was a good swimmer and had easily passed his lifeguard certification test. That was a great summer. Pretty girls flirted with him because he was the best looking lifeguard at the pool. They bought him Coke and candy from the vending machines and invited him to go out on dates, their treat. He hated it when summer ended and the pool closed.

For several years he bummed around, taking and losing job after job. His mother would threaten to throw him out when he lost a job but would always relent and let him stay if he promised to get another one.

Sean's first steady girlfriend had been Debra. He was twenty-six and she twenty-one when they started dating. Debra was different from his other girlfriends; she understood him. When he lost a job, she didn't care. She made enough money to support them both. A couple of months after they started dating, Debra invited him to move into her apartment. He was grateful for the opportunity to get out from under the watchful eye of his nagging mother. The constant criticism had become unbearable.

The down side of moving in with Debra was that he had no interest in having an intimate relationship with her. If he wanted sex, he preferred to get it from strangers, prostitutes. Afraid that he might jeopardize the living arrangement by being honest, Sean decided his best strategy would be to stall. He told Debra that since they had only been dating for a couple of months, he didn't feel that they should sleep together until they got to know each other better. He went on to say that having sex too early in a relationship could ruin its potential for success. Although disappointed, Debra reluctantly agreed.

Within a couple of days, Sean began to feel tied down. He mentioned to Debra that he wanted a car. She suggested he buy a used car and gave him five hundred dollars for a down payment. Even though he would have preferred a new car, he decided he would have to settle for a used one for the time being.

He finally settled on a 1989 Chevy he found at a used car dealership two blocks from Debra's apartment. The sticker price was three thousand five hundred dollars.

Sean was prepared to bargain. "I'll give you two thousand dollars for the car, with a five hundred dollar cash down payment. I'll finance the rest."

The salesman recognized Sean. He remembered the neighborhood bully who had beaten his son up because his son would not give him his lunch money. There was no way the salesman was going to bargain with the thug standing before him.

The salesman replied, "The price is three thousand five hundred dollars. If you can pay the sticker price, we have a deal."

It wasn't the response Sean expected. He tried once more. "Okay, I'll give you two thousand five hundred and five hundred dollars down."

"Face facts, Sean, you can't afford this car and you can't bully me into selling it to you for less than the sticker price."

Sean had been furious. How did this asshole know what he could afford, and what right did he have to refuse him? He gave the salesman a hard shove. The man lost his balance and fell over backward, cracking his head on the sidewalk. Sean, taking advantage of the salesman's vulnerable position, jumped on top of him and continued his assault.

After a few blows, a pool of blood gathered under the salesman's head and he lost consciousness.

"Call the police," a passerby screamed.

Sean scrambled to his feet and started running. His clean yellow shirt was soiled with the blood of the man he had just killed.

Moments later, several squad cars, with sirens howling, were bearing down on him. Two officers got out and took chase. One slammed Sean to the ground and handcuffed him on the lawn in front of Debra's apartment.

Sean pleaded not guilty. As he expected, his mother refused to give him money for a lawyer. Debra didn't have enough money to hire an attorney for him, so the judge appointed a public defender to represent him. The jury found him guilty. Sean had been on probation when he killed the salesman so they gave him the maximum sentence allowed by law.

Three years prior to killing the salesman, Sean had gone door to door in a retirement community telling people he was a former private detective who had become a security consultant. He offered to do free home security checks. During his presentations, he flashed a phony badge to make his scam look more authentic.

After Sean completed a security check, he would recommend the installation of a security system. He'd then tell his victims they could purchase systems for a mere four hundred dollars; two hundred dollars to be paid in advance, and two hundred after units were installed. Sean used a brochure he had picked up at a security control equipment store to show how the system worked. Most people were persuaded to buy the product, and they happily wrote out a check for the down payment.

Sean would tell his customers he had a backlog of orders and it could be three to four weeks before the systems could be installed. He'd sold twenty units.

It was Sean's plan to milk the scam for a month, then leave town; however, the son of one of his victims became suspicious and called the police. Without really thinking, Sean had used his real name and deposited the money in his checking account. It had been easy to track him down.

During his trial, the victims he had bilked begged the court to keep him out of prison so he could pay them restitution. The court agreed. He did a month in jail and then went on probation and was ordered to get a job.

Sean's mother had been horrified when she learned what he had done, but she allowed him to move back in with her. She did everything she could to make his life as miserable as possible, though. She called his probation officer regularly to make sure her son was making his restitution payments. The probation officer assured her that he was.

Sean lied to his mother and probation officer about having a job. He had found a fence willing to give him fair prices for hot goods. Because his probation officer was overloaded with case files, he hadn't had time to verify Sean's employer. All the probation officer knew was that the restitution payments were being made. What he didn't know was that Sean's income was coming from the pockets he picked and the merchandise he stole.

Debra hadn't known Sean was on probation when she invited him to move in with her. After the killing, the truth came out. She had been very upset, but Sean had finally been able to sweet talk Debra into coming to visit him in prison.

The first year Debra visited Sean every Sunday, but she began to tire of the trips. In spite of Sean's objections, her visits dwindled to once a month. When she discovered he wouldn't be getting out of prison until he served his full sentence, she stopped coming to see him altogether.

Sean's mother visited him occasionally, but she always rubbed it in about how she no longer had any friends as a result of his criminal behavior. She said people on the street whispered when they saw her coming and ducked into doorways to avoid her. On her last visit to the prison, she told him she was moving to Tucson, Arizona, because she could no longer tolerate the cold winters. When he pleaded with her to stay so he would have visits, she had said, "Maybe this will teach you to stay out of trouble."

The years in prison had passed slowly. When Sean came up for parole, he was sure he'd be released early since he had been a model inmate with very few incident reports. But in spite of his exemplary record, Dr. McGuire had testified he shouldn't be released until his sentence expired.

He smiled when he thought of McGuire. It had been easy for Sean to settle the score with him. After he was released from prison, he looked up the address of Dr. McGuire's mental health clinic in the phone book. He had waited in the café across the street from the clinic and watched for McGuire to leave. The flirtatious waitress didn't seem to mind that he sat at a table by a window for over three hours. She kept filling his cup with coffee. He knew the psychiatrist was in his office that afternoon; he had made an anonymous call to make sure. Sean had waited until five minutes to seven. Since Sean hadn't seen him leave, he decided it was time to check and see if he was in.

He had paid for his coffee and walked across the street to the office building. The sign indicated Dr. McGuire's office was on the first floor and down the hall near the exit to the parking lot.

Sean had reached inside his jacket and felt the bulge on his right hip. The knife was secure in the leather sheath. Knowing what he wanted to do, he started down the hallway toward Dr. McGuire's office, without hesitation.

And now, Sean thought, *I'm all cozy in my nice warm bed and McGuire is lying frozen in the trunk of his car; a shrink on ice.* He chuckled at the thought and drifted off to sleep.

12

SEAN QUICKLY SHOWERED, SHAVED and got dressed. The smells coming from the kitchen were making him hungry.

When he emerged from the bedroom, he saw Mary standing over the stove. She was humming softly as she cooked. "Damn it," she cursed. Some bacon grease had spattered out of the frying pan and landed on her arm.

"I'm shocked at your language," Sean said, coming up behind her.

His presence startled Mary, and she let out a gasp. She had lived alone for so many years, having a boarder was going to take some getting used to. Mary turned around and smiled. "I get pretty vulgar when I'm frying bacon. How did you sleep?"

"Best night's sleep I've had in a long time. What's for breakfast besides the damn bacon?"

"An omelet. Guess I should have asked if you like eggs?"

"Sure do. In fact, I'm so hungry I could eat a horse."

"People around these parts don't take kindly to having their horses eaten," Mary teased.

"In that case, I'll settle for the omelet. I don't want to upset the neighborhood."

"You look beautiful today," he said, giving her platinum hair a gentle tug. "Is this your natural color?"

"I'm blond, but I get a little help to lighten it up."

"Mine is starting to lighten up without any help." Sean laughed at his wit.

"Don't ever get rid of the gray; it's a nice contrast to your black hair. The gray makes you look very distinguished."

"Does it really?" he asked, catching a glimpse of his reflection in the door of the microwave.

After they finished breakfast, Mary rinsed off the dishes and put them in the dishwasher. "If you want to ride to work with me, you're welcome to." She took off her apron and hung it on a hook inside the pantry door.

"Thanks, but I'd better drive in case I have to work late. Is there a gas station on the way to the prison? My tank is empty."

"There's one a few blocks from the prison. If you follow me, I'll show you where it is."

Sean waved Mary on as he pulled into the gas station. Hopefully, it would have an automated teller machine. He needed to withdraw some cash.

The ATM card reminded him of the last time he and his mother had been together. After Sean killed Dr. McGuire, he had gone to the Greyhound bus depot in Saginaw and purchased a ticket for Tucson. Even though he had no real desire to see his mother, she was the only person who had stayed in contact with him during his last few years in prison. Sean needed to get out of Michigan and didn't know where else to go.

When Sean arrived in Tucson, he called his mother from the bus station. It had been a shock to Loraine Byrnes to learn her son was in Arizona. She knew he had been released from prison but assumed he would be staying in Saginaw. After his call, Loraine drove to the bus depot to pick him up. She decided to take Sean out to dinner that night. On the way to the restaurant, they had stopped to get money at an ATM. Sean watched closely as his mother withdrew her money. He noticed his mother's personal identification number was the year of her birth, 1935. When Loraine realized Sean was looking over her shoulder, she directed him to step away and quit snooping.

After he had been with his mother for a couple of days, Sean asked to borrow her car to run a few errands. In fact, he planned to go to Mexico and had no intention of returning. He had no guilty feelings about not returning the vehicle because his mother owed him a car. She should have bought him one when he graduated from high school.

Instead of letting him take her car to run a few errands, she had said, "If you want a car, get a job and buy one yourself. Besides, you don't even have a driver's license."

Her refusal had made him so angry he played the father card for the first time in his life. He glared at her. "I really paid the price growing up without a father. My father would have seen things more my way than you ever did. If he were still alive, I'm sure he'd let me use the car."

Then, after years of lying, Sean's mother told him the truth about his father. "Oh he would, would he? I guess you're old enough to hear the truth about your father. He didn't die in the Korean War. We'd been married less than six months when I discovered I was pregnant. Instead of being happy with the news, he told me he didn't want to have children and ordered me to get an abortion. In those days, abortions were illegal."

Her bottom lip quivered as she paused a moment to regain her composure. "After I told him I was going to have my baby, he left town, and I never heard from him again. Your father never gave me so much as a penny to help raise you. That's who your father really was. He was a loser, and you're no more than a chip off the old block, his block that is."

Sean had been stunned. His mother had lied to him all these years, and now she was calling him a loser.

The fight that followed had gotten out of hand. He called his mother a lying bitch. She slapped him across the face like she had done so many times when he was a child. All the fury he felt towards her erupted. He had grabbed her around the neck, and she had kicked him in the shin. Sean tightened his grip around her throat until he felt a bone snap. When he released her, she fell limply to the floor. He hadn't planned to kill his mother, but she'd started the fight and he'd been forced to finish it.

That night, Sean took his mother's body out to the garage and stuffed it into the trunk of her Buick Regal. For the next couple of hours, he dug through her personal belongings. He'd found his birth certificate and the title to her car in the file cabinet.

His mother had kept good financial records. The thousands of dollars she had put aside for his college education were still listed in her ledger as a future expenditure she expected to pay out. *She must have put every penny she hadn't needed for necessities into her savings account*, he thought. Now that Sean had his mother's ATM card, he could access the large amounts of money in her checking account and maybe even her savings. For the first time in his life, he appreciated his mother's ability to manage her money.

The morning following the deadly fight, Sean went next door and introduced himself to his mother's neighbor. He told her he was taking his mother to Mexico for an extended vacation. The neighbor had said what a nice son he was and agreed to take in the mail and look after things while Sean and his mother were gone.

He was about thirty miles from the border when it struck him that the border patrol might decide to check the trunk of the car. He turned off the interstate and onto a narrow, paved road going west. An hour later he came to the small, isolated town of Empalme. It was late in the afternoon, and he was thirsty. The little town cantina looked inviting. He decided to stop and have a few drinks. After dark, he'd figure out a way to dispose of his mother's body.

Only one other patron had been in the cantina that day, a woman named Josie. He took the stool beside her. She had asked him what he was doing in Empalme. On the spur of the moment, he had decided to assume Dr. McGuire's identity. He told Josie that he was a psychiatrist on leave from his mental health clinic and that he was looking for a quiet place to do research. Josie, who waited tables at the café across the street from the cantina, had suggested he stay in Empalme.

Sean was in no particular hurry to get to Mexico because it was highly unlikely Dr. McGuire's body would be found, at least not in the foreseeable future. He decided it might be interesting to hang out in Empalme for a week or two and pretend to be a psychiatrist.

When Sean asked Josie if she knew of a place where he could stay, her answer came as no surprise. She offered to give him room and board for three hundred dollars a month. Sean doubted he'd ever have to pay her.

Josie wasn't a pretty woman, but he knew she was easy and could be used. Unlike his mother, she seemed to appreciate him, which was one thing in her favor.

After Josie had gone to bed that night, Sean slipped out of the house and drove to the small cemetery he had noticed when he came into town earlier in the day. Even though he was still angry with his mother and felt she had deserved what she got, Sean did not feel right about dumping her body in the middle of the desert. He opened the gate and slowly drove down the narrow, dirt path to the far end of the cemetery.

The moon was full that night as he stood surveying his surroundings. Most of the graves had stones piled on top of them. Sean rubbed his chin; the setup was perfect. Instead of digging a new grave, he would remove the stones from one of the graves, put his mother there and cover her back up.

He selected a spot in the far corner by the fence. Removing the stones was harder work than Sean had anticipated. He stopped to have a cigarette. After one last drag, he dropped the cigarette butt to the ground and continued clearing the stones off the top of the grave. He retrieved his mother's body from the trunk of the car and put her down on the gravelly ground. Her normally well-coiffed hair had fallen over her closed eyes. He smoothed it back, away from her face. Too bad she couldn't appreciate all the fuss he was making. He lit another cigarette. If it hadn't been so late, he would have conducted some kind of service, but he needed to get back to Josie's before she discovered he was gone. He dropped a second cigarette butt to the ground, and piled the stones on top of his mother's body. To make sure she was totally covered, he took some additional stones off a nearby grave.

When Sean had disposed of his mother's body, he thought that would be the end of it. He had no way of knowing coyotes would smell her body and dig it up and that Warden Logan would make the gruesome discovery.

The good news was that no one in Empalme would ever think the reputable Dr. McGuire was a murderer.

Sean topped off the tank, walked briskly inside the station and paid for the gas. He wanted to be on time for his eight o'clock meeting with Kitt.

As he drove toward the prison, he thought about how proud his mother would have been to know he had a job as a prison psychiatrist.

13

MARY'S FACE BRIGHTENED WHEN SHE SAW Charles approaching her desk. "Hi. I picked you up some lunch tickets." She handed the tickets to him and nodded toward Kitt's office. "She's ready for you."

"Thanks, Mary. I'll catch you later with the money." He tapped on the open door and entered the warden's office.

"Good morning," Kitt said, looking up. "Sorry I missed you yesterday afternoon, but I had to leave for a Pardon Board meeting in Phoenix."

"No problem. By the way, Dr. Reynolds and I will be meeting later this morning to discuss the Smith case."

"Good." Kitt poured a cup of coffee and handed it to him. "How did your first day go?"

"Great. I didn't realize how much I missed the hands-on piece of psychiatry until yesterday. Maybe I'll forget the research altogether and go back to my practice when I'm done here." Sean was amazed at how well his responses flowed. It was almost like he really was Dr. McGuire.

Kitt glanced at the clock on the wall. "It's eight thirty. We had better get over to the morning meeting. I'm a stickler for everyone being there on time. It wouldn't look good if we're late."

"Will you want me to come to the morning meetings every day?"

"Only if a specific problem arises or we're debating a policy change that affects your area."

That was a little deflating, Sean thought. If Kitt knew how

much he could help her understand inmates and their behaviors, she'd want him in every meeting.

Captain Mahoney nodded when they entered the room. The chatter stopped, and all eyes were on Dr. McGuire. He took a seat next to the warden.

Kitt looked around the table and mentally took attendance. "For those of you who haven't met him already, this is Dr. Charles McGuire."

The staff responded with smiles and hellos. "We'll start with introductions," Kitt said, looking first at Captain Mahoney.

"We've already met," was his gruff response. "Move on to Dale."

Sean thought Mahoney could have said something about how nice it had been to meet him yesterday, but then what could you expect from a pompous ass?

"I'm Dale Whipple, the deputy warden," said the soft-spoken man beside the captain. "I supervise the assistant wardens of administration and operations and assume the warden's responsibilities when she is gone."

Sean studied the thin man with glasses who was introducing himself as Dale Whipple. *A classic example of a nerd*, he thought, biting his cheeks to stifle a smile.

Most of the people in the room were wearing glasses. Maybe he should buy a pair with clear glass lenses. It might make him look more like a prison psychiatrist.

After the introductions were completed, Kitt turned to him. "I gave your credentials to everyone last week when I told them you were coming. The floor is yours if there's anything you want to say."

Sean cleared his throat. "I'm happy I can be here to help out, and I look forward to working with all of you." Not knowing what else to say, he stopped.

After making certain that this was going to be the extent of his comments, Kitt said, "You're welcome to stay for the rest of the meeting if you'd like, Dr. McGuire. It might give you a flavor of some of the things we're dealing with."

"That would be helpful." He clicked the ballpoint pen he was holding a couple of times.

Kitt turned her attention to the captain. "I understand we had an incident yesterday. What happened?"

"A fight erupted between two gangs, the Bikers and the Bloods," the captain responded. "It started out in the yard late yesterday afternoon but we were able to de-escalate the thing before it got out of control. The inmates didn't realize the K9 unit was on the other side of the yard. Within seconds, the unit was on the scene. When the inmates saw the dog, they scattered like roaches when the lights go on. We're still interviewing a couple of snitches to find out how the thing got started. I ordered a lockdown of the prison until we sort it all out and make sure there is nothing else going on."

"Sounds like everything is under control," Kitt said, as she put on her reading glasses and glanced down at the next item on her agenda.

She looked back up. "As you all know, last session the legislature mandated we have to be smoke-free by June. Going smoke-free will, in the long run, lower our health care costs, but it's not going to be an easy sell to either staff or inmates. Many of our staff are as upset as the inmates about the new mandate. There's a chance some will quit their jobs over this. Do we have any statistics on how many of our staff smoke?" Kitt asked. She looked over at the director of Human Resources.

"I don't have the exact number, but I'll venture a guess that it's about half. I'll follow up with accurate numbers for you," she replied.

"I'd also like to know how many staff have taken the smoking cessation classes we've been offering."

"Training should have that information," Dale said. "I'll check with them."

"How about the inmates? Are they attending the classes?" she asked Dale.

"Some have, but most are opting for nicotine patches."

Captain Mahoney interrupted the dialog between Kitt and her deputy. "I'm hearing that a few of our regular troublemakers are trying to use the smoking ban as a reason to agitate. I've decided to stage a mock riot so we can practice our Incident Management System. The sheriff's office, fire department, local police department and the state patrol will be participating in the drill. When the inmates see the multi-agency response to the staged incident, it might be enough to put the kibosh on any thoughts they're having about a riot."

"That's a good idea," Kitt said. "Will we have advance notice?"
"No. We need to be prepared to manage a riot anytime, day or night. And one more thing; I'd like to purchase another dog for the K9 unit before the smoking ban goes into effect. Every dog is worth several officers when it comes to managing incidents. We have a number of officers who have been trained to handle dogs, so it wouldn't take long to get the dog and officer working together."

"Go ahead and get another dog," Kitt concurred. "Anything else . . . anyone?" The only sound in the room was the clicking of Sean's ballpoint pen. She took off her glasses and looked around the table at her managers. "If not, see you tomorrow morning."

Finally, thought Sean. The discussion about a riot was interesting, but the rest of it was boring. He wanted to get back to his office and make a decision about the pervert who had stuck a light bulb up his ass.

14

NANCY LOOKED UP AND SMILED when she saw Dr. McGuire standing in her doorway.

"How did the morning meeting go?" she asked.

"Very well."

"Dr. Reynolds told me to call him when you got back to your office. He said he'd come right over."

"Before you call him, I'm interested in hearing what you think we should do with Mr. Smith, Nancy. Should we post a guard outside his cell to make sure he doesn't try to put things where the sun don't shine?"

Nancy laughed. "A psychiatrist with a sense of humor; I like that. Most of the psychiatrists I've worked with have been so serious."

Sean wasn't sure what it was she found so humorous. He'd been serious about posting a guard outside Smith's cell. Maybe she was laughing about his reference to the rectum as a place where the sun didn't shine. It *was* pretty funny, so he laughed along with her.

"All kidding aside, what would you recommend we do with Mr. Smith?" he asked.

Nancy wondered why he was so interested in what she thought about Smith's case. Maybe he was testing her. "We're not equipped to handle Mr. Smith here," she said. "There's no question he needs intensive therapy, the kind he would get at the state hospital. If it were up to me, I'd try to get him transferred to the State Security Hospital."

Nancy noted that Dr. McGuire seemed to be sincerely interested in what she was saying, like he was weighing her every word. "Transfers," she continued confidently, "can be a major hassle, but if Warden Logan calls the hospital administrator, the two of them might be able to agree on an inter-agency transfer. Otherwise, it's a long, drawn-out process. Getting Mr. Smith out of here would free you up to spend more time with other inmates who need your help."

"That's exactly what I expected you'd say. Your experience is showing through. Now go ahead and call Dr. Reynolds. Tell him I'm back and ready to meet with him."

A few minutes later Reynolds poked his head in Nancy's office, "Where are we meeting?" He noticed the newly employed psychiatrist standing off to the side. "Oh, I didn't see you. Excuse me for not introducing myself. I'm John Reynolds. I presume you are Dr. McGuire."

"You presume right," Sean said, shaking the extended hand.

"The small conference room is open if you'd like to meet there," Nancy offered.

The two men exchanged pleasantries while they walked over to the room.

"Well, let's see what we can do for Mr. Smith." Sean took a seat at the head of the table.

"I know this is only your second day on the job, but have you had a chance to read his file?" Reynolds asked.

"Yes. I reviewed it yesterday. In my opinion, Mr. Smith needs intensive treatment, but I won't have the time to give it to him. There are too many other inmates who need my help. I think we should try to get an inter-agency agreement and send him to the state hospital." He quoted Nancy almost word for word.

Dr. Reynolds nodded. "That's the same conclusion I reached."

"I'll talk to the warden later today and see if she will make a call to the hospital administrator. That should help speed things along," Sean said confidently.

"Good. I'll scratch the Smith case off my list. Unless there's something else, I'll take my leave."

"It's been a pleasure doing business with you," Sean quipped.

After Reynolds left, Sean walked back to Nancy's office and told her that Reynolds had agreed with the decision to transfer Mr. Smith to the state hospital. The nurse replied that she had expected he would.

"I need to get a few minutes with the warden to let her know what we've decided. Give Mary a call and see if she can arrange it." Nancy left the room to make the call. Sean liked the idea of having someone to do his bidding. Usually he was the one getting bossed around. Now he was the one doing the bossing. It felt good.

Nancy was back with a report a few minutes later. "Mary scheduled you for one fifteen."

"Thank you."

Time passed slowly for Sean. He was having trouble finding things to do. After practicing his new signature for a while, he tore the paper into tiny pieces and tossed it in the trash. Sean glanced at his watch. It was eleven fifteen. Maybe Nancy would want to take an early lunch. He stood up, stretched his back, and walked over to her office.

"I'm hungry, are you?" Sean asked Nancy.

"You go ahead. I need to prioritize the list of inmates who have requested to see you so you can begin meeting with them tomorrow."

Sean had no interest in going to the lunchroom without Nancy. He didn't like eating alone. "You shouldn't work during your lunch time. In our kind of work, it's important to take a break from the stress. Besides that, I like your company. Come to lunch with me and then, after my meeting with the warden, we'll go over the inmate requests together."

"You don't have to twist my arm," Nancy said, clearly delighted that her supervisor said he liked her company. "Did you get some lunch tickets?"

He pulled two tickets out of his pocket. "I certainly did, and today I'm treating you to lunch, just like we're on a date." He observed color creep into Nancy's cheeks. *Another woman who can't resist me*, he thought.

The meeting with Kitt that afternoon went well. She had agreed to call the superintendent at the state hospital. With a little luck, he wouldn't have to worry about Smith putting light bulbs up his rear end any longer. The employees at the state hospital would have that pleasure.

Sean didn't feel like going back to his office. Nancy would be able to prioritize the list of inmates without his involvement. If she couldn't, she had no business working in the mental health wing. He decided to feign a headache and leave.

When he left Kitt's office, he grimaced and put his hand up to his eyes.

"What's wrong?" Mary asked, with concern in her voice. "How did your meeting with the warden go?"

"The meeting went fine," he said, squinting his eyes. "It's just that sometimes I get bad headaches that come on very suddenly."

"Maybe you should go home and rest," Mary suggested.

"That's a good idea. Would you please call Nancy and let her know I won't be back in the office this afternoon? Tell her to work on the list and we'll go over it tomorrow morning. She'll know what list I'm talking about." He squeezed his face into another grimace while he gave Mary her marching orders.

"I have some Extra Strength Tylenol if you want it," Mary offered.

"Thanks, you're a lifesaver." He took two of the red and yellow caplets.

"I have to stay longer today to get a report done, so dinner will be a little late. Hope you don't mind. I'll be home around seven."

"No problem. I'll probably spend most of the afternoon resting. If I'm asleep when you get home, wake me up."

Sean tossed the Tylenol caplets into the trash barrel outside the front door of the prison. It was a hot afternoon, but the air conditioning in his car would cool him down in a hurry.

After Sean arrived at Mary's, he quickly drained a bottle of beer, grabbed a second one, and went into his bedroom to change clothes. He selected a pair of Levi's and a tee shirt.

The house was too quiet, and he wasn't in the mood to stay inside on such a beautiful day. Dr. McGuire's credit cards were burning a hole in his pocket. Assuming the doctor paid his credit card bills before he had planned to leave for California, there should be plenty of money to spend. Florence didn't offer the kind of shopping Sean had in mind, so he decided to drive to Phoenix. He should have time to get there and back before Mary got home. Just to be on the safe side, he left a note on the kitchen table saying he'd gone to Phoenix to see a neurologist about his headache.

Two hours later, Sean pulled into a large shopping mall.

The first store that caught his eye was a trendy optical shop.

The young, attractive clerk walked up to Sean and asked, "May I help you?"

"I'm looking for a pair of sunglasses, really good ones."

"We have a large selection, everything from Foster Grants to Serengettis."

"Show me your Serengettis," Sean directed.

"They're the top of the line," the clerk warned. "A pair of Serengettis runs anywhere between two and three hundred dollars."

"Price is no object," he replied sternly. *How dare she question whether he could afford Serengettis.* When he opened his wallet to pay for them, he made sure she saw the credit cards and large amount of cash he carried.

Sean positioned the new sunglasses on top of his head. He hadn't felt this good in a long time.

The AT&T shop was his next stop. Browsing the store, he picked up a cell phone, even though he had no intention of buying one. Kitt had told him she would get him a cell phone to use while he was working at the prison. Sean had never used a cell phone before and he needed to figure out how they worked.

He studied the cell phone in his hand.

"Are you finding what you need?" the clerk asked.

"I'm just getting an idea of what you have," he said. "Up until now, I have refused to own a cell phone, but my fiancée is putting pressure on me to buy one. She likes to keep tabs on me, if you know what I mean."

"I understand completely." The pleasant, middle-aged man chuckled. "Here, I'll show you how this one works."

After a thorough explanation, Sean thanked the clerk and said he would be back to buy the phone after he finished the rest of his shopping.

A large department store at the end of the long hallway caught his eye. He selected a couple pairs of Bermuda shorts, some polo shirts, three pairs of Levi's and a pair of silk pajamas. On his way out of the store he noticed a black leather jacket displayed on a mannequin. "Has my name on it," he muttered aloud. It would look great with his new pair of black Levi's. The clerk found him a size forty-two. It fit perfectly.

The time was four o'clock. Sean calculated that if he started back for Florence by four thirty he could get his new purchases put away before Mary got home from work.

He passed a jewelry store and noticed a beautiful turquoise belt buckle displayed in the showcase window.

Going in, he asked the clerk to take the belt buckle out of the display case for him to examine. "It's on sale today; twenty percent off," the clerk told him.

"Well, that's a deal I can't refuse. I'll take it."

"Can I interest you in anything else?"

Sean's eyes fell on a pair of turquoise and silver earrings. He'd noticed that Mary liked to wear Indian jewelry. Maybe she'd forget about the rent he was supposed to pay at the end of the week if he bought them for her. "I'll take those earrings, too. Gift wrap them, please."

One last stop, Sean thought as he turned into a music store. The only compact discs his mother had in her car were classical music; Mozart and Beethoven. He'd rather have silence than listen to that crap.

Sean scooped up ten compact discs, whipped out a credit card and paid the woman at the cash register.

It was getting late. He'd have to step on it to get back to Florence before Mary got home. Sean set the cruise control ten miles above the speed limit and pushed the Bee Gees CD into the stereo. It was amazing how he remembered the words to "Stayin' Alive." He cranked up the volume and sang along in his clear tenor voice.

His reverie was interrupted by the scream of a siren. He looked into his rear view mirror and saw a highway patrol squad car, lights flashing, right behind him. It made the skin on the nape of his neck crawl.

Knowing he had no choice, Sean hit the brake and pulled over to the side of the road. The squad car followed him to the shoulder of the road and stopped.

Stay calm; don't panic, he thought, as he rolled down the window and smiled at the state trooper. The officer was in his late fifties. His stomach hung over his belt a bit, and he walked with a swagger. The reflective sunglasses he wore reminded Sean of the stereotypical Southern sheriff.

"I was over the speed limit, Officer, I'm sorry," he said, wishing he could get a read on the officer's eyes. All he saw was his own reflection in the sunglasses. Sean took off his Serengettis, hoping the trooper would do the same. He didn't.

"You were ten miles over, sir," the trooper said, adjusting his sunglasses. "May I see your driver's license?"

Sean's mind was racing. He had destroyed McGuire's driver's license because of the photograph.

He opened Dr. McGuire's wallet and started thumbing through the cards. When he came to the honorable discharge card from the Army, Sean paused to make sure the trooper got a look at it.

"I can't believe it," Sean said, shaking his head in bewilderment. "My license isn't here. I used it when I cashed a check earlier this afternoon in a department store. Either I left it there or I dropped it when I was putting it back in my wallet. I can show you other proof of my identification. I have my social security card and a prison employee identification card with a photograph of me on it."

Without waiting for an answer, Sean handed the trooper his prison ID card. "I'm employed as a psychiatrist at the Florence Prison Complex. Just before you stopped me, I received an urgent page. That's why I was exceeding the speed limit. I don't have my cell phone with me, so I was rushing to get back to the prison to see what's going on."

The officer looked at the photo on the ID and then back at Sean, "I'm going to let you off with a warning this time, but make sure you keep it closer to the speed limit in the future. Be sure and check with that department store to see if anyone found your driver's license. There's a lot of identity theft going on these days. If you don't locate your license, notify the authorities that it's lost. Would you like an escort back to the prison?"

"Thank you, but it isn't necessary. I'm sure Captain Mahoney has everything under control."

"Tell the good captain hello from me. My name's Burke. He and I served in Vietnam together."

"I'll make a point of telling him I met you." *A snowball's chance in hell I'm going to tell the captain I met Burke*, thought Sean, as he pulled back out onto the highway and set the speed control two miles under the limit. Mahoney would wonder under what circumstances he had met Officer Burke. The trooper turned his car around and went in the opposite direction.

The driver's license thing was a problem, and Sean knew he needed to get it figured out. He had to find someone who could make him a fake one. In the meantime, he had to be more careful.

Mary's car wasn't in the carport. After looking to make sure she wasn't on approach, Sean took the packages out of the trunk. He tore up the note he had left on the table and took the new purchases into his bedroom.

After perusing his new clothing, he selected a pair of Bermuda shorts and a light blue polo shirt. When he inspected himself in the mirror, he noticed the color of his shirt matched his eyes. He could see why the women all fell for him.

Sean had a hard time believing that women had fallen for the real doctor McGuire. He hadn't been the least good looking and had looked old for his age. At the time of his death, the psychiatrist had just turned fifty-one years old.

With all the rushing around and stress of being pulled over by a cop, Sean needed a drink. He opened the refrigerator door and took out a beer. Mary's car pulled up in the driveway. He took out a second beer and held it out to her when she came through the door.

"For you," he said, handing her the beer. "How's this for service?"

"Great." Her face brightened into a big smile. "How are you feeling?"

"Much better. The Tylenol kicked in so I had a nice, relaxing afternoon. I'm sure my headache was stress-related. Even though I don't like to admit it, working with mentally ill inmates is stressful. It gets a little overwhelming at times, but don't tell anyone. Psychiatrists aren't supposed to get overwhelmed."

"Having a new job is very stressful in itself," Mary said, "and having the responsibility of working with mentally ill prisoners, well, it's no wonder you had a headache. My advice is to try to leave the work at the prison and come home to relax."

"I know, Mary. I've given that same advice to many people but it's easier said than done. Let's forget about work and practice relaxing."

"Before I do that," Mary said, taking a swallow of her beer, "I'm going to get out of these clothes and into something more comfortable." She put her beer down on the coffee table in the living room and disappeared into her bedroom.

Sean went into his room and finished putting away his new purchases. When he was done, he took the small box containing the earrings off the dresser and walked into the living room.

Mary was sitting on the couch, legs drawn up under her, drinking her beer. She had on a red shirt and white shorts. He noticed a rose tattoo on her ankle.

114

"I have a presentation to make to you."

Mary gave him an inquisitive look.

"You have gone out of your way to help me get settled in my new job, and I want to give you a little token of my appreciation." He handed her the box, which she opened immediately.

"Oh, Charles, they're beautiful, but you certainly didn't need to get me anything."

"I want you to have the earrings. Now try them on."

Mary took off the cheap hoop earrings she was wearing and went over to a mirror. "How do I look?"

"Like they were made for you. I knew that when I bought them."

After one more look, she turned away from the mirror and walked over to him. "Thank you, Charles. I love them."

He leaned down and gave her a light kiss on the cheek. "You're welcome," he said. Then Sean cupped Mary's face in his hands, "I have something very important to ask you."

"What?" she asked hesitantly, but with curiosity.

"When will dinner be ready?"

Sean laughed.

15

MARY TOUCHED THE SIDE OF HER CHEEK where Charles had kissed her the previous night. *What did the kiss mean? Was it kiss of friendship, or was it more than that?* She picked up the small box containing her new earrings and walked into the bathroom. She slid them through the holes in her ears and they dangled halfway down to her shoulders. She turned her head from one side to the other, admiring the intricate Zuni workmanship. A ray of sunshine reflected off the silver and made a flash of light on the wall. They were the most beautiful earrings she had ever owned. She wondered when Charles had bought them. Was it before he started working at the prison? Had he purchased them to give to another woman, or did he pick them out specifically with her in mind? Maybe he bought them after his headache subsided yesterday afternoon, but where?

Mary carefully outlined her lips with bright pink lipstick and smoothed her green, broom-style skirt. She went to the full-length mirror in her bedroom, turned sideways and looked closely at her profile. Many women her age had "baby baskets," but she was fortunate. Childbirth had not given her a big stomach, and she still didn't have one, not yet anyway. She went out into the kitchen.

Charles was seated at the table drinking a glass of orange juice. He looked up and flashed a smile. Oh, those incredible eyes. She could feel the heat of a blush creeping into her face. She hated it when she blushed. It was a dead give-away to what she was thinking.

"Good morning, Mary. Nice earrings."

"Thanks to you."

"I've gotta get going," he said. "I told Kitt I would draft some talking points for her about the Smith case. We're going to try and

116

do an inter-agency transfer with the state hospital, if we can. When you see her, tell her that I'll have everything ready for her later this morning."

"Will do. I'm leaving after I grab a bite of breakfast. Did you find anything to eat?"

"A bowl of cereal and a banana was all I wanted. I don't eat like a horse all the time," he laughed. "Speaking of eating, how about I take us out to dinner tonight? I hate for you to work all day, then come home and have to worry about getting dinner ready."

"You're paying me for room and board, so I expect to cook." She paused then said, "On the other hand, it would be nice to go out to dinner tonight. Can I change my mind?"

"You certainly can. We're going out and that's that. Speaking of paying room and board, are you okay with waiting for the money until I can get to the bank and transfer money from savings to checking?"

"Of course," Mary said, smiling, "I know you're good for it."

He stood up and walked over to where she was standing. Without saying anything, he looked into her eyes, smiled and gave her a hug. His lips brushed the side of her cheek, then he moved past her and out the door.

Mary's heart was pounding. She sat down at the table. What was she getting herself into? She was falling for a guy she barely knew. Mary had always prided herself on moving slowly when it came to relationships with men. Why was Charles different from the others? Was it because he was so handsome and considerate, or because he was so highly respected in the field of psychiatry? It was all of the above, she decided.

Did Charles give kisses and hugs as a show of friendship to other women, she wondered, *or did he consider her special?* Mary had no way of knowing. Even though it had only been a week since Mary first laid eyes on Charles, she found herself thinking about him more than she wanted to. In a few weeks, he would finish his work at the prison. Then what? Kitt mentioned that he had been living with a woman named Josie in Empalme. What was his relationship with Josie? He hadn't mentioned her to Mary. Would he go back to her?

Mary dug her elbows into the table and dropped her head into her palms. "Shut up," she said aloud to stop her mind from racing.

Mary had lost her appetite. She shoved a banana in her purse and left for work.

16

"Morning, Nancy," Sean called out. The nurse was walking down the hall in front of him. She stopped and turned around. "Good morning, Dr. McGuire."

"I hope I didn't leave you in the lurch yesterday afternoon, but I developed a splitting headache. Did Mary call you?"

"Yes, she did. How are you feeling today?" Nancy asked with concern in her voice.

"Much better, thank you. Warden Logan asked that we draft some talking points for her on the Smith case. She needs them before she calls the state hospital to see about the interagency transfer. Will you have time to do that for me this morning? She wants to make the call this afternoon, if possible."

"I'll do it right now," the diligent nurse replied. "By the way, I called our technology supervisor yesterday morning and told him to get your computer installed. It's all set up."

"Thank you for taking care of everything. It's a great comfort to have such a capable person working with me in the unit."

"That's my job." She smiled and turned to go back to her office.

Sean had taken a computer class when he was in prison. He'd learned the basics of word processing, but inmates weren't allowed to go on-line because one of the inmates, a child molester, had been caught using the Web to find child pornography sites. The administration found out, and somehow so did the press. When legislators read about it in the paper, they insisted the prison change their policy so inmates couldn't access the Internet. The change had ruined everything for him and a lot of other inmates who weren't interested in viewing child pornography.

The computer was on his desk. He sat down and looked it over. One of these days he'd have to learn how to send e-mails.

Sean swiveled around in his chair a couple of times. He felt in the mood to start seeing some inmates. After Nancy got through with her assignment, he'd tell her to get some appointments scheduled.

Nancy obviously did a lot of clerical work. That concerned Sean because, when he started seeing mentally ill inmates, he would need her to help him come up with treatment plans. He was betting Nancy would be grateful to be relieved of the clerical work. Kitt had told him several times to let her know if he needed anything. Sean needed a secretary. He decided to ask Kitt for one next time he saw her. *Guess I'll make Nancy's day and share my brainstorm with her.*

He walked down the hall to Nurse Mirabal's office. "I'm going to ask the warden for some secretarial help," he said, entering her office without knocking. "You are a nurse, and you shouldn't have to do all the clerical work for the unit. What do you think?"

She folded her arms and beamed. "You just made my day. I've asked for help several times in the past but, with the fiscal problems due to budget cuts, my small voice was never heard. I could do my job so much better if we had clerical help."

"Say no more. I will ask Warden Logan about it when I see her this afternoon. Do you have the talking points on the Smith case finished yet?"

"I'm almost done. I'll have a draft ready for your review in a few minutes."

"Good. I'll be in my office."

Ten minutes later, the draft was in his hands. Sean glanced at it briefly. "I think you've covered everything. Attach a short memo from me and I'll walk it up to the warden."

He dialed Mary's extension. "Any compliments on the earrings?"

Mary laughed. "Several people have commented on them, but I didn't mention where they came from. The rumor mill around here is unbelievable."

"I understand. I have the stuff ready that the warden wanted. Is she in?"

"If you come over right away, you can catch her."

Sean liked the idea of having immediate access to Kitt. Mary was the gatekeeper, and no one could see the warden without going through her. He knew Mary would do anything she could to accommodate any of his requests. Sean noticed the blush on her face when he had kissed her the night before and again this morning. She was falling in love with him.

"I'm going over to the warden's office, Nancy. When I get back we can talk about which inmates I need to see. I'd like to get started this afternoon."

"I'll have the list ready for you."

Sean shoved the report into his briefcase and started for Kitt's office. When he got there, he leaned down by Mary's ear and whispered, "Hey, beautiful, can I go in?"

She jumped. "Oh, you scared me!"

"Sorry, you were so intent on your work, I couldn't resist sneaking up on you. Now, can I go in?"

"She's waiting."

Half an hour later, he was back in his office. "How'd your meeting go?" Nancy asked.

"Great. She'll let us know how her call goes to the state hospital. Is there anything else you'd like to know about the meeting? For instance . . . something about getting clerical help?"

"Well, I didn't want to seem too pushy."

"Warden Logan said she'd see what she could do. She doesn't have the money to create a new position, but she'll try to reassign someone to our unit. Let's go over that list, and then we can go eat," he said.

Sean stared down at the Salisbury steak, peas and mashed potatoes on his plate. It was typical prison food, generous portions but tasteless. The din of the dining room was getting on his nerves. This would be the last time he would subject himself to eating the same food the prisoners ate. In the future, he'd either go out for lunch, bring something or go without.

Nancy must have been reading his mind. "Not very appetizing, is it?"

"No, it's not." He didn't mention that he wouldn't be dining with her in the future. "Any advice before I see inmates this afternoon?"

"I guess I'd suggest that you start with Mr. Hoffman. You encountered him during your tour with the warden. He was the inmate on suicide watch in segregation."

"The guy who bangs his head against the wall?"

"He's the one. We're keeping him on suicide watch because he's still very agitated. Mr. Hoffman isn't on any medication but probably should be given something to relieve his anxiety. I'll pull his file for you."

"Let's make sure we finish lunch in time so that I can read his file before I see him."

When Sean returned to his office, he got Hoffman's file and began to read. Hoffman's offense was assault and battery related to a drug deal that had gone bad. The inmate had not been diagnosed with a mental illness. *It's up to me to decide what's wrong with him,* he thought with confidence. His guess was Hoffman had fried his brains on drugs.

Sean scanned the titles of the reference books on the shelf beside his desk. *Psychiatric Diagnosis* by Goodwin and Guze sounded like it had potential. He flipped it open and skimmed the chapters. All sorts of disorders were covered: schizophrenia, obsessive-compulsion, manic depression, panic attacks and the antisocial personality. Realizing he could never learn about all the disorders before he saw Hoffman, Sean decided to worry about the diagnosis after he met with the prisoner.

He flipped to chapter twelve; it dealt with how to conduct psychiatric examinations. The authors suggested that the examining psychiatrist exchange friendly greetings at the beginning of the session and then start asking open-ended questions. Sean knew what an open-ended question was. He'd say something like, "Tell me about your childhood."

There were hundreds of drugs for people with mental illnesses. How would he ever decide what to give Hoffman? *I'm putting the cart before the horse,* he realized. *First comes the diagnosis; I'll figure out the medication later.* This job was going to be one of the easiest jobs he'd ever had.

Nancy tapped lightly on his office door. "It's two thirty. Are you ready for Mr. Hoffman?"

"Give me about five minutes." Sean didn't want to seem overly anxious to start the session, even though he was looking forward to conducting his first psychiatric examination.

"Do you want security to bring Mr. Hoffman here or to the conference room where you won't have any interruptions?"

Sean looked up from the book. "I'll see him in the conference room."

The inmate was seated at the table when Sean entered the room. He nodded to the guard. "You are free to go now. Nurse Mirabal will call you when we're done."

He took a seat across from the prisoner. "Mr. Hoffman, I'm Dr. McGuire. Would you like a cup of coffee or a glass of water?"

"No."

Sean took a swallow of his coffee. The inmate could have at least said, "No, thank you." He moved on to his next question, "How are you doing today?" That seemed like a good question, open ended and all.

"Same as every day."

Maybe it wasn't such a good question after all. "So, what can I do for you?"

"I thought you were the one who knew what I needed," mumbled Hoffman.

Sean felt himself immediately become impatient. Here he was trying to help this loser and all he got was a lot of lip. He took a deep breath. If the inmate didn't answer his next open-ended question, he would call the officer and tell him to take Hoffman back to his cell. There were a lot of other inmates who would appreciate his help.

This was definitely going to be his last try. "Why do you keep trying to kill yourself?"

Mr. Hoffman looked surprised and then burst into tears. "The whole world is going to hell in a handbasket, and no one seems to care."

"I care," Sean replied, wondering what in the hell a handbasket was. He shoved the box of Kleenex Nancy kept on the table for such emergencies over to the inmate. *How am I going to get this guy to stop bawling? Maybe I should hypnotize him.* Sean wondered what he could swing back and forth in front of Hoffman's eyes to get him hypnotized. Unexpectedly, the inmate quit crying and blew his nose.

"Can you help me, Dr. McGuire? I haven't slept in weeks."

"I'll do everything I can, but you have to work with me. First, I need to ask you a few specific questions. Don't be distracted; I'll be taking notes," Sean said, remembering the book had suggested the psychiatrist should mention the note-taking to the patient. His eyes searched the room looking for paper and a pen. Seeing none, he lifted the phone and called Nancy. Moments later she appeared with a note pad and a pen.

When she'd closed the door behind her, he said, "I see that you were married, Mr. Hoffman. Tell me about it."

"Well it wasn't much of a marriage. When I was a senior in high school, I got my girlfriend pregnant, so we got married. She said she wanted a divorce two months after the baby was born. I was glad because the kid screamed day and night. The whole experience kind of soured me on the idea of marriage."

"Did you continue to see your child?"

"No. The judge ordered me to pay child support, but I left the state instead."

This shit is just like my father, Sean thought. He stifled his desire to confront Mr. Hoffman, took another deep breath and continued the examination.

"What kind of family did you grow up in? How did you feel about your mother? Did you have any friends?"

Mr. Hoffman looked bewildered with the barrage of questions coming at him. "What should I talk about first?" he asked.

"Start with your family, and we'll take it from there."

"My parents were alcoholics. Dad ran off with a younger woman when I was just a kid. Never saw my old man again. Mom had lots of boyfriends. She called them my uncles. When I was nine, my grandma took me in. She just died a couple weeks ago, and I wasn't even able to go to her funeral. That's why I tried to kill myself. Grandma was the only person who ever cared about what happened to me."

Sean was so involved in taking notes that he didn't realize Mr. Hoffman had stopped talking.

"Oh," he finally said. "That's too bad. If I had been here then, I would have persuaded the warden to let you go. Do you hear voices?" Sean asked abruptly.

"You mean people talking?"

"Damn it," Sean cursed. The pen he was using had run out of ink.

"What?" asked the startled inmate.

"Not you. My damn pen isn't working."

Mr. Hoffman watched, wide-eyed, as his psychiatrist threw the useless pen into the metal wastebasket in the corner.

"Now, where were we?" Sean said.

"Do you want to get another pen?" Hoffman asked.

"No, I'll rely on my memory." *What the hell was my last question? Oh, yeah it was about voices.* "Do you hear voices in your head telling you what to do?"

"I hear people telling me things to do."

"Anything else you want to say?"

"I . . . I guess not," the inmate stuttered.

The doctor closed his note pad. "I don't have any more questions. We're done."

Hoffman slowly stood up, trying to process the sudden end of the session. Because the psychiatrist apparently had no more to say, the inmate decided it must be up to him to give some closure to the session. "Thanks for saying you would have tried to get me to my grandma's funeral. It's nice to know someone around here cares."

"Of course I care about you." Sean was fighting to keep a straight face. "I think this session went very well. I'll review my notes and then decide what medications I'm going to prescribe for you."

"Thanks."

"You're welcome. Be sure to let Nurse Mirabal know if you want to see me again."

Sean dialed Nancy's extension. "Mr. Hoffman and I are finished. He's ready to be escorted back to his cell."

Nancy watched as the officer took the inmate out of the room and down the hallway. "What kind of magic did you do? He seems so much calmer."

"After I created a safe environment for him," Sean said, parroting a line from the *Psychiatric Diagnosis*, "Mr. Hoffman began to talk to me. He's a very sick man. I'll review my notes tonight and decide what medication he needs. Who do I see tomorrow?"

"Bruno Keppel. He suffers from everyday acute agitation, which as you know, sometimes results in violent outbursts. Dr. Shelton prescribed Valium for him, but Mr. Keppel is refusing to take his medication. Captain Mahoney called and asked if you would try to get Bruno back on his medication so he can be taken out of segregation and returned to the general population. When Bruno takes his Valium, he's no problem. I have him scheduled for nine o'clock tomorrow morning, if that's okay."

"That'll be fine. I'll take his file home with me tonight. Anyone else for tomorrow?"

Nancy sorted through the stack of inmate files until she found David Hunter's. She handed it to him. "I'll schedule Mr. Hunter for tomorrow afternoon."

Sean plucked a couple books out of the bookcase and put them and the two inmate files into his briefcase. "Since I'll be working late into the evening tonight, I'm going home now. Page me if you need anything."

"Don't work too late on those cases. I don't want you burning out the first week on the job."

"No chance of that," Sean replied with a wink.

17

SEAN PUT HIS SCOTCH AND SODA on the dining room table and opened up Bruno Keppel's file. He took a swallow of his drink and read Bruno's vital statistics. The inmate stood six feet four inches and weighed two hundred and fifty pounds. Sean flipped through the record until he came to the previous psychiatrist's personal notes.

Bruno had been raised in an abusive family. His mother was a prostitute when she became pregnant with Bruno. She hadn't known who had fathered her son. He had been three years old when his mother married Bruno's stepfather.

After that, life apparently had become even more difficult for Bruno. His mother's new husband had been physically and emotionally abusive.

When Bruno was eight years old, his stepfather's brother came to live with the family. According to the notes, one night when Bruno and the uncle were home alone, the uncle got drunk and raped him. Bruno was terribly ashamed about what had happened but decided to risk telling his mother, hoping she would do something. Her only response had been to tell Bruno to stay away from the uncle.

During his freshman year of high school, Bruno began hanging out with a group of kids who were troublemakers. One night, he and three of his friends broke into an older couple's home. The thugs beat up the couple and threatened to kill them if they reported the crime. Ignoring the threat, they had called the police. From the descriptions given by the victims, the police knew who the perpetrators were. They were arrested and prosecuted. Bruno was sent to a juvenile facility where he remained until he was eighteen years old.

Sean took another swallow of scotch and read on. He was surprised to learn that Bruno had shared such personal information with the former psychiatrist.

After Bruno's release from the juvenile facility, Bruno had had no interest in seeing his mother or stepfather, but he did pay a visit to the uncle who had assaulted him that memorable night so many years ago. This time the uncle was on the receiving end. Bruno knew the uncle would not be stupid enough to report it.

One night Bruno was in a neighborhood bar drinking with one of the troublemakers he had hung out with in high school. The guy, who was familiar with Bruno's family history, asked him if his mother was still a hooker. It took several men to pull Bruno off his former friend. An ambulance came and took the badly beaten man to the hospital.

The police took Bruno to jail. He was convicted of assault and sent to prison for six years.

This guy doesn't sound so bad, Sean decided. *If I were in his shoes, I would have done the same thing.*

He had to admit that he was enjoying reading about Bruno. Sean finished his scotch and continued.

After Bruno's release from prison, he tried to get a job, but his prison record prevented him from finding anyone willing to hire him. In order to survive, Bruno began robbing people who were under the influence of alcohol. He'd stake out a bar and watch for people who were drinking heavily. Just before the bar closed, he would go outside and wait under the cover of bushes or behind trees for a victim who had decided to do the responsible thing and walk home.

Bruno would follow his prey from a respectable distance until the person approached an alley or dark street. He'd slip on a ski mask he carried in his pocket and close the distance. A shove from behind usually sent the inebriate reeling to the ground. He'd gotten away with cash a few times.

One eventful night, Bruno underestimated the intoxication level and the strength of a man he attempted to rob. Instead of falling, the man turned around and threw a right cross that nailed Bruno on the chin. The blow had stunned Bruno and the man apparently pulled off the ski mask, saw the assailant and got away. Having survived the attack, the victim was later able to identify Bruno from a mug shot. The police picked Bruno up two days later. He was convicted of assault and robbery and sent back to prison.

Sean closed the file. Bruno Keppel was an interesting case. He had been so absorbed in the inmate's file that he hadn't heard Mary come in the back door.

"I'm home. I'll go freshen up a little, then we can go," Mary called as she headed for her bedroom.

It took a minute for Sean to remember where they were going.

She reappeared a few minutes later. "Reading files, huh? That can be very depressing."

"It's depressing, but necessary. I need to understand the histories of the inmates I'm trying to help in order to be successful."

"Of course you do. Whose file is this?" she asked, looking over his shoulder.

"Bruno Keppel."

"Oh, I know Keppel. He's a very scary guy. Have you met him yet?"

"No, but I'm scheduled to meet with him tomorrow morning at nine."

"Be prepared. He's huge and always frowning – brooding is probably a more accurate description. You should consider having an officer or two in the room with you during the session."

"I'll think about it. Let's forget Mr. Keppel and go to some nice place for drinks and dinner. Have you decided where you want to go?"

"I didn't know I was supposed to choose."

"I've only lived in Florence for a few days, so I don't have a clue. You decide which is the best restaurant in town. That's where we're going."

"The L&B Inn is nice. It has great Mexican food."

"Sounds good to me. I'll drive," he said, taking his keys off the table.

As Mary buckled her seat belt, she noticed Charles wasn't wearing his. "It's against the law in Arizona not to buckle up."

"So what?" he answered defiantly. "They're uncomfortable, and in my opinion the government has no damn business mandating silly things like wearing seat belts."

Caught off guard by his angry response, Mary quickly changed the subject. "Take a left at the next block. I want to show you our historic courthouse."

The two-story building was Victorian in design, constructed of red brick with white trim around the windows. Tall pine trees interspersed with fruit-bearing trees adorned the front yard of the courthouse. The pine trees seemed out of place in the small desert town.

"Construction was completed in February of 1891," Mary said. "The clock on top is made out of wood. The time painted on the face is eleven forty six. That's the exact time it opened for business on February 2, 1891."

Spare me, he thought. "Interesting," he mumbled.

The L&B Inn was a cozy restaurant. It was an off-white, adobe structure with the customary red tiled roof. The host met them as they walked in the door.

"Hi, Mary," he said, giving her a big grin. "Long time, no see."

"Yeah, it has been awhile. Mario, I want you to meet Dr. Charles McGuire. He's a psychiatrist and just started working at the prison this week."

"Nice to meet you," the two men said simultaneously.

"Do you have anything open outside on the patio?"

"Sure do," he said. "Follow me."

Walls painted with murals of desert cacti enclosed the patio. A waterfall cascaded over a tower of rocks in the corner. The atmosphere was relaxing and romantic. Mario seated them at a table beside the waterfall.

Mary ordered a glass of cabernet sauvignon. Sean ordered a double shot of scotch and a chaser. After the second round, Mary suggested they order dinner. Sean would have liked a third drink, but decided he was really hungry and would eat instead.

Mary continued her history lesson during dinner. She told him how Tom Mix, the western movie star, had gotten drunk in a Florence bar on October 12, 1940, and was killed later that night in a car accident eighteen miles east of town. The arroyo where he was killed was now called the Tom Mix Wash. A monument, with a metal, riderless horse, had been constructed at the site in memory of him.

When the waiter presented the bill for the evening, Sean pulled out a credit card. In spite of Mary's objections, he insisted on paying the tab. He knew she would be impressed and wouldn't forget his generosity.

After they settled the bill, Sean put his arm around Mary and guided her out the door of the restaurant to the car. He unlocked the passenger door first and helped her in. Sean was pleased with his gallantry. His mother had taught him well in the ways of a gentleman.

When he slid behind the wheel, Mary gave him a peck on the cheek. "Thanks for a wonderful evening, Charles."

"You're very welcome," he said, touching his hand to her cheek. He turned the ignition and started for home.

Once they arrived home, Mary flipped on the kitchen light.

"Well, tomorrow's going to be a big day," Sean said. "I better try and get some sleep, but first . . ." He pulled Mary into his arms and gave her a lingering kiss on the lips. *That ought to give her a thrill*, he thought.

"See you tomorrow," he said.

Sean let go of Mary and went down the hall to the bathroom. He glanced in the mirror at his reflection. Some of Mary's bright pink lipstick remained on his lips. Sean picked up the bar of soap and scrubbed it off. He didn't like kissing, but it was part of the ritual he had to go through to manipulate a woman. The taste of soap on his lips reminded him of his mother. It had been his mother's preferred tool of punishment. When she had overheard him tell a kid to go to hell, she said the soap would clean out his filthy mouth. Fortunately, she didn't know anything about the baseball mitt he had been trying to take away from the kid, or his punishment would have been worse.

Sean carefully hung up his clothes in the closet and put on the silk pajamas he had bought in the Phoenix department store. The silk felt good against his skin. He guessed that Bruno Keppel would never have the opportunity to wear silk pajamas.

Mary felt warm all over. The evening had been wonderful. She touched her fingers to her lips, remembering the kiss Charles had given her when they had said goodnight. Should she be worried about how fast things were happening? She really knew so little about him. For a change, she decided to throw caution to the wind, take a risk and see what happened.

18

MARY HAD ALREADY LEFT FOR WORK when Sean emerged from his bedroom. He poured himself a bowl of Frosted Flakes, topped it off with milk and carried it into the dining room. Nancy would be expecting a diagnosis for Hoffman. Sean had an hour and a half before his nine o'clock session with Bruno. That should give him plenty of time to figure out Hoffman's diagnosis. He opened the psychiatric reference book he had brought home from work.

Sean spooned Frosted Flakes into his mouth and paged through the chapters of the book. The chapter on schizophrenia seemed to have possibility. After reading about the disease for a few minutes, he decided Hoffman was definitely a schizophrenic. He moved onto the drug section of the chapter. His finger stopped at Haldol, a drug commonly used for prisoners who were schizophrenic. The normal protocol was to give the first dose of Haldol intravenously and then switch to oral doses. Sean saw no reason to give Hoffman an intravenous dose of the medication. That was simply too complicated. He was certain he could get the same result by giving Hoffman a large oral dose instead. The clock on the wall showed eight forty-five. Sean had spent way too much time on Hoffman's diagnosis and was going to be late for his appointment with Keppel.

It was ten after nine when he poked his head in Nancy's office. "Everyone needed to talk to me on my way in, so I'm a little late. Hope you didn't think I'd forgotten my appointment with Mr. Keppel."

Nancy smiled broadly. "No, I wasn't worried. Do you want me to call security and have them bring Mr. Keppel over now, or would you rather have a few minutes in your office?"

"Give me a little time, then make the call."

He sat down at his desk and took another look at Keppel's file to refresh his memory. He didn't want to ask any stupid questions, especially since Nancy told him the captain wanted one of his security officers in the room at all times.

Sean heard loud voices in the hallway. "I don't need a damn shrink. Just take me back to my cell and leave me the hell alone."

"You have an appointment with Dr. McGuire, and you're going to keep it," came the surly voice of an officer.

Nancy entered the office with a concerned look on her face. "I told the officers to put Mr. Keppel in the conference room. He's not having a good day. His mood swings are dangerous when he's off his Valium. You may want to keep more than one officer in the room with you."

Sean slowly got up from his desk, picked up the file and walked to the conference room. Maybe this wasn't going to be as much fun as he'd anticipated.

One of the officers was posted inside the door of the room. Two others had taken a seat in the common area down the hall.

Bruno was seated at the table, which was too small to accommodate his large frame. His arms were folded tightly to his chest, and his long legs were stretched out under the table.

The inmate had dull, black, brooding eyes. Sean looked at the table and wished it were larger. He selected the chair nearest the door in case the inmate decided to try to grab him.

Bruno was slovenly in his appearance. His thinning brown hair looked greasy, like it hadn't been washed in a couple of weeks, and he needed a shave. Keppel had a foul body odor that permeated the room.

"Good morning, Mr. Keppel, I'm Dr. McGuire."

"Fuck you," Bruno growled.

"Watch your mouth, Keppel," warned the officer standing by the open door.

Bruno glared at the officer but said nothing.

"Would you like some coffee, Mr. Keppel?" Sean tried to keep his anger in check.

"Yeah, and I want it with sugar and cream," the inmate sneered.

"Officer, would you please get Mr. Keppel some coffee with

cream and sugar?" Sean had an edge to his voice.

The officer tightened his jaw and shook his head. "The captain said we weren't supposed to leave you alone with Mr. Keppel."

"And I said to go get the coffee," Sean insisted sternly. "I'm the one calling the shots here."

The officer mumbled something on his way out the door.

"Aren't you smart enough to be afraid of me?" Bruno sneered.

Unable to contain his frustration any longer, Sean stood up and pounded his fist on the table. "You listen to me and you listen good. I don't care about you or your troubles. You can go straight to hell as far as I'm concerned." Sean's temper had overcome his concern about his physical safety. He leaned forward across the table and closed the distance between himself and the inmate, "I have a job to do here, and if you try messing with me again, you'll regret it . . . trust me."

Keppel was momentarily stunned. Normally, he was the one who did the threatening. Something about Dr. McGuire unnerved the inmate. Maybe it was those icy, pale blue eyes. He wasn't like the other psychiatrists he'd seen over the years. Whatever it was about McGuire, Bruno decided to take the threat seriously. He found himself wishing the officer would hurry back with the coffee.

"What do you want?" Bruno asked in a subdued tone.

At that moment the guard returned with the coffee. He looked surprised at the change in Keppel's demeanor. "Thank you, officer," Dr. McGuire said, the anger gone from his voice. He nodded at Bruno to do likewise.

"Thanks," Bruno replied.

"Now, Mr. Keppel, I have read your file, and I see that you've spent most of your life behind bars. Tell me about yourself." The doctor paused and looked up at the officer. "Officer, you can go. We'll be speaking confidentially."

"But Captain Mahoney said. . ."

"What is it about 'leave us alone' you don't understand?"

The officer slammed the door behind him.

Bruno couldn't believe what he'd just witnessed. This new psychiatrist didn't seem to be afraid of anyone. With the officer out of the room, the inmate was expecting another tongue-lashing. Instead, the psychiatrist appeared to have made a one hundred and eighty degree about-face.

"Now tell me why you're in segregation and causing trouble." Sean said, making eye contact with the inmate.

"I'll tell you, but you won't understand. I don't mean to diss, I mean, disrespect you," Bruno hastened to add, "but you can't understand unless you've been locked up."

Little does he know, thought Sean, coughing to stifle his urge to laugh. "Try me," he said.

For over thirty minutes Sean listened to the inmate talk about his life, inside and outside of prison. Nothing the inmate said surprised him. *Why would it?*

After Keppel had finished, Sean said, "I understand you're refusing to take your medication. Why?"

"It makes me feel like a zombie. I can't remember things and I get all spaced out. I need to be alert at all times, or someone may try to take me down. I don't have many friends here."

"I understand what you're saying, but do you think you can contain your anger if you don't take Valium?"

"If I want to. When I give people trouble, it's because I want them to leave me alone. I make a conscious decision to raise hell sometimes, you know, like to scare guys, so they get out of my face."

Sean understood what the inmate meant about keeping other inmates out of his face. What seemed strange to him was that Bruno apparently hadn't tried cheeking his medication. Because Bruno preferred to stay to himself, maybe he had never overheard other inmates talking about how to do it. If Sean could get something in return, he would be willing to educate Bruno on the technique. *What could the inmate give him in return?* The answer was simple. *Protection, that's what he could get from Keppel.* It would be comforting to have a large, intimidating inmate like Bruno watching his back. If he helped Bruno get back in the general population without taking the Valium, Bruno would owe him.

"Do you like being in lockup?" Sean asked.

"Hell, no. They only let me out of my cell one hour a day. I'm not crazy, but I will be if I don't get out of segregation pretty soon. But," Bruno added, "I'm not going to take those tranquilizers. I'd rather be crazy than dead."

"Well," Sean said, his left leg beginning to twitch. "I can understand your position, but in order for you to get out of segregation, you have to take your medication."

Bruno started to object, but Sean held up his hand to stop

him. "Hear me out. I'm going to let you in on a little prison secret. Have you ever heard of cheeking your meds?"

"No." Bruno perked up.

"It's when you pretend to take your medication. I will tell you how to do it if you promise to control your temper and stop putting on shows to make people afraid of you."

"Yeah, okay."

"Okay, so when the nurse gives you the pill, flick it up inside your cheek and don't swallow it. You have to do it carefully so she doesn't get suspicious and ask you to open your mouth. Spit the pill out after she leaves. If she catches you cheeking, she'll stand there to make sure you swallow it. If she does discover you're cheeking, swallow the pill and when no one's around, stick your finger down your throat and puke it out."

The inmate's eyes narrowed, "Why are you telling me this, Dr. McGuire?"

"Let's just say I have sympathy with your situation. Now, if anyone asks why you agreed to go back on Valium, say that I persuaded you to so you could get out of segregation, okay?"

"Okay."

"And, if in the future, I need a favor from you . . . ?"

"You got it," Bruno replied. "I owe you one."

Dr. McGuire stood up and walked over to the door. He called down the hallway for the officers to escort the inmate back to his cell.

Nancy was standing outside the door to the conference room, shaking her head. "Another miracle. Did he agree to go back on his medication?"

"Yes, he did. He had to get it through his head that taking the medication was his only ticket out of segregation."

He handed Keppel's file to Nancy. "Can you come over to my office for a minute? I want to talk to you about Mr. Hoffman."

"Sure," she responded.

"Have a seat," he told her, as he nestled into his leather chair. "After careful review of Mr. Hoffman's file and the notes I took yesterday during our session, it is clear Mr. Hoffman is suffering from schizophrenia."

"He is?" Nancy sounded astonished.

"Yes, his situation is rather unusual, but I've seen a few cases similar to his. I really don't have time now to get into the details of my diagnosis."

"Oh, I didn't expect you to. I guess I was just a little surprised that Mr. Hoffman is schizophrenic."

"You may want to follow his case because it is interesting. Anyway, I am prescribing a large initial dose of Haldol. Normally, I would first give him an intravenous dose then follow up with the oral but, in his case, I think an initial large oral dose would be more appropriate. I'd like him to take one hundred milligrams a day to begin with because his symptoms are severe. We'll cut back as he progresses."

"How much did you say?" Nancy wanted to make sure she had heard correctly. A hundred milligrams of Haldol was an extremely high dose.

"One hundred milligrams," he repeated. *Did she need a hearing aid or was she questioning his decision?* "Please prepare the prescription for my signature."

"You want me to write it up for you?"

"Didn't you write the prescriptions for Dr. Shelton?" He sounded accusing.

"No, I didn't, but if you want me to do it, I will. You will double-check that it's written correctly before you sign your name, won't you?"

"Of course I will. The only reason I'm asking you to fill it out is that I'd like to rely on you, Nancy, and give you more hands-on training."

Nancy was wondering how writing out a prescription for Haldol would give her more hands-on training. Why didn't Dr. McGuire just do it himself?

"When do you want to schedule Mr. Hoffman's follow-up?" she asked.

· "A week from today."

Nancy made a note to schedule the appointment.

Dr. McGuire was prescribing a very large dose of Haldol for Hoffman. She knew the drug was toxic and could cause serious side effects. Dr. Shelton had avoided using Haldol on inmates. *But* then, *who was she to second-guess McGuire? He was the expert.*

"When do you want me to schedule Mr. Hunter?" Nancy asked, looking up at the clock on the wall.

"Make it for one thirty this afternoon. I have a meeting outside the prison and need to leave in a few minutes, but I'll be back before then."

136

"If you can wait a minute, I'll get Mr. Hoffman's prescription filled out and you can sign it before you go."

"Fine."

Sean was relieved to get back home. The meeting with Bruno had been draining. He went over to the refrigerator and reached for two beers and the doggie bag containing what was left of his Mexican combination plate from the night before. After taking a couple gulps of beer, he began reading David Hunter's file.

Inmate David Hunter was one of two children, twins, and had been born into a wealthy family. His grandfather had made a fortune as a top executive in one of the big Arizona copper mines. Even though the copper-mining business had been depressed for many years, David's father had managed the family investments wisely. The Hunter family had homes in Arizona, New York and Grand Cayman.

David Hunter was handsome, drove a sporty car and had money to burn. He began smoking marijuana during his senior year of high school. The school police liaison officer caught him with a reefer, but he was never charged with possession because of the large charitable contributions his father made to the school's athletic department. David applied for and was accepted into Yale.

At age twenty, Hunter was introduced to cocaine and began using it on a regular basis. According to the notes, one night he and his girlfriend, who was also a user, decided to elope. David's father cut off his son's monthly allowance. As a result, David dropped out of school.

It wasn't long before the novelty of being married wore off. His wife wasn't interested in being married to a man with no income, and David, having become bored with his new wife, began seeing some of his old girlfriends.

Unwilling to work, the only way David could have the lifestyle he'd grown accustomed to was to sell drugs. One of his customers ended up being an undercover cop. The transaction was filmed, and Hunter went to prison.

Adjusting to prison had been difficult for him. Most drug pushers enjoyed respect from the other inmates, but not David. It seems many resented him for having been born with a silver spoon in his mouth. They made his life miserable by stealing the few belongings he had in his cell. According to David, the guards also made life difficult. They shook him down after his visits because they assumed the women who visited Hunter were mules and were smuggling drugs into the prison for him.

He asked to be placed in protective custody, but the administration refused since other inmates needed the cells more than David did. Hunter had written a conciliatory letter to his father and asked him to pull some strings and get him into protective custody. His father didn't answer his letter.

According to Dr. Shelton, David Hunter suffered a "feigned" nervous breakdown. But, feeling that it was wise to err on the side of caution, he decided to have him transferred to the mental health wing for observation.

Hunter was now making a request to be evaluated by Dr. McGuire. The inmate claimed to need drugs to calm his nerves.

Sean closed the file. He smiled as his mind began to drift. The session with David Hunter might have some interesting possibilities. He threw the two empty beer bottles in the trash and headed back to his office.

19

Sean waited until Nancy finished her phone call. "I'm ready for Mr. Hunter. Tell Security to bring him to my office." He didn't want Nancy, or anyone else, to overhear the conversation he intended to have with the inmate.

"Okay," Nancy replied. "I'm sure you read that most of us think Mr. Hunter faked a nervous breakdown to get into the mental health unit. He's a smart, spoiled, rich kid used to getting his way. He'll try to get you to prescribe some medication for him."

What did she know about his ability to identify someone running a scam? Sean considered Nancy's comments inappropriate; she was only a nurse and not a trained psychiatrist, but he held his tongue. He didn't want to reprimand her and give her reason to turn against him. On the other hand, if he let her comments go without saying something, she might feel she could call the shots.

"I'm aware of Mr. Hunter's history, but I would never rely on other people's opinions to decide whether Mr. Hunter had a real nervous breakdown. I have to see him to make that determination. He deserves the same treatment other prisoners get, and just because his family has money shouldn't be a factor in his case at all."

"I apologize. I was repeating what Dr. Shelton said the last time he saw David Hunter. You certainly know a lot more about nervous breakdowns than I do."

"There's nothing to apologize for, Nancy," he said, giving her arm a squeeze. "I value your advice and hope you'll continue to make your observations known to me."

"I'll try to," Nancy responded, confused by the mixed message she was getting. She picked the phone up and dialed security. "Dr. McGuire is ready to see Mr. Hunter. Would you bring him down?"

Sean took out a notepad and pen, then looked at the top of his desk. It didn't look like a busy person's desk. He put David Hunter's file in front of him and scattered some important-looking papers from his in box on his desk. Moments later, a security officer and a young, handsome inmate entered his office.

"Mr. Hunter, I'm Dr. McGuire. Please have a seat." The large officer was the same one who had brought Bruno Keppel. Sean said, "I'll call you when Mr. Hunter and I are finished. Please shut the door on your way out."

The officer glared and slammed the door shut.

"Make yourself comfortable, Mr. Hunter. Would you like a cup of coffee?"

"No thank you, sir, I'm trying to give up coffee because of my nerves. It makes me more jittery and depressed than I already am."

Sean summoned up a look of concern. "Tell me about your depression."

His plan had been to spend the first few minutes making Hunter feel comfortable, but it appeared that he could cut right to the open-ended questions since the inmate had already mentioned his depression. No need to dance around wasting time with small talk if the poor, little rich kid was ready to discuss his emotional problems.

"I don't know where to begin," David said, shaking his head.

"Start with your adjustment to prison. I've read your file. I know about your history of drug abuse and why you were sent here."

"Prison for someone like me is very difficult. My family has money, so most of the cons in here seem to think they can help themselves to my things. When I was in general population, my cellmate took my stuff and traded it for cigarettes and drugs. You notice I'm not wearing a watch. I forgot to put it on one day, and the next thing I knew, it was gone."

"Have you reported the thefts to the administration?"

"No way. I value my life. My cellmate threatened to kill me if I reported him."

"Is that why you requested to be placed in protective custody?"

"Yes. Trust me, Dr. McGuire, if you were in my position, you would, too."

"Fortunately, I haven't ever been incarcerated," the psychiatrist lied. When Sean had been in prison, he hadn't worried about inmates stealing his valuables because he didn't have any. He had been one of the inmates who did the stealing.

"How are things going for you now?" he asked. "I read in your file that you had a nervous breakdown."

"Yeah, I was a basket case, and the previous shrink didn't believe me. Sorry to say it, but the whole incident caused me to lose faith in your profession, Dr. McGuire."

"I'm sorry to hear that, Mr. Hunter. Maybe I can help restore your faith in psychiatry."

"If you really mean that, you could give me something to calm my nerves."

Sean had to fight back a laugh. The session was comical, but he was the only one in the room who could appreciate the humor of a con trying to manipulate a con.

"I really wish I could give you something, but everyone seems to think you were faking your nervous breakdown. You were transferred into the mental health unit for observation only. Dr. Shelton decided you were not to be given any medication, and the administration agreed."

Sean let his words hang in the air a moment, then continued, "The truth is, I tend to disagree with the previous doctor's opinion. I believe you are suffering from clinical depression as a result of your breakdown. The problem is, I've only been employed here a few days. If I prescribe something, the administration might question why I am disagreeing with my predecessor."

David started to say something, but saw that McGuire had rested his chin on his hand and appeared to be pondering the dilemma. He remained silent.

Sean looked back at Hunter. "Let me think out loud with you for a minute. If you were my patient on the outside, I'd be able to prescribe something appropriate for you, providing you had the money or health care coverage to pay for the medications."

Sean sighed loudly and shook his head. "Between you, me, and the fence post, prison administrators really aren't very compassionate. All they seem to care about is making ends meet, financially. It's not fair, but that's what we're dealing with here."

"If it's a matter of money, we don't have a problem. I have access to as much money on the outside as I want," David replied, sensing drugs of some kind were in his future.

"What do you mean by that?" Sean asked with sincere interest.

"My twin sister is rich. She'd give me money. All I have to do is ask."

"It's against prison policy for someone on the outside to give money for an inmate's medication," Sean said, not having a clue if it was or wasn't, "but I appreciate your trying to help me come up with a solution to your dilemma."

Sean sat quietly for a few moments twisting a lock of hair around his finger, giving Hunter the opportunity to make a suggestion. He didn't want to make an offer unless it was absolutely necessary.

This shrink is a pushover, David thought. *Time to lay it on him.* "What if," Hunter began slowly, "my sister gave you money and you got the medication and brought it in to me? I'm sure you could get pills inside. They wouldn't go off in the metal detector. I'd make it worth your while. You're my only hope, Dr. McGuire. Would you please consider doing this for me?" David pleaded.

"What kind of medication has worked for you in the past?" Sean asked.

"Well, I've used cocaine; it helps me relax and gives me confidence."

"Cocaine is an illegal drug," Sean said, trying to sound shocked. "However, there are some prescription drugs available which do pretty much the same thing."

Hunter had never heard of prescription drugs that gave a person the same kind of high as coke.

Sean rubbed his chin thoughtfully, "Besides thinking about an appropriate medication to prescribe for you, I must weigh the ethics of your proposal. Personally, I think I can justify it because I know you are clinically depressed and could be helped with medication. On the other hand, if the administration found out we had this agreement, we'd both be in serious trouble. I'm taking a big risk. I could lose my job and reputation."

"My sister would advance you money, like maybe five thousand dollars to pay for the pills. No one would be the wiser. I promise."

"Your sister? How do I know I can trust her?"

Hunter laughed. "She's a junkie. That's why you can trust her."
Works for me, Sean thought.

Sean nodded. "Well, the drugs I am thinking of are very expensive and I'll have to make many trips to Phoenix to pick them up; I won't be able to get more than thirty or forty pills at a time."

"I realize that it will be costly. How about ten thousand dollars? Would that be enough?" David paused, then said, "Look at it this way. There are doctors who help their patients commit suicide; Dr. Kavorkian, for instance. Getting me a few pills doesn't compare with what he does to help his patients."

Sean knew the inmate had taken the bait. Now it was time to close the deal.

"You make a good case, Mr. Hunter. I think we can work something out. Talk to your sister and see how she feels about it. If she agrees with you, I'll meet her somewhere and she can give me the ten thousand dollars. When are you seeing her again?"

Sean knew that he probably could have gotten more money if he would have held out longer. On the other hand, he had to start somewhere. There must be other inmates who would be interested in a similar arrangement. Sean's temporary job had the potential of being extremely lucrative.

"Della, that's my sister's name, is visiting me this weekend. She lives in Vegas but she flies to Phoenix every other Saturday, rents a car and comes to see me. I'll tell her what we've worked out when I see her this weekend. I'll ask her to bring the money a week from this coming Saturday. I think she'd be willing to come and see me two weeks in a row; in fact I know she would. Della owes me."

Owes him for what? Sean wondered. "All right then. Talk to her about it on Saturday. But," Sean cautioned, "use discretion. Don't let anyone hear your conversation. Remember, phone conversations are taped, so if you call her before Saturday, don't mention anything about our arrangement. You must tell her in person. Do you understand the need to keep this thing quiet?" Sean asked.

"I certainly do. I'm sure as hell not going to jeopardize this deal."

"Okay. Then have your sister bring the ten thousand dollars a week from Saturday. I'll meet her at Gibby's Old Town Cantina at noon. You won't get your drugs," Sean purposely used the word drugs instead of medication, "until after I get the money, which means it'll be two and a half to three weeks. I assume you have no problem with the time table."

"I'd like it sooner, but it appears I have no other choice."

"We have a deal." Sean stood up indicating they were finished. "I'm going to warn you again not to mention a word of this arrangement to anyone other than your sister or everything's off."

"Are you kidding? I don't have any friends in here to talk to, and I'm sure as hell not going to tell any staff. I need these drugs, and you're my only hope."

"Oh, I almost forgot; tell your sister to bring cash. Nothing bigger than fifty dollar bills." *If the sister balks at the deal, I'll blackmail her,* Sean decided, *a plan B for blackmail. Brilliant!*

"I'll tell her."

Sean lifted the phone and dialed Nancy's extension. "Mr. Hunter and I have concluded our session. He's ready to go back to his cell. I'll want to see him this same time next week."

He turned back to the inmate, "A week from today you can confirm to me that your sister will meet me with the money the following Saturday."

"I'll see you next week." David smiled broadly at the officer who came into the room to collect him.

"How did it go?" Nancy asked, after Hunter was out of sight.

"I convinced Mr. Hunter that medication isn't in his best interest. He didn't pressure me for it after I told him about the bad side effects many of the drugs have. I gave him some suggestions about how to manage his bouts with depression. He appreciated the fact that I was willing to see him again next week."

It was only two-thirty, but Sean decided it was quitting time. He picked up his briefcase and told Nancy he was leaving for the day. "Page me if you need anything," he said on his way out the door.

The timing on this deal is perfect, he thought as he walked towards the car. He'd get the money in less than two weeks, stall Hunter another week and then he'd be on his way to Mexico. He knew he couldn't risk staying any longer than that. No muss, no fuss and ten thousand dollars richer.

This was cause for celebration. Sean had never been inside Gibby's Old Town Cantina, though he'd passed it on the way to dinner with Mary, and he wanted a drink. He could kill two birds with one stone; quench his thirst and scope out the establishment where he would be receiving the money.

He parked in front of the reddish brown adobe building on the corner. The smell of pine cleaner met him as he entered the bar. It reminded him of his mother. She had always used it to clean the floors of their house.

A man and a woman were seated beside each other at the long bar. No conversation passed between them as they methodically lifted their drinks to their lips. Sean took a stool in front of the bartender, an attractive woman with long, red hair and a warm, friendly smile.

"What can I get you?" She placed a coaster in front of Sean.

"I'll have a Mexican beer. Make it Dos Equis."

"Haven't seen you in here before. Are you just passing through?" the bartender asked, putting the bottle of Dos Equis in front of Sean.

"I'll be in town for about a month. My name is Dr. Charles McGuire. I'm working at the prison."

"No kidding. My dad works there. He's the captain."

"Captain Mahoney is your father?"

She nodded affirmatively.

"All I can say is you're a lot prettier than he is."

"I'm glad to know that," she said with a laugh.

"I have the highest regard for your father. He's taught me a lot in the short time I've been on board."

"I'll tell him. It'll make him feel good."

"I normally don't get away this time of day, but I'm taking the afternoon off." Sean wanted to cover his tracks. Mahoney would wonder what he was doing in a bar at three o'clock in the afternoon if his daughter said she'd met him.

Sean decided to change the subject. "This is an interesting building. What's the history?"

"Well, it's old, as you can see. Some people claim it's haunted by the ghosts of people who were shot in gunfights back in the early days."

"Gunfights?"

"Yep. Miners used to come into town on their days off. It got a little dicey at times." She laughed. "One time there was a gunfight out on the street between the governor and a judge; can't remember who walked away from it."

She leaned her elbows down on the bar and lowered her voice for effect. "There was a brothel next door. The customers would come in, have a few drinks, then slip out the back door and spend time with the ladies of the night."

"You said this place is haunted," Sean said. "Have you seen any of the ghosts?"

"I see them all the time. There's one sitting right beside you," she teased.

"I don't believe in ghosts, but some day I'll come back and let you try to convince me. In the meantime, I better get going. I've enjoyed visiting with you."

"Don't be a stranger," she said warmly.

20

KITT TOSSED THE EXTRA PAIR of shoes back into the closet. No way they were going to fit into her jam-packed suitcase. She closed the suitcase and put a tie band between the two zippers. The days of locked luggage were gone, but she didn't mind. Safety was the issue.

"How you doing, Cord? About ready to go?" she called.

"Yes, I am," he shouted in response. He was standing within six feet of her.

Kitt jumped. "You scared me. I didn't hear you come in."

"You started the hollering. I decided I'd better yell in case you've become hard of hearing."

"Very funny. For your information I had a hearing test a couple of months ago, and my doctor said it's normal for a woman my age."

"Does that mean you're getting old?"

Kitt took a deep breath and blew it out her mouth. "You're a fine one to talk, Mr. Social Security. Besides, I'd rather have some hearing loss than the selective hearing problem you've had ever since I've known you."

"Uncle," Cord surrendered and swept her into his arms. "Enough already."

They were looking forward to their trip to Minnesota, even though March in Minnesota is usually a month of gray skies and blizzards. They weren't going for the weather. The American Correctional Association was holding a national seminar for wardens in St. Paul. While Kitt was at the seminar, Cord would hang out with some friends he hadn't seen in a long time. During the evenings, they would spend time with their children and grand-children. The St. Paul Hotel, the location of the seminar, was a very old and magnificent structure. It had always been a classy place to stay. Even though their children had wanted them to stay with them, Kitt preferred to stay where the seminar was being held, and Cord wanted the privacy of a hotel room.

"Where did you put my glasses?" Cord asked, as he searched the top of his dresser.

"Same place I always do," she replied with a chuckle. It was a standing joke. Every time Cord misplaced his reading glasses, he'd accuse Kitt of moving them.

"If you don't start keeping track of your glasses, I'm going to buy you a chain so you can hang them around your neck when you aren't using them. Remember the kids and their mittens?" She stopped, realizing he was ignoring her. His selective hearing had kicked in.

The plane departed on time. Kitt pulled out her new Janet Evanovich novel. With all the heavy reading she had to do for her job, Evanovich's novels were a wonderful escape. Cord had closed his eyes. He nudged Kitt when she laughed out loud as she read.

"Keep it down, Red. I'm trying to get a little shut-eye here."

As the plane began its descent into the Minneapolis/St. Paul airport, Kitt looked at Cord. "Help me remember to ask Charles if he's heard from Josie when we get back home. Eddie called yester-day and asked if he'd heard anything from her."

"Okay. What else did Eddie have to say?"

"She wants us to come down one of these weekends. I told her we'd get something set up after we get back from Minnesota."

"Sounds good to me."

Once they landed, it took a few minutes to deplane. When they reached the baggage area, their son, Nathan, greeted them with big bear hugs. "Annie got off work. She's circling the airport because we can't park at the curb anymore. Of course, Muffin insisted on coming along."

After grabbing their bags and stepping outside, they saw Annie pull up alongside the curb in her Ford Explorer. Nathan and Kitt slid into the middle seat beside four-year-old Muffin, who was buckled into her booster seat. Cord hopped in the front seat. "I'll ride shotgun," he announced.

"Hi, Grandma. Hi, Pompa," Muffin said.

Cord reached back and gave Muffin's leg a tug, "Hey, Tiger. Thanks for coming to get us."

"You're welcome. Did you tell Uncle Nathan and Mommy thank you?"

"Thank you, Annie and Nathan," Cord and Kitt said in unison.

Kitt leaned over and gave Muffin a peck on the cheek. "Hi sweetie pie, how are you doing?"

"Not very good," she said, as her beautiful, dark brown eyes filled with tears.

"Why?" Kitt asked, suddenly concerned.

"Well, I cut my hair and Dad's real mad. See." Muffin turned her head to show Kitt her new asymmetrical hairstyle.

It was everything Kitt could do to keep a straight face. Cord swiveled his neck around to take a look then quickly turned face forward. His shoulders began to shake.

"Don't worry, it will grow out again," Kitt reassured her namesake.

"I know, and I'm not ever, ever, ever going to cut it again," the four-year-old proclaimed. Her eyes dried and a smile returned to her face.

Kitt gave Annie's shoulders a squeeze. "So how you doing, Annie?"

"A lot better now that my mommy and daddy are here," she answered with a chuckle.

Cord leaned over and glanced at the speedometer, "You're over the speed limit, Annie."

"Like father, like daughter," Annie said. "Remember, I learned everything I know from you, Mr. Leadfoot." The good-natured bantering had begun and would probably last all the way to the hotel.

"See you tomorrow night," Annie said, as she pulled up in front of the St. Paul Hotel to let them off.

21

THE ALARM WENT OFF PROMPTLY AT SIX. The warden's breakfast was scheduled for seven, so Kitt had plenty of time to dress and get downstairs. She was looking forward to seeing everyone from Minnesota.

The conference room was already buzzing when Kitt got there. Her eyes fell on the two tallest men in the room. Fred, the former commissioner of the Minnesota Department of Corrections, and Dennis, the deputy commissioner, were deep in conversation. Kitt walked over to them.

"I bring sunshine and warmth from Arizona," she announced, giving each a hug.

"Don't rub it in," Fred teased. "We ordered up this cold weather especially for you so you don't forget what Minnesota winters are like. You guys in Arizona have it way too easy."

"Work-wise or weather-wise?"

"Both."

"If I have it easy work-wise, it's because you guys taught me well."

Fred raised his eyebrows in surprise. "Would you please repeat what you just said, Warden Logan? I thought I heard a compliment."

"It was a compliment, but don't let it go to your head."

Fred and Dennis had mentored Kitt and helped her through some difficult times after she was first named warden of an adult male prison in Minnesota. She had always enjoyed listening to the stories they told about their experiences working inside the prison walls. Now she had some of her own stories to share. She couldn't wait to tell them about the light bulb incident.

"Did Cord come with you?" Dennis asked.

"Yep. He's here. Maybe we can have a drink together. He's anxious to see you both again."

"Looks like they're getting ready to start serving," Fred said. "Since I'm a hot shot, I have to sit at the head table."

"They've assigned seats for the rest of us," Dennis said. "Same old strategy: let's make everyone meet new people."

"Whatever. I'm hungry." Fred set off for his table.

"Later, Kitt," Dennis said, as he went in search of his seat.

Five wardens and a representative from the American Correctional Association were seated at Kitt's table. Sheila Franks, the warden from a Michigan prison in Saginaw, was seated beside Kitt.

Kitt was trying to remember the Michigan prison where Charles had contracted for his services. *It wasn't Saginaw?*

"Sheila, do you by any chance know a Dr. Charles McGuire?"

"I certainly do. We contracted with him for years. I hated to lose him, but I understood why he didn't renew his contract. He wife suffered such a long, painful death. Why do you ask? Do you know him?"

"Dr. McGuire's filling in for us until the new psychiatrist I've hired comes on board. He agreed to help me out for thirty days."

"You're very fortunate. He's an excellent psychiatrist and will serve you well, but I didn't know he was going to Arizona. Last I heard, he was taking a month's leave of absence from his practice in Saginaw and going to Carmel, California. He must have changed his mind. In any event, you're lucky to have snagged him."

Kitt was surprised to hear Charles had recently lost his wife. He didn't seem to be in a state of grief; in fact, quite the opposite. But maybe that was his way of coping with a loss. When she got back home, she'd ask Mary if he'd mentioned anything to her about losing his wife.

Sheila had said Charles was only taking a month leave of absence from his practice; she must have meant a year's leave. Kitt didn't have time to ask Sheila to clarify, as the keynote speaker was being introduced. She'd try to remember to ask Sheila about it later in the day.

That afternoon, the seminar participants had two hours for lunch on their own, and Kitt had arranged to meet Louise. They would have a chance to reminisce about their trip to Mexico. Louise was picking her up outside the hotel at noon.

"Where are we eating?" Kitt asked, as she climbed into Louise's car.

"The Lex, where else? I thought about Mexican food, but it wouldn't be as good as what we had in Puerto Penasco. What a ball that trip was. Let's do it again next winter."

"You're on," Kitt said.

The Lexington, or the Lex as everyone in the Twin Cities called it, was an old, well-established, classy restaurant with excellent food and service. It was always one of Kitt's favorite places to eat.

"We have reservations in the no smoking section," Louise told the hostess, who was dressed in a white blouse and black skirt. "Could we have that table in the back?"

The hostess looked over at the table, then down at the seating chart in front of her. "Sure, this way."

"So, tell me more about the body you found when you were stranded in that little town," Louise said, after they were comfortably seated.

"I can't remember what I told you on the phone. Did I tell you about Eddie, the person who stopped to help me when I was stranded?"

"You mean the one you thought was a man but was really a woman?"

For the next fifteen minutes, Louise sipped her ice tea while Kitt told her about finding the body. After she finished, Louise said, "So you hired a psychiatrist you met while you were in Empalme? How's he working out?"

"Well, he's only been at the prison for a week, so it's a little early to tell. He certainly comes highly recommended. I talked to a warden from Michigan this morning and she said Dr. McGuire was on contract with her prison for many years. And she told me some things I didn't know about him, like he recently lost his wife to cancer and that he was supposedly going to Carmel, California, to spend some quiet time and grieve the loss of his wife. I don't know how he ended up in Empalme, but I guess it's none of my business."

"It does sound a little strange. What's he like?"

"Good-looking and smart. Mary, my secretary, is quite taken with him. He's renting a room from her for a month. I have the feeling that Mary will be surprised to find out there was a Mrs. McGuire. The guy doesn't seem to be grief-stricken. Maybe it was such a blessing when she died that he's relieved her suffering is over. I don't know what it is, but there's something about him that doesn't add up." She stopped. "Excuse the rambling. I'm thinking out loud, as usual."

"Kitt, you have a good sense of intuition. If your gut is telling you something about McGuire, pay attention."

The waitress placed their food in front of them. "Is there anything else I can get you besides more iced tea?"

"No thanks, just the refills."

Kitt's pager went off. She looked down and saw it was Mary's number.

"My secretary just paged me. This can't be good news. I'll go outside to call her so I don't disturb anyone. I hate listening to people talk on their cell phones while I'm trying to enjoy a meal." Kitt pushed back her chair, made her way out of the restaurant and dialed her secretary.

Mary picked up the phone on the first ring.

"Hi, Mary, it's Kitt. What's up?"

"The deputy warden is here and he wants to talk to you. Hang on while I forward your call to the private line in your office."

Kitt felt a knot in her stomach. *It must be serious*, she thought. Dale was standing by to talk to her.

Dale didn't bother with any pleasantries before getting straight to the matter at hand. "Warden, we had a serious assault about an hour ago. I hesitated to call you but decided you'd want to know about it."

"I'm glad you called. What happened?"

"Two inmates got into a fight, and one of them is in really tough shape."

"What do you mean by tough shape?" Kitt interrupted.

"He's in the hospital and on a respirator."

Kitt took a deep breath. "Anyone else hurt?"

"The other inmate didn't suffer any injuries but one of our officers, Sergeant Tripp, has a broken nose. Naturally, he's traumatized, but other than that, he's okay. He'll be taking some time off. Before I forget, Captain Mahoney wants you to call him. He locked down the cell hall right after the fight."

"Do you know if he's in his office now?"

"He's waiting for your call."

"Before you hang up, tell me who the inmates were."

"Keppel and Harper."

"Did you stay Keppel, as in Bruno Keppel? We've had trouble with him before."

"Yeah. I need to warn you that the captain has gone ballistic. He let Keppel out of segregation after Dr. McGuire told him he'd make sure Keppel stayed on his medication. As it turns out, Keppel was cheeking his Valium."

Kitt pursed her lips and let out a quiet whistle. "Thanks, Dale. Would you transfer me to Captain Mahoney?"

"Mahoney," the captain snarled.

"Captain, it's Kitt. Dale just briefed me on the incident that occurred this morning. He said you wanted to talk to me."

"First of all, let me say I have a real problem with your Dr. McGuire. He convinced me Keppel was going to take his medication, so I took him out of segregation and put him back in the general population. Seems like your psychiatrist is pretty naïve for having had years of experience working in prisons. My reading of McGuire is that he's a quack."

"Let me begin by saying that he's not my psychiatrist, he's our prison psychiatrist," Kitt fired back. She knew she needed to get some responsibility back on the captain's shoulders, or he'd keep up the barrage of observations and complaints. "And furthermore, I don't want you to refer to Dr. McGuire as a quack."

"Okay, I suppose you're right," he said, humbled by his supervisor. "I guess there's no use in crying over spilt milk and honestly, I'm the one who should take responsibility. I decided to put Keppel back into the general population. I should have trusted my instincts and kept him in segregation."

"It's not a matter of blame," Kitt said, feeling a slight twinge of sympathy for her captain, "it's a matter of dealing with the situation. Has Dr. McGuire been notified of the incident?"

"No. He's not at work and he's not answering his pager. I don't know where the hell he is."

"Really? Maybe Mary knows. Transfer me back to her. I'll see if she can find him. Before you do that, how's Sergeant Tripp doing?"

"He's doing all right physically, and I'm sure he'll regain his composure in a few days. Mr. Harper, on the other hand, is hanging on by a thread. Dale told Harper's family you're out of town and that you'd call them when you get back. Make sure you meet with our legal counsel before you talk to them. They'll sue us sure as hell."

It irritated Kitt that Mahoney felt compelled to advise her how to proceed. She was well aware of the threat of lawsuits. "Just transfer me back to Mary."

"You survived your conversation with the captain," Mary said, when she picked up the phone.

"He's really riled up. Do you know where Charles is? I told Mahoney I'd find him."

"No, I don't. After I heard about the assault, I called Nancy. She said Charles wasn't planning to come in until this afternoon. He's not answering the phone at home. He must be out somewhere."

"This is just why I needed to hire him. Keep trying to reach him. If you find him, page me. I need to talk to him as soon as possible."

Kitt walked back to the table. "Sorry, Louise."

"From the look on your face, everything is not okay."

"There was an incident at the prison this morning. An inmate assaulted another inmate and one of my staff. Doesn't look good for the inmate who was on the receiving end. He's in critical condition. The injured officer was on the squad and trying to break up the fight. He has a broken nose and will be off work for awhile."

"Bummer," Louise said.

"I guess I'm going back to Arizona as soon as I can catch a flight."

When Kitt returned to the room, she found Cord stretched out on the bed. She stooped down and gave him a peck on the cheek.

"How was your lunch?" he asked sleepily.

"Lunch was good, but Mary paged me and said there was a serious assault at the prison this morning, and I think we should go back." Kitt explained what had happened.

"Do you want me to check with the airlines to see if we can get a flight while you're at the seminar?"

"That would be helpful. Give the kids a call and tell them what's going on. Oh, I almost forgot. Fred and Dennis want to have a drink with us after we're done today. Is that okay with you?"

"Sure."

Kitt took out her cell phone and tried Mary again. "Any luck finding Dr. McGuire?" she asked.

"Not yet. I'll keep trying and page you when I get him."

"We're coming home tomorrow, if we can get a flight. Tell him to be in my office at two o'clock tomorrow afternoon. If for some reason I can't get back by then, I'll give you a call."

"Okay. Do you want me to check with the airlines for you?"

"No, thanks. Cord said he'd take care of it."

22

CORD WAS ABLE TO BOOK an early morning flight back to Phoenix, and they arrived home that afternoon. Having time for lunch, Kitt washed down a sandwich with a Diet Coke. "I'm off," she said to Cord, as she started for the door.

"Give 'em hell," he called as he watched her back out of the driveway.

Mary was at her desk when Kitt arrived at her office. "I'm sure sorry you had to cut your time in Minnesota short. How were the kids and grandkids?"

"Everyone was fine. Our grandchildren are growing like weeds." She sat down in the chair by Mary's desk. "Were you able to reach Charles?"

"Yes. He called just after you did. We couldn't find him yesterday because he had a doctor's appointment in Phoenix. Charles said he turned his pager off when he was in with the doctor, then forgot to turn it back on again." A worried look crossed Mary's face. "I'm a little concerned about him."

"Why?" Kitt asked.

"After Charles saw the doctor, he came home and poured himself a stiff drink. He said the doctor's assessment of his condition wasn't very good. I didn't realize that he's been having chest pains."

"Really? He does seem pale and he smokes a lot, doesn't he? Did he say if the doctor diagnosed his condition?"

"No. I got the distinct feeling he didn't want to talk about it. He asked me not to mention anything about his chest pains to anyone because he prefers to keep his health matters private. I struggled with whether to tell you, but I decided you needed to know why he couldn't be reached yesterday. You won't tell anyone, will you?"

"I won't say a word about it to him or anyone else," Kitt assured Mary.

"On another subject," she said, remembering her conversation with Sheila Franks, "has Charles ever said anything to you about being married?"

"No." Mary put her chin in her hand then, raised her eyes to meet Kitt's. "Is he?"

"I'm sorry, I didn't mean to say that he is married but that he was married. His wife died after a long battle with cancer. I was wondering if he said anything to you about it?"

"No, but maybe that explains why he seems so distracted at times, like he's in his own world. How did you find out about his wife? Did he tell you?"

"No, Sheila Franks, the warden from Michigan, sat beside me at the seminar. I asked her if she knew Charles and, of course, she did. Sheila was surprised to hear that he was in Arizona because she'd heard he was planning to go to California. Guess he must have changed his mind."

"Here he comes now," Mary said quietly.

"Let him tell you about his wife. I don't want to have him think I'm spreading his private matters around."

"Welcome back, Warden Logan," Sean said with a big smile. "Mary said you wanted to meet with me regarding the Bruno Keppel incident."

"Come on in. Would you like something cool to drink?"

"I'd take a soda if you have one."

Kitt opened the door of her small refrigerator, pulled out a Coke and handed it to him. She popped open a Diet Coke and sat down behind her desk.

"Before I forget, Charles, Eddie called last week. She's worried about Josie. No one has heard from her since she left town. Eddie was wondering if you've heard anything."

"Not a word since she went back East to see her mother. But, now that I think about it, Josie doesn't know where I'm staying or how to reach me. If she wrote, she would have sent the letter to her house. I didn't bother to have the mail forwarded because I'm only going to be here in Florence such a short time."

Sean took a couple of swallows of his Coke while he thought about what else he should say so Kitt wouldn't get suspicious. He realized he should mention something about why he hadn't contacted Josie.

"When Josie left," he continued, "she didn't leave an address or phone number, so I don't know how to get in touch with her. She did say she'd call me after things settled down, but if she has tried calling the house no one would be there to answer. I've been thinking about going back to Empalme a week from this coming Saturday to check on things. Maybe there'll be a message on her answering machine or a letter there for me."

"I think that's a good idea. Let me know if you hear anything. Now, back to the business at hand."

To Sean's relief, Kitt had changed the topic. "I called Captain Mahoney yesterday after I heard about the incident between Keppel and Harper. You saw Mr. Keppel last week, didn't you?"

"Yes I did. At the time I thought the session had gone very well. He told me he didn't want to take his Valium because it dulls his senses and interferes with his ability to keep himself safe. I told him the only way he'd get out of segregation was to go back on his medication. When Mr. Keppel left my office, he promised to take his Valium. I was certain he would do it, or I never would have told the captain I thought it was all right for him to go back into the general population."

Kitt was surprised to hear that Charles believed Keppel would take his medication because the inmate promised he would. "Was anyone checking to make sure he actually took it?" she asked.

"I assumed Nancy was double-checking to make sure he was taking it, but I guess she wasn't. I'll follow up with Nancy to see what went wrong."

"The truth is," he added, "I'm very disappointed with Mr. Keppel. From now on, I will make sure he takes his Valium if I have to force it down his throat myself."

His reaction sounded dramatic – strange – to Kitt. Charles certainly knew that federal law prohibited prison staff from forcing an inmate to take medication. She pondered his comments while she finished her soda.

"For the time being," she said, "Captain Mahoney is going to keep Mr. Keppel in segregation. In the meantime, I want you to get paperwork started for commitment to the state hospital. I'm not sure we can pull off the commitment, but it's worth a try."

Sean left the office in a sullen mood. Mary looked up as he walked past without acknowledging her. His mind was on Bruno Keppel and how he had lied to him about being able to control himself. The inmate had made him look like an idiot. Bruno had sold him down the river. Sean couldn't wait to see the look on Keppel's face when he was told he was being transferred to the state hospital. With a little luck, they'd give him shock treatments or a lobotomy while he was there.

Nancy was at her desk when he returned to the wing. She looked up. "How did it go?"

"The warden supports my decision to try and get Mr. Keppel committed to the state hospital. I won't need to see him again because he'll be in segregation for the remainder of his time here."

"I hope you don't take this matter too seriously. These things happen," she said encouragingly.

"Yes, I know," he unenthusiastically responded. "When's my next session with David Hunter? I forgot."

"I'll have to check. It's either tomorrow or Thursday."

"Let's make it tomorrow morning. Reschedule it, if you have to." Sean was anxious to hear how David's conversation with his sister had gone.

"You're scheduled to see Mr. Hoffman this morning. He's been on his medication for a week."

"All right," Sean grudgingly confirmed. He would rather have gone home and had a drink, but he decided to stay and see the pathetic inmate.

Hoffman had an unsteady gait as he approached the conference room. His complexion had a yellow tint.

Nancy helped the inmate get seated, then asked Dr. McGuire, "May I speak with you privately?"

"Excuse me, Mr. Hoffman," Sean said, as he reluctantly trailed Nancy out into the hallway.

"Mr. Hoffman seems to be having some pretty serious side effects from the Haldol. He looks jaundiced, and he's having trouble walking," the nurse began.

"That's to be expected," Sean snapped. He didn't like the idea that Nancy was second-guessing his decision to put the inmate on Haldol. "Anytime a new drug is introduced into the body," he said slowly, emphasizing each word, "the body must take time to adjust.

You must have noticed that Mr. Hoffman is calm, which means the drug is beginning to manage his schizophrenia."

"I suppose you're right, but he looks so sick. How long do you think it will take for his body to adjust to the drug?" Nancy probed. She was still very concerned.

"It varies. In Mr. Hoffman's case, it'll probably take two or three weeks. Now, I better get back in the room or he's going to wonder what's going on."

When Sean entered the room, the inmate was resting his yellowed, jaundiced face in his palms.

"Mr. Hoffman, how are you feeling today?" Sean asked, noticing the whites of the inmate's eyes were yellow. It took him by surprise.

"Not very good. I feel like I'm going to throw up."

Sean quickly pushed the wastebasket over to Hoffman. "Use this if you think you're going to puke." He couldn't stand the sight of someone heaving his guts out. The session with Hoffman was going to be a short one.

"What you're feeling is perfectly normal. It's just that your body is getting used to the medication. Have you heard any voices lately?"

"I hear a lot of people talking, but they're not talking to me."

"A very good sign. You'll be feeling better in no time. Now, it would be best if you go back to your cell and get some rest."

The inmate let out a groan.

Once he had Hoffman escorted back to his cell, Sean reported to Nancy that the medication was working because Mr. Hoffman wasn't hearing voices anymore. He also told her Hoffman had an upset stomach and to give him some Tums to help it settle down.

A feeling of apprehension flooded through Nancy as she returned to her office. She knew Tums wouldn't make Hoffman feel better. Lieutenant Taza was leaning against the wall near her office door. His face showed no emotion, but she could see concern in his eyes.

"It needs to be taken care of," he said calmly.

"Come on in." Nancy knew it would take some time to find out what Taza was thinking. He had probably noticed Hoffman's change in appearance. "I could use a little company. Want some coffee?"

He shook his head no and sat in a chair next to Nancy's desk. She waited for him to say something. He didn't.

"I know Mr. Hoffman is really sick, but Dr. McGuire says its just his body getting used to the drugs."

The lieutenant remained silent.

"Look, you said it has to be taken care of. What do you suggest I do? Dr. McGuire knows a lot more about treating inmates than I do. He's the psychiatrist; I'm only the nurse. Who am I to second-guess him?" Nancy's frustration was boiling to the surface.

"It's bigger than Hoffman, Nancy."

"What's bigger?"

Taza's dark, American Indian eyes seemed to bore right into Nancy's brain, but she wasn't unnerved like McGuire had been. "What's bigger?" she repeated softly.

"McGuire."

"What do you mean?"

"He isn't who he says he is."

"Who told you that?" As the words flew out of her mouth, she realized no one had told Lieutenant Taza anything. "No one told you. You feel it, don't you?"

He nodded.

"When you and Dr. McGuire met his first day on the job, he told me you made him nervous."

"He knows I know. That's why I make him nervous."

Nancy studied Taza, a man she admired greatly and trusted completely. She knew he would never say something he didn't believe to be true.

"You feel it, too, don't you, Nancy?"

"I don't know what I feel right now." She paused, not expecting Taza to respond. "Dr. McGuire has made some decisions, especially in Mr. Hoffman's case, that have concerned me, but I wouldn't go so far as to say he isn't who he claims to be."

Nancy looked directly into the lieutenant's dark, all-knowing eyes. "If you're right, and I pray that you aren't, what should I do?"

"You don't need to do anything except answer honestly when you are asked the questions. You'll have a chance soon."

"Who will be asking me the questions?"

Ignoring her question, Lieutenant Taza, with a hint of a smile and soft eyes said, "You'll know when the time comes." He stood, gave Nancy a long, assuring look and walked out of the office.

What an intuitive man, Nancy thought as she watched him until he was out of sight. *What does he know that I don't know and when would the time come that he alluded to?*

23

"MAHONEY." KITT HEARD THE CAPTAIN'S typically gruff greeting on the other end of the line.

"Mahoney, it's Kitt. I'm calling to let you know I met with Dr. McGuire. We've decided to start civil commitment procedures for Bruno Keppel."

"Wonderful," said the nonplussed captain.

Kitt slammed down the phone and yanked open her desk drawer. She was going home. She'd had a gutful of Mahoney and his snide comments.

"Mary," she said, locking the door to her office, "arrange a meeting for me with our legal staff first thing tomorrow morning."

"What time? Seven thirty or eight?"

"Either time is fine. I'll be here before seven thirty. Do we know anymore about Harper's status?"

"He's still in intensive care, but I guess he's doing a lot better than they thought he would."

"It's nice to get some good news for a change. Well, I'm out of here. Everything else can wait until tomorrow."

Walking through her parking lot to her car, Kitt caught a glimpse of Charles pulling out of the parking lot and waved him over. He drove up beside her and rolled down the window.

She leaned down to talk to him. "Mr. Harper is doing better than expected and might make it after all."

"That's good news," Sean said, making sure Kitt saw the relief in his eyes. He wished it were Keppel in the hospital fighting for his life instead of Harper.

Yes, Kitt thought as she climbed into her car, relieved to be going home.

"Cordell Logan, where's my drink?" she called as she dropped her briefcase. "I thought you'd have it waiting for me."

He looked at his watch. "You're earlier than I thought you'd be. If you hold your horses a minute, I'll get it for you."

Kitt collapsed onto the couch.

Cord handed her a brandy on the rocks. "To us." He clinked his glass against hers. "So?"

"Everything's under control, as far as I know. In our meeting this afternoon, Charles and I decided to try to get Keppel committed to the state hospital. That makes two inmates in two weeks we're trying to ship out."

She silently studied her drink for a few seconds. "What's bothering you?" Cord asked.

"What are you, a mind reader? You always know when something's bugging me."

"Answer my question."

"I'm not sure what's going on, but my gut is kicking up a storm," she said. "When I met with Charles today, he said some things that struck me as really strange, especially coming from an experienced psychiatrist. There's something unsettling about him, and I'm trying to sort it out."

She told Cord how Charles had been disappointed with Bruno because he had cheeked his medication. "I can't put my finger on what's going on with Charles. He should have known better than to trust an inmate." Her voice trailed off.

Kitt shook an ice cube from her glass into her mouth.

"It is surprising that he would trust an inmate to that extent. Want another drink?" Cord asked.

"No, thanks. I'd be out for the count if I did." She put her glass on the end table and asked, "Do you want to go to Empalme this weekend?"

"Sure."

"Good. I'll give Eddie a call to see if it works for her," Kitt she said, reaching for the phone.

Eddie sounded out of breath when she answered the phone.

"Hi Eddie, it's Kitt. You sound a little winded. What did I take you away from?"

"I was out in the yard pulling some weeds. It's good to hear from you."

Eddie was delighted to hear Kitt and Cord would be spending the weekend with her. "What time do you think you'll get here?"

"If I can get out of my office by one thirty Friday afternoon, we'll be there around six o'clock. We'd like to hang out in the cantina before dinner."

"That's a good idea; everyone will want to see you again and meet Cord. I'll spread the word that you're coming. Maybe I can persuade grouchy old Clyde to come over for a beer. By the way, he asked about you a couple days ago."

"He did?"

"Yeah, I know you think he doesn't like you, but he does. He's a grizzly bear on the outside but a teddy bear inside."

"You'll have to do a little more convincing to persuade me of that."

"We'll spend Saturday at the ranch. You can stay until Sunday, can't you?" Eddie asked.

"We can if it's not too much bother for you."

"Bother? You should be ashamed of yourself for saying that."

"It's a go," Kitt told Cord after she hung up.

Kitt was anxious to see Eddie and the others again, but she also wanted to poke around Empalme a little bit. Sheriff Martinez had called her last Friday to say the body she found in the cemetery had been identified and that his office would be doing a press release soon. The victim was an older woman named Loraine Byrnes from Tucson. The neighbor living next door to Ms. Byrnes had become concerned when Loraine and her son had not returned from Mexico, and she had contacted the sheriff's office. The neighbor told Sheriff Martinez that Ms. Byrnes was widowed and lived alone. It was unclear whether Loraine had any family, other than the one son.

Vinny also said they had done background checks on the two card players and, as Kitt had guessed, they had prison records, but they were property crime offenders. Neither of them had a history of violence.

24

SEAN STRETCHED OUT ON THE COUCH and flipped on the television. Mary was in the kitchen fixing dinner. He was just beginning to nod off when he heard a reporter say, "Today, the sheriff's office released the name of the homicide victim found in the Empalme Cemetery. The victim is Loraine Byrnes from Tucson, Arizona. Police are asking for help in locating her son, Sean Byrnes, who was last seen with her over a month ago. He is wanted for questioning."

Sean sat bolt upright on the couch. His mother had been identified, and now they were looking for him. Sean's heart started racing. He was driving her car. The authorities would easily be able to track down the license plate number. He would have to switch license plates with those from someone else's car. Odds were the person wouldn't notice the plate had been exchanged, at least not right away. For the time being, the car was safely parked in front of Mary's car in the driveway. No one could read the license number from the street.

Sean was also concerned about the conversation he'd had with Kitt that day. She'd asked whether he'd heard anything from Josie, and he said he hadn't.

Kitt had gone on to say that people in Empalme were wondering why Josie hadn't been in touch with anyone. Just when things seemed to be going so well, all hell was breaking loose. Now his evening was ruined because of nosey people and a damn license plate.

Sean's mind drifted back to his last day with Josie. After she left for work that afternoon, he'd gone to the cantina to celebrate his new job. He was drunk when he went back to her house. Josie had to close up the café after her shift that night, so he knew she would be coming home later than usual. He dreaded going into the house when she was gone since her dog, Rusty, always growled at him and usually acted like he was going to attack. Sean had asked Josie several times to get rid of Rusty, but she wouldn't. The dog was the only problem with his living arrangement with her.

When Sean stumbled through the door that night, Rusty had snarled and bared his teeth. The dog's aggressive nature had been the final straw. He decided to take care of the problem once and for all. Sean went to the bedroom and took the Bowie hunting knife out of the drawer. When he returned to the living room, the dog was standing in the same place, studying his every move, still growling.

"Come here, Rusty," he said.

The dog curled his upper lip and bared his teeth again.

The dog wasn't going to come to him without some bait. Sean went into the kitchen and took a fresh rib eye steak out of the refrigerator. He unwrapped the steak and went back into the living room.

"Dinner time, Rusty," he said, extending his hand with the meat in it toward the dog's nose. In his right hand, behind his back, was the knife.

The dog cocked his head slightly, then slowly walked over and sniffed at the steak. Just as Rusty started to take a bite, Sean grabbed the dog by the nape of his neck and, in one swift motion, slashed the dog's throat. A river of red pulsated out of the wound and onto the snow-white hair of Rusty's chest. The dog whimpered and lay down on the floor to die.

Even in his blurred state of mind, Sean knew he needed to get things cleaned up before Josie got home. He went to the linen closet, took out a towel, and wrapped it around Rusty's throat to stem the flow of blood that was pooling on the floor near the dog's head. He found a large trash bag in the pantry. Sean slid the limp, lifeless dog into the bag, face first, then hoisted the bag off the floor and carried it outside behind the house. A trail of bloody footprints marked his every step. He went back inside to clean up the living room floor.

Sean was down on his hands and knees scrubbing the floor when Josie came home.

"What happened? Are you hurt?" Josie cried, staring first at him, then at the red water in the pail beside him.

"No, I'm okay, but Rusty tried to bite me. I told you to get rid of that dog."

"But why is there blood on . . ." Josie stopped mid-sentence. "Where's Rusty?" she asked, in a voice filling with panic.

"Outside."

"Outside where?"

"Outside in a garbage bag. I killed him. It was self-defense."

"You killed him?" She was stunned.

"That's what I said," came the drunken, slurred response. "I suppose it doesn't bother you that he tried to bite me. Besides, you're better off without that damn dog. Just think – if he bit a stranger, you'd get sued."

"Rusty has never bitten anyone, including you," she said, in a voice filled with rage. She was standing directly in front of him. "What kind of psychiatrist are you anyway? I want you out of my house."

Still on the floor, Sean wobbled to his feet. "Let me see if I understand the situation correctly. You want me to leave because I killed your dog in self-defense? I thought I meant something to you. Just this morning you told me you cared a lot about me."

"Maybe I did, but if you had any feelings at all for me, you never would have killed Rusty. You know how much he means to me."

"Yeah, I know how much he meant to you, more than I ever did. That's for sure." Sean voice was measured and his icy eyes were on fire.

"Get your stuff and get out now," she repeated in a throaty, grief-stricken voice. She turned to go outside and look for her dog's body.

Sean reached for the knife, which he had wiped off and and laid on the coffee table. He followed her out the door.

Josie sensed he was behind her, but she didn't turn around. "Get away from me, I hate you," she said sobbing.

The blood rushed to Sean's head. As she stepped out into the yard, he grabbed her around the neck and swiped the blade of the knife across her throat. She fell to the ground. "How dare you think more of a dog than you do of me!" he snarled.

He looked around and saw that no lights were coming from

any of the neighboring houses. He went back into the house for a blanket and a couple more trash bags. He wrapped Josie in the blanket, then put one trash bag over her head and pulled the other up over her legs. He unlocked the trunk of his mother's car and put Josie inside. He threw the bag containing Rusty on top of her. By this time, he was sobering up.

The ground where Josie had collapsed was soaked with blood. A shovel was propped up alongside the house. He covered up the blood with dirt from Josie's nearby garden, then walked over the dirt so the ground would look undisturbed. He went back inside the house and poured a double shot of scotch. After gulping his drink, Sean drove to an arroyo about three miles outside of town and buried Josie and Rusty in a shallow grave. The hard, clay-like desert soil made the digging very difficult. He stopped digging a couple of times for cigarette breaks.

Sean was pulled back into the present by Mary's call from the kitchen. "What do you want to drink with your dinner?"

"What did you say?"

"I asked what you want to drink for dinner."

"Wine."

"Wine sounds good to me, too. I'll open a bottle of chardonnay."

He watched Mary setting the table. *Had she overheard Kitt ask him about Josie? Should he say something to her about Josie?* No, he'd wait and see if she mentioned it.

"Dinner's ready," she said, walking over to the stereo to put on some soft music.

It was obvious that Mary had gone out of her way to create a romantic atmosphere. There were fresh-cut flowers on the table. She lit the candles and turned off the dining room light.

She's hooked, he thought. That was okay, as long as she didn't expect any romance from him. He pulled out Mary's chair and seated her.

"Looks delicious." Sean gave Mary a peck on the cheek before he took his seat. "I don't know how you always put together such nice meals, especially after working all day."

"Years of practice, I guess. It's nice to have someone to cook for again."

"You haven't mentioned anything about your neighbors," he said, trying to steer the conversation away from the two of them, "and I haven't been around long enough to get acquainted."

"Well, the Larsons live next door. They're a young couple with no children. Mrs. Price, an older woman, lives in the house behind me. She has trouble getting around these days because of her arthritis. I run errands for her sometimes when her daughter is unavailable."

"That's too bad about her arthritis. Is she able to get around, to drive?"

"Only if she absolutely has to. She still has a car but she's not that comfortable behind the wheel any more."

Bingo. Mrs. Price's car plate would do nicely. "I need to do some work on my car tonight," he said, abruptly changing the subject. "Do you have any tools?"

"Depends on what you need."

"Just the ordinary; wrenches and a screw driver. Stuff like that."

"There's a tool box in the closet by the kitchen door. I'd be glad to help you if I can."

"No, I won't need any help. The truth is, I enjoy tinkering with my car. It's therapeutic for me." *That ought to keep her away*, he thought. *She wouldn't want to interfere with my therapy.*

After they had finished their dessert, Mary put her apron back on. "You go ahead and get started on your car. I'll clean up the kitchen."

Sean couldn't risk having Mary come out and see him removing the license plate. He'd do it after she went to bed. "No, I'll help you with the dishes and work on the car later."

After the dishes were done, Mary went into the bedroom, then reappeared dressed in a robe. She sat down beside Sean on the couch. The robe was loosely draped, partially revealing her breasts.

Hadn't he made himself clear? Why did she keep trying? He didn't want an intimate relationship with anyone, man or woman. He'd had sex with women before he went to prison, but it wasn't anything he particularly enjoyed. When he wanted sex, he preferred soliciting it from a prostitute, no strings attached.

Mary was coming on to him, and he needed to put a stop to it in a way that wouldn't jeopardize his living arrangement.

Sean moved over and put his arm around Mary. He gently turned her face towards him and said, "You are one beautiful woman inside and out and I haven't been this happy in a long time."

He stopped to let his words sink in, then continued, "I do have a confession, though," he said sheepishly. "I have considered trying to seduce you, but after thinking about it, I came to my senses. I realized how much I respect you, and decided I wouldn't want to do anything like rush into a sexual relationship because it might jeopardize what we have going. When a relationship has as much potential as ours, we can wait. If things work out the way I think they will, there will be plenty of time for lovemaking down the road."

Mary smiled. "You're a very special man, Charles. To tell the truth, I've been wondering how you feel about me. Now I have a confession. I was attracted to you the first time I laid eyes on you. This hasn't happened to me before; not like this, anyway."

"Mary," he said, giving her a lingering, closed-mouth kiss on the lips. "Now, don't tempt me. Let's see if there's a good movie on television before things get out of control."

Mary handed him the remote control, drew her robe tighter around her and snuggled up to his shoulder. It had been a long time since she'd been this happy. Charles had shared his feelings about her so openly. He still hadn't said anything about losing his wife to cancer, but maybe that was another reason he wanted to go slowly. He hadn't mentioned Josie, either. She remembered Kitt saying she didn't know what kind of relationship Charles had with Josie. Evidently they were only friends; she'd overhead Charles tell Kitt he didn't know how to contact Josie. They couldn't have had a very meaningful relationship if he didn't know how to reach her.

Mary soon nodded off on Charles' shoulder and he gently shook her awake. "You're sleepy. Why don't you go to bed?" Sean kissed the top of her head. "I'm going out to work on my car."

"See you tomorrow morning," she said sleepily.

Sean perused the toolbox until he found a screwdriver and a flashlight. He waited half an hour to make sure Mary was asleep. He went out to the carport where his mother's car was parked. He removed the license plate from the back of the car and stuck it inside his jacket. Arizona law required only one license plate on a vehicle. That made the job easier.

No lights were on in Mrs. Price's house. It was dark in her carport since there was no streetlight in front of the house. He took the flashlight and screwdriver out of his pocket and exchanged the plates.

Mission accomplished, he thought, as he started back through Mrs. Price's back yard toward Mary's house. Suddenly, the light outside the door switched on.

"Who's there?" called the elderly lady.

She had seen him. He didn't dare run. "Hello, Mrs. Price," he said, checking to make sure the license plate was out of sight. "It's Dr. Charles McGuire. I'm renting a room from Mary. I'm sorry if I frightened you. I was out for a walk and decided to take a short-cut through your yard."

"Oh, Dr. McGuire. Mary mentioned you were staying with her. It's nice to meet you."

"Mary was just telling me over dinner tonight how much she enjoys having you as a neighbor. I apologize for being lazy and cutting through your yard."

"You may pass through my yard anytime you like. One of these days you and Mary must come over for a cup of tea. I don't know if she told you, but I make a great carrot cake."

"My favorite," he said dramatically. "We'll take you up on your offer real soon."

"Just let me know when you're coming so I can get the cake baked."

"We sure will. Good night now. Sleep well."

"Good night, Dr. McGuire. I'll be looking forward to our tea."

Sean quickly put the stolen license plate on his car and went back into the house.

Mary was standing in the kitchen. "What's going on?" she asked. "I had my bedroom window open and heard you and Mrs. Price talking."

"After I fixed my car, I decided to take a walk. I cut through her yard on the way back and she saw me, so we visited for a few minutes. She invited us over for tea and carrot cake."

"She's a dear. Maybe we can go over this weekend sometime. I want her to know you aren't a prowler out to do her harm. Rest well, Charles," she called over her shoulder as she padded back down the hallway to her bedroom.

I'll damn sure rest better now that I have a new license plate, he thought.

25

KITT ARRANGED THE PAPERWORK on her desk so she could pick up where she left off on Monday morning. She lifted the phone. "Hi, I'm on my way home. See you in about ten minutes."

"Good," Cord said. "I'm all ready."

"Have fun this weekend," Mary said, as Kitt passed by on her way out.

"Thanks. You have a good weekend, too."

Cord had piled their bags by the door. "I'll get changed and then we can leave." Kitt gave him a kiss and headed for the bedroom.

"Do you want to take your car or the pickup?" he asked.

"The pickup. My Chrysler stands out like a sore thumb in Empalme. Your pickup will blend right in."

Cord was dressed in Levi's and cowboy boots. He had grown up in a family that had run a large cattle operation in North Dakota. He was no drugstore cowboy; Cordell Logan was the real deal.

Kitt re-appeared carrying her overnight bag and two large bottles of water. Walking over to the truck, she tossed her bag into the back seat and climbed in.

"Did you pack a pair of jeans and your boots?" Cord asked, settling in behind the wheel.

"Sure did. Eddie said we can go for a ride tomorrow morning, if we want to."

"Tell me about these people I'm going to meet," he said, as they headed south on the highway towards Empalme.

"I've already told you a lot about Eddie, so I'll start with Jeb. He's a miner and has a sharp wit. He's short and thin, probably about seventy. You'll recognize him right away because he has a really long, gray beard. The first time I went to the cantina, Sal, the bartender, asked me to give her my gun. When I took out my Smith & Wesson, Jeb made fun of it. Called it a starter pistol. Under normal circumstances, I might have found his comment humorous, but I was in such a foul mood because of my car trouble, I snapped at him and told him to mind his own business. He's a crusty old fart with a weird sense of humor. Jeb claims to be a great nephew of Ike Clanton. Ike was one of the shooters in the Gunfight at the OK Corral."

"Is he married?"

"Jeb was married, but his wife got tired of life in Empalme and moved to Colorado. Want some water?" she asked, opening one of the bottles.

"Yeah, thanks. So, tell me about Sal."

"Sal runs the cantina. She's a little rough around the edges but seems to have a heart of gold. Don't know too much about her except her husband died of a heart attack a few years ago and she has a teenage daughter to support."

Kitt opened the other bottle and took a swig. "Then there's Clyde. He's a retired marine. Clyde runs the gas station. You'll recognize him because he's the only guy in town with a marine buzz cut. He's short, stocky and has beady little eyes. It took me awhile to get comfortable being around him. He was rude to me when we first met but after I lost my cool and yelled at him, he simmered down. Maybe it was a test to see if I could hold my own. We get along fine now."

"Sounds like yelling at people helps build friendships in Empalme," Cord chuckled, "at least with Jeb and Clyde anyway."

"Whatever works. Let's see, who else? Oh, yeah, there are two drifters who hang out in the cantina. From the looks of their tattoos, they are Hell's Angels bikers."

Kitt tipped her seat back a couple of notches. "Sheriff Martinez did a criminal history check on them, and they've both done time for property crimes. They don't have a history of violence in their records, but it's possible they might have murdered the woman, Loraine Byrnes, whose body I found. There are a lot of suspicious-looking characters I saw in Empalme. It's the perfect place for a person to drop out of sight."

Kitt yawned. "Can I take a nap now, or do you need more information?"

"I have all the information I can handle for now. Before you go to sleep, put in a Willie Nelson CD."

Kitt slipped in a disc and closed her eyes.

"Mamas, don't let your babies grow up to be cowboys," Willie sang. *Why shouldn't they?* Kitt wondered, just before she drifted off.

She awoke abruptly when the pickup came to a stop. "What's happening?" Kitt asked, as she snapped her seat back into an upright position.

Cord had pulled into a gas station. "I'm going to fill up the tank, empty my tank and get a Coke. Do you want anything?"

"A Diet Coke, with caffeine, and something salty. Peanuts."

Kitt sipped her soda and munched her peanuts as the desert rolled past. A herd of cattle grazed on open range. It reminded her of the time a herd had gone down the main street of Empalme. Cord laughed when she told him about it.

The now familiar, run-down adobe buildings ahead indicated they had arrived in Empalme.

"Where to?" Cord asked.

"We may as well go straight to Eddie's house. I'm sure she'll be there waiting for us."

Eddie opened the door before they had a chance to knock. "Come in, come in," she said, giving Kitt a warm hug. "And you're Cord, I presume. It's good to meet you."

"Same here, even though I feel like I already know you." Cord extended his hand.

"Oh for Heaven's sake, give me a hug," Eddie said.

"Eddie," Cord said releasing her from his bear hug, "I want to thank you for all you did for Kitt last time she was here. What a coincidence – you were on the road when her car broke down. It's comforting to know there are still some good samaritans willing to help out people in trouble, and Kitt was certainly having her share of troubles that day."

"I'm glad I could help," Eddie said. "You know, Cord, I don't believe in coincidences. Everything that happens, good or bad, is part of a larger plan. Kitt's path crossed with mine for a reason."

She looked at the clock on the mantel above the fireplace. "Go on and take your bags into the bedroom. The gang should be assembled at the cantina by this time. I told them to be there by six o'clock."

"Do you want to walk or ride over?" Eddie asked, after they came back out into the living room.

"Let's walk. I'm stiff from sitting in the pickup for three hours," Kitt said. "It's only a short walk," she explained to Cord.

When the trio entered the cantina, Jeb was the first to hop off his stool. "Kitt, how ya doin'?"

"Great. It's so good to see you," she said, catching Jeb off guard with a hug.

"Don't forget to give that little starter pistol to Sal," Jeb said with a wink.

"Hey, I've told you before not to make fun of my gun." She gave his thin arm a soft punch. "This time I brought reinforcements. Meet my husband, Cord."

"A pleasure," Jeb said, shaking hands with Cord. Kitt introduced him to the others who had gathered around.

The two card players were sitting at a table in a dark corner of the bar. They looked up but remained seated, showing no interest in joining the reunion. Kitt glanced over at them without smiling.

"Come on, everyone," Sal rasped, "these guys are thirsty."

"How was the trip down? No problems with the alternator, I presume?" Clyde asked with a smile.

"We drove down in Cord's pickup but my car is running like a dream, thanks to you. I'd refer all my friends to you if it wasn't such a long drive to Empalme."

Clyde puffed up like a peacock. "I'm good. I admit it."

"Well, I'm surprised you can get your damn head through the door, it being so big and all," Jeb piped up.

Everyone laughed.

"How about a round on the house?" Sal asked. A resounding cheer went up from the patrons. "You want a Corona, Kitt?"

"You've been reading my mind," Kitt quipped.

"I'm a psychic bartender. Didn't anyone tell you?" Sal laughed. "What's your poison, Cord?"

"Brandy on the rocks El Presidente, if you have it."

After everyone had their drinks and things quieted down, Eddie asked Kitt if she had a chance to talk to Charles about Josie.

"I saw him yesterday morning," Kitt said. "I told him people are getting concerned because no one has heard from her. Charles said Josie had so much on her mind that she left without giving him a phone number or address where he could reach her. He said he's coming down next weekend to check her mail and phone messages."

"It's awful strange," Jeb said, carefully licking the paper of a cigarette he had rolled, "that Josie hasn't gotten in touch with anyone to tell us how her mother is doing. She's like family, ya know?"

"What about her dog?" Clyde asked. "Is anyone taking care of him?"

Silence. No one had thought of Josie's dog, Rusty.

Kitt looked over at Clyde. "I didn't realize Josie had a dog. I'll ask Charles where the dog is on Monday."

"I would have taken care of Rusty. He knows me real well because I take him hunting sometimes." Clearly, Clyde was disappointed that Josie hadn't asked him to take care of the dog. "Rusty better not be in some strange kennel somewhere."

Murmurs of agreement circled the table.

Kitt nudged Cord when Jeb started to light his cigarette. That was his cue.

"Jeb, does that beard of yours ever catch on fire?" Cord asked.

"I've got a funny feeling you know about the time I set it on fire," Jeb drawled, giving his beard a loving stroke.

"Yeah, Kitt told me about the fire," Cord admitted. "It certainly grew back in fine style. Don't think I've ever seen one that long before. It's even longer than Santa's."

"Say, Kitt," Clyde interrupted, " I heard on the news that the body you found was a lady named Loraine Byrnes. Sounds like they think her son did it. If I could get my hands on the son-of-a-bitch, I'd kill him. You know anything more about what they think happened?"

Everyone, including the two card players, stopped their conversations to listen to what Kitt had to say. "I've talked to Sheriff Martinez a couple of times about the case, but you probably know as much as I do. He told me the investigators collected some evidence near the body, which will help with a conviction once they charge a suspect."

"What kind of evidence did they find?" asked one of the tattooed card players.

Interesting question, thought Kitt. "The sheriff didn't tell me." She'd mention to Vinny that he might want to take a closer look at the bikers. Just because they had never been convicted of a crime of violence didn't mean they had never committed one.

"The café has set up a buffet dinner for everyone," Eddie announced. "It's ready, so let's get over there."

"The bar is closed," Sal announced in a loud voice. "I'm going to go eat."

Kitt watched the two card players as they shrugged their shoulders and stood up. They turned in the opposite direction when they walked out the door. Apparently, they were declining the invitation to dine with her and Cord.

After dinner, Eddie led the way back to her house. The cool evening air was refreshing, and the stars twinkled brightly in the heavens. Coyotes were howling in the distance. With a shiver, Kitt realized the howls were coming from the direction of the cemetery.

"I'm assuming you'd like to spend tomorrow at the ranch," Eddie said, as they approached her house.

"We sure would," Kitt replied.

"Hello, Mama. Hello Mama," came the hoarse, loud call when the three walked through the front door.

Cord looked puzzled. "I forgot to tell you," Kitt whispered, "Eddie has a son named Pete. He's kind of a loner – doesn't go out in public very often."

Kitt had a hard time keeping a straight face. Pete's hoarse voice made him sound like someone dying of consumption.

"I'll introduce you to Pete," Eddie said, picking up on Kitt's game. "We'll have to go into his room because he's limited in his ability to move around."

Cord gave Kitt a look that said, *Why didn't you tell me about this guy?*

Kitt and Eddie burst into laughter when they saw the relief on Cord's face as he gazed at the cage containing the macaw. "Wow, what a beautiful bird." He was both awed and relieved.

"He thinks he's human, so you better refer to him as Pete," Kitt advised. "Has he had his dinner yet?"

"I fed him before you guys came." Eddie put a blanket over Pete's cage. "Good night, Pete."

"Good night," Pete croaked.

They went back into the living room. "How about a nightcap?" Eddie asked. "Rumor has it you sometimes enjoy an after-dinner drink on special occasions, Cord."

"You sure seem to know a lot about me, Eddie," he said, with a smile towards Kitt. "I'll have brandy on ice if you have it."

"How about you, Kitt? What would you like?"

"The same."

They sat in the living room, sipping their drinks and visiting for over an hour.

Eddie's eyes were heavy, and she noticed Kitt was having trouble staying awake. She stood up. "I'm going to call it a night. What time do you guys want to get started tomorrow morning?"

"It's up to you. Anytime works for us."

"If we leave early, we can go for a ride before it gets too hot. I understand you're a good horseman, Cord."

"I can hold my own, I guess, although it's been awhile since I've been on a horse."

"Well, let's make it six tomorrow morning. We'll have a bite to eat and then get going."

"I didn't pack an alarm clock. Give us a holler to make sure we're up." Kitt picked up the three empty glasses and carried them out to the kitchen sink.

26

THE SMELL OF FRESHLY BAKED cinnamon rolls greeted them as they went through the door of the ranch house. Even though they had already eaten breakfast at Eddie's, Kitt and Cord eagerly wolfed down the rolls and coffee Juanita had prepared in anticipation of their visit.

"Let's take a ride before it gets too hot," Bennie suggested.

"Can I have Chico again?" Kitt asked. "I feel like we know each other."

"Sure," Bennie said, and led the way out of the kitchen toward the corral.

"I'm guessing you want a horse with some spirit, Cord?" he asked over his shoulder.

"Definitely!"

"I was afraid he'd say that," Kitt whispered to Eddie.

Once they were all in the saddle, Bennie and Cord took the lead. The two women hung back a little so they could talk.

"I told Cord about the strays; hope that was okay," Kitt admitted to Eddie.

"That's fine. Now he'll know what we're doing when we put out the bottled water. By the way, I like Cord a lot. He's polite, interesting and real good-looking to boot."

"I knew you two would get on." Kitt looked at the men riding ahead of them. "Bennie and Cord have certainly hit it off."

Eddie smiled and nodded.

"This business of Josie being incommunicado really has me bothered," Eddie said. "I was sure she'd either write or call me because we've been close over the years. It's totally out of character for her to do this. On the few occasions Josie has left town in the past, she always gave me a phone number where she could be reached."

Eddie fell silent for a moment, then continued, "Clyde has always taken care of Rusty when Josie has been away. He loves that dog darn near as much as Josie does. If you find out from Charles where Rusty is, let me know. I'll go get him and bring him back to Clyde's house."

At that moment, Cord's horse reared up. Kitt watched with her heart in her throat as he struggled to keep from being thrown off.

Bennie called back over his shoulder. "Hold up. It's a rattlesnake." He pulled a shot gun from a case on his saddle and fired a shot toward the ground. After the dust settled, he said, "You can come on through now."

Kitt had jumped at the sound of the shot, but Chico stood still.

"Bennie has trained the horses not to spook when they hear a rifle shot. He fires off a round every so often when he's out riding so the horses get used to hearing the sound," Eddie explained.

Kitt looked for the remains of the rattler as they passed through the area where it had caused Cord's horse to spook. There was no sign of the snake anywhere.

Eddie smiled and pointed, "The shot blew it over there beside that rock. Bennie never misses," she said with pride. "Cord sure proved himself to be an excellent horseman. I'm not sure I could have hung on."

"I'd be on the ground right now if it had been me," Kitt replied, holding the reins a little tighter.

After dinner that night, Kitt and Cord went for a walk. "I love this place," he said. "It reminds me of home. I always dreamed of having a ranch, but it's a lot of hard work and at this stage of my life, I wouldn't be willing to put in the time."

"I wouldn't want the responsibility of running a ranch, either."

Kitt felt a chill. It always amazed her how quickly the desert cooled off after the sun went down. "Let's go back inside and sit by the fire."

27

IF EVERYTHING WENT AS PLANNED, David Hunter's sister, Della, would be waiting for Sean at Gibby's in fifteen minutes. He would have to make up an excuse to tell Mary about why he was going out. He grabbed his briefcase and went into the living room where Mary was sitting on the couch reading the paper.

"I have to run over to my office and get Bruno Keppel's file. After I get back, we'll do something fun like take a run up to Phoenix."

"Sounds great," Mary said enthusiastically. "I'll be ready to go when you get back."

"See you in about an hour."

Gibby's was swarming with people when Sean walked through the door. He searched the crowd until he saw a young woman sitting alone at a table in a dark corner of the bar. *Perfect setup,* he thought. She had picked a private place. He walked over to her table.

"Ms. Hunter?"

The beautiful, dark-haired woman smiled and stood up to shake his hand. "Dr. McGuire, I presume. I'm Della Hunter."

"You look like your brother, Ms. Hunter, and that's a compliment," Sean said, flashing his charming smile.

"Thank you," Della said sitting back down. "Order a drink, then we can talk business."

Sean wanted to order a double scotch on the rocks but opted for a beer instead. He would have plenty of time to drink later in the day.

"Your brother has asked me to do something I thought I would never consider doing," he began, "and I've really had to ponder the ethics of his request. To be honest with you, drug offenders are often discriminated against in prison. Many times they have real psychological problems, but prison administrators think they fake their problems so they can get prescription drugs and space out."

"Really," Della said. "I had no idea."

"David," Sean continued, "is suffering from a very serious depression. I don't mean to alarm you, but he is suicidal. Prison life has been an extremely difficult adjustment for your brother."

"Suicidal?" she asked, a hint of a smile on her face.

"Your brother has some serious mental health problems, Della, but I don't want you to worry. I'm going to do everything I can to get him the medication he needs to stop his suicidal tendencies."

"Thank you for taking a personal interest in my brother," Della said.

Personal interest only because of your family's money, thought Sean. David Hunter was not really suicidal. Even if Hunter were suicidal, it wouldn't matter to Sean. It would serve the poor little rich kid right to pay for drugs he'd never get.

"It is frustrating." Sean paused for effect. "If David were to commit suicide, I could never forgive myself. That's why I am willing to risk my reputation to work something out for him."

Sean was becoming bored with the compassionate psychiatrist routine and wanted to get down to the critical issue of money. He looked at Della and said, "It's very difficult for me to have to accept money from you but it's the only way we'll be able to get your brother the help he needs. I wish I were in a position to pay for the medication myself."

"Oh, please, let's just cut the crap," Della said as she lifted the wine glass to her bright red lips.

"Sounds good to me. You do understand that I'll need some time to get his drugs. I told David that I'll call the prescription in this coming week, but I won't be able to get to Phoenix to pick it up until next Saturday."

"David didn't mention anything about having to wait. Well, whatever it takes."

His mind drifted to a beach in Mexico. The money he was about to get from Della Hunter would keep him going in Mexico for a long time.

"I have a busy day," he said, "and I'm sure you want to get over to the prison to see David. If you're ready to go, I'll pay the tab and we can do the transaction."

"I'll get the tab," she said, taking a fifty-dollar bill out of her purse. He didn't argue.

Once she laid down the bill, the two got up and exited the bar. Della opened the doors of the rented Cadillac, slid in and reached for the briefcase in the back seat. She handed it to Sean who had slipped into the passenger seat. "David said you wanted small bills, so that's what I got. I'll wait while you count it."

"Why would I want to count it? I trust you." *What was ten thousand dollars to this rich, cocaine-sniffing bitch.*

"As I've said before," Sean warned, "our agreement must remain confidential. Don't tell anyone, and remind David not to say a word to anyone about it either." He finished transferring the money to his own briefcase.

"You needn't worry. Our lips are sealed."

Sean got out of the Cadillac and strode confidently to his car. He threw the briefcase into the back seat. "It's been a real pleasure doing business," he said under his breath and gave Della a final wave.

Mary was looking out the kitchen window when Sean pulled into the carport. "Is everything a go for Phoenix?" she asked with anticipation.

"It sure is," he replied cheerfully. "I'm going to change clothes, and then we can take off."

"What should I wear?" she asked.

"Put on your party clothes. We're going to celebrate."

Mary wondered what they were celebrating, but she decided he'd probably tell her later. She pulled a low-cut, white silk blouse and a black skirt out of her closet. After pondering her accessories, she decided on a silver concho belt and the earrings Charles had given her. At her neck she wore a narrow silver and black neckerchief.

Sean stuffed the money from his briefcase under his cotton knit shirts in the large bottom drawer of his dresser. Five hundred dollars went into his wallet for the trip to Phoenix. If he wanted to spend more than that, he'd use McGuire's credit cards.

Mary was standing in the kitchen drinking a glass of water. He picked her up and swung her around. "Are you ready to party, my beauty?" She laughed as the water splashed out of the glass and onto her blouse.

28

"GOOD MORNING, KITT," MARY SAID with a bright smile. "How was your weekend in Empalme?"

"We had a really nice time. I put work out of my mind, kicked back and relaxed. How was your weekend? Did you do anything special?"

"Charles and I drove to Phoenix on Saturday afternoon. We went shopping, then out to dinner at a very fancy restaurant."

"Is that a new turquoise ring I see on your finger?"

Mary blushed. "Charles bought it for me. When he saw it in the display case, he said it had my name on it. He is a very generous man."

"Did he say anymore about his health? I've been wondering how he's feeling."

"No, he hasn't said anything, and I haven't asked." She paused, wondering if she should speculate to Kitt. "The restaurant we went to on Saturday night had live music. When the band started playing, he got quiet and listened to the music. At first I thought he was tuning me out, but then I realized he probably has a lot on his mind with his chest pain, losing a wife and the stress of a new job."

Mary couldn't put the conversation she'd overheard last Friday between Kitt and Charles out of her mind. Kitt had asked Charles if he had heard from Josie. She was curious about the woman Charles had been living with in Empalme.

"Last Friday, I heard you ask Charles about a woman named Josie. Has anyone heard from her yet?"

"No," Kitt said, "and people are starting to worry. Charles said he is going to Empalme next weekend to check on things. I'm hoping there'll be a letter from Josie or a message on her answering machine."

Mary was surprised to hear Charles was going to Empalme on the weekend. He hadn't mentioned anything to her about the trip. Maybe it had just slipped his mind.

"What kind of relationship do you think Charles and Josie had?" Mary heard herself ask.

"I think it was strictly platonic, since he doesn't seem to be overly concerned that he hasn't heard from her. If it was a romantic relationship, I'm sure they'd be communicating regularly with each other."

Mary was relieved to hear the warden say she thought the relationship was platonic. Her feelings for Charles were growing more deeply every day, even though there hadn't been any intimacy other than the kisses between them.

The phone rang. Mary put the caller on hold. "It's Warden Franks. Do you want to take it?"

"Yes. Transfer it into my office."

Once at her desk, Kitt picked up the phone. "Sheila, good to hear from you. Sorry I had to leave Minnesota without saying goodbye, but there was a serious assault while I was gone and I felt I needed to get back."

"Been there, done that. Hope everything is okay."

"Yes and no. One of my inmates assaulted another inmate and an officer. The inmate who was assaulted is in critical condition, but it looks like he's going to recover, thank God. The officer suffered a broken nose. I'm trying to get the inmate who perpetrated the assault transferred to the state hospital. So, how's everything in your neck of the woods?"

"So far, so good, but I say that knowing all hell can break loose at a moment's notice. The reason I'm calling is that I bumped into one of Dr. McGuire's partners, Dr. Sobel, at a concert Saturday night. I mentioned to him that Charles was working for you on a temporary assignment. I could see he was a bit taken aback. Apparently, he was expecting McGuire to return to work last week. Sobel said Charles hadn't contacted him to say he was going to take more time away from the practice than originally planned. He asked me if I knew how he could get in touch with Charles. I told him I'd give you a call and have you ask Charles to contact him. Hope you don't mind "

Kitt ran her fingers through her hair. She wasn't crazy about asking Charles to call Dr. Sobel. "This is all news to me, Sheila. Charles told me he was taking a leave of absence from his job to work on a research project. He didn't say for how long, but from the way he talked, I assumed it was an extended leave, not just a few weeks but more like a year. Either there's been a real breakdown in communication with his partner or someone's lying."

"I don't want to get in the middle of it," Sheila said, "but it might be good if you could find a tactful way to tell McGuire that he should get in touch with Dr. Sobel."

"I'll think about it, but I don't know if I want to get in the middle of this thing between them, either. Do you think they had some sort of falling out before Charles left?"

"I can't imagine a falling out. They have always seemed to have a good working relationship, but who knows? Stranger things than a falling out with a business partner have happened. Anyway, it's off my desk and on yours. Now you get to worry about it."

"Thanks a lot," Kitt said with a laugh. "Let's stay in touch."

Kitt put down the phone. *What on earth*, she wondered, *was going on with Charles? Why hadn't Charles been up front with his partner?* She didn't want to tell him how to run his affairs but, on the other hand, Charles should know that Sobel was concerned that he hadn't heard from him.

29

When Sean arrived at his office Monday morning, Nancy was clearly stressed. Her face was drawn, and she exhaled loudly when she saw him. He was about to say good morning when she said, "I was just going to page you."

Sean did not appreciate having to deal with some kind of crisis the minute he got to work. Certainly, whatever it was could wait while he got his coffee and settled in.

"I'll go get a cup of coffee, and then we can talk."

"This can't wait," Nancy replied.

"What's so damn important that I can't even get a cup of coffee?" Sean snapped.

"It's Mr. Hoffman." The nurse was not going to be intimated by him. "I went in to check on him a few minutes ago, and I could not wake him. You need to go see what's wrong with him."

"Did you call Dr. Reynolds? I'm a psychiatrist, not a medical doctor."

"Yes, but he's not in yet." Nancy's voice had a distinct edge to it.

Give me a break, Sean thought. *Hoffman probably just wanted to sleep in.* With an exasperated sigh, he started down the hall toward Hoffman's cell. The inmate was on his side with his face turned toward the wall of his cell when Sean arrived.

"Mr. Hoffman, it's time to get up."

There was no response. Sean rolled the inmate over on his back and shook him, gently and then roughly after he didn't respond. The inmate still didn't stir. What if Hoffman was dead? That's all he needed, a dead schizophrenic.

Nancy, who had been standing just outside the cell observing Dr. McGuire, stepped over to the bed. She knew continuing to shake Hoffman was an effort in futility.

"Check his pulse," she said, taking charge.

Sean moved aside. "You do it."

Nancy leaned over and placed her fingers on the inmate's neck. "My God, I'm barely getting a heartbeat. This man is dying."

She stood up and began giving orders. "Call security and tell them we have an unconscious inmate. Make sure they bring a stretcher and some oxygen. While you're doing that, I'll try Dr. Reynolds again and call for an ambulance."

Nancy dashed down the hall toward her office. Sean stood dumbfounded.

"What's going on?" asked the inmate in the cell next to Hoffman's.

A chorus of other voices started yelling. "Yeah, what's wrong with him, Doc?"

"Is it catching?" asked another.

"All you guys shut the hell up. Your shouting is not helping Mr. Hoffman one bit," he barked as he left the cell.

A hush came over the mental health wing. Not only were the inmates worried about what was going on with Hoffman, their psychiatrist sounded more angry than concerned.

Sean marched down the hall and back to his office to notify security. What a way to start out the week, he thought. This job was getting to be a pain in the ass.

Nancy's face was flushed when she entered his office. "The ambulance is on the way, but I can't reach Dr. Reynolds."

"He's a typical doctor. Never around when you need him." If Hoffman died, it would be Reynolds' fault, not his, Sean decided.

The squad arrived within minutes. They loaded Hoffman onto the stretcher and started the oxygen. Sean was relieved to get him out of there. The inmates in the wing watched in silence as the squad rolled the stretcher past their cells and down the long hallway to where the ambulance would be waiting.

"If you haven't notified the warden," Nancy said, "you'd better do it right away."

Nancy was no longer the blushing nurse infatuated with him. She had developed an attitude. She was giving the orders.

"For your information, Nurse Mirabal, I'm going up to see her right now," he snarled.

Back at her station, Nancy took a deep breath and poured a cup of coffee. She needed a few minutes alone. It was obvious that Dr. McGuire had been totally unprepared to deal with the emergency. *He must have encountered similar emergencies when he was working in the Michigan prison,* she thought. *Why was he at such a loss about how to manage Hoffman's situation?*

When Dr. McGuire prescribed the Haldol for Hoffman, she had questioned the dosage. Now she wished she would have followed her instincts and challenged his decision more strenuously. But then, he was the psychiatrist. He was supposed to know about drugs and dosages.

There were other things about McGuire that were beginning to bother Nancy. Besides seeming unconcerned about the side effects Mr. Hoffman was having from the Haldol, why did he ask her to write out the prescription for the drug? And why did he often ask her what she would do if she were the psychiatrist? At first she had been flattered by his questions and thought he was testing her knowledge. Could it be he didn't know how to care for mentally ill inmates? Nancy gently slapped her face and whispered aloud, "Get a grip, Mirabal." *Was stress over the Hoffman matter causing her mind to run amok, or was it the conversation she'd had with Lieutenant Taza?*

Nancy's mind kept racing. *Dr. McGuire often left for meetings outside the prison. What kind of meetings was he attending? Last week when he had returned from one of his meetings, there was alcohol on his breath.* A gnawing anxiety was building in the pit of Nancy's stomach.

Charles was still angry at Nancy when he got to the warden's office. Mary looked up at him as he rounded the corner.

"Hi! You didn't call to say you were coming. Are you here to see me," she asked hopefully, "or to see the warden?"

"The warden. We have an emergency in the mental health wing. Is she in?"

Mary dialed Kitt's extension. "Dr. McGuire's here. He needs to talk to you right away."

"You can go right in," she said, hanging up the phone. She was disappointed that he had been so curt with her.

When he walked in, Kitt could see from the look on his face that something was wrong.

"We had to call an ambulance for a schizophrenic in our wing. He's been in the mental health unit since he tried to commit suicide. We saw him my first day here when you were giving me a tour of the prison. He was bloody from hitting his head on the wall." Hearing the words tumbling out of his mouth, Sean realized he needed to think before he talked. He was sounding out of control.

"Slow down, Charles. Start from the beginning."

"Sorry. I just need a minute to catch my breath."

"Would you like a cup of coffee?" she asked.

"Please," he said, grateful he would have a minute to get back into the role of a psychiatrist in control.

"Let me start from the beginning," he said, having regained his composure. "Mr. Hoffman is a schizophrenic. I had to medicate him because he was out of control, and I was worried he would try to kill himself again. Normally, the drug works very well and Mr. Hoffman was doing well on the medication until this morning, when he started experiencing some negative side effects. I thought it best to get him to the hospital. You know, to be on the safe side."

"Good. It's always better to err on the side of safety. What drug was he taking?"

What was the name of the damn drug? It started with H. Sean leaned back in his chair and coughed to buy a little time. Then he remembered. "Haldol. It's a drug commonly used for schizophrenics. Fortunately, I decided to check on Mr. Hoffman when I came in this morning. If I hadn't stopped by his cell, he might have died."

"Well, keep me apprised about how Mr. Hoffman is doing," Kitt said, concerned.

"I'm sure he'll be just fine, but I will get back to you after I speak to the doctor who is treating him. By the way, I'm sorry about barging in on you like this, but I knew you'd want to be in the loop."

When he walked out of the warden's office, his face looked more relaxed. Mary ventured a question. "Everything okay?"

"It is now. We had to call an ambulance for Mr. Hoffman. He had a bad reaction to some medication he's taking. He's on the way to the hospital."

"I'm sorry. This isn't a good way to start the week."

"In my business, you never know what will happen next. It's

just lucky I stopped by Hoffman's cell to check on him this morning, or he could have died."

"Dr. McGuire, could you come back in here for a minute?" Kitt asked, poking her head around her door.

"Sure."

Kitt had decided to mention the call she had received earlier from Warden Franks. She hoped she wasn't making a mistake.

"I got a call this morning from the warden at Saginaw Prison in Michigan, Sheila Franks. By the way, she said to greet you for her," she began.

Sean's heart stopped. *Warden Franks? Why in the hell would that bitch be calling Kitt?* He saw her once while she was giving a group of legislators a tour of his cell hall. When he tried to talk to her for a minute, she had ignored him and kept on walking.

He sat down. He jittered his leg as he smiled and asked, "I had no idea that you knew her. How is she?"

"She's fine. I met her while I was at the warden's seminar. After she mentioned she was from Saginaw, I asked her if she knew you and, of course, she said she knew you well. Sheila spoke very highly of you. I told her you were filling in for us."

Kitt was trying to get a read on Charles. He nodded but said nothing. She continued, "Anyway, she said she ran into your partner, Dr. Sobel, at a concert Saturday night, and she told him you were here working for us. He asked if she knew where you could be reached. Apparently, he's anxious to talk to you."

His lungs began expanding again. He could handle this problem just like he had handled all the others. He place his hands on his knees and leaned forward.

"Knowing my good friend and associate, Dr. Sobel, as well as I do, my guess is he's afraid I'm going to make a permanent move and leave the practice. I'll get in touch with Dr. Sobel tomorrow and let him know what's going on."

He stood up to leave. "One more thing before you go," Kitt said. "My husband and I were in Empalme this past weekend. Eddie and some of the others are worried because they haven't heard from Josie. I told them you haven't heard from her either, but that you plan on going back to check on things this weekend. Are those still your plans?"

"Yes. I'm going on Saturday."

"Clyde asked about Josie's dog. No one seemed to know who's taking care of him."

Sean sniffed and coughed again to stall for time. This meeting with Kitt was beginning to feel like an inquisition. He fiddled with his coffee cup while his mind raced. "We took Rusty along to Phoenix with us the morning I dropped Josie off at the airport. Josie didn't want to ask anyone to take care of him because she didn't know how long she'd be gone and didn't want to impose on anyone. She asked me to find a kennel in Phoenix for her dog, so I did."

That's odd, Kitt thought. *According to Eddie, Clyde enjoyed keeping Rusty when Josie was out of town, and Eddie had said Josie would never want Rusty in a kennel.*

"Well, when you see Clyde and Eddie, tell them where the dog is."

"I certainly will. If Clyde really wants to take care of Rusty, I could go get him, but I won't have time to do it before this Saturday." Sean put down his coffee and quickly left, passing Mary's desk without looking at her.

Even though Sean had been able to diffuse this most recent situation, things were beginning to heat up. A few days ago, the authorities had identified his mother and were now looking for him. The real Dr. McGuire's partner was starting to get suspicious. The good news was he had ten thousand dollars in untraceable cash to work with. He could bail anytime he wanted to. Since Kitt thought he was going to Empalme on Saturday, that would be the perfect time to leave for Mexico. When he didn't show up for work on Monday morning, it wouldn't matter if they were suspicious. He'd be on a beach in Mexico.

It was time he told Mary about his weekend plans. If she wanted to go along with him to Empalme, he'd make up an excuse about why he had to go alone. Sean decided he had covered his butt enough for one day. He had plenty of time to dream up a reason why Mary couldn't accompany him to Empalme on Saturday.

Everything was under control for the time being. Sean knew he could manage the lies through Friday. In the meantime, he needed a drink. Nancy would never know if he took half an hour to run home and belt down a couple of scotch and sodas. He'd tell her that the meeting with Kitt went longer than he had expected it to.

30

KITT SAT STARING AT THE CHAIR Charles had just vacated. She thought of the first time she had seen him in the cantina. His penetrating eyes had briefly unnerved her, but the following day when they had been the only two patrons in the cantina she had enjoyed talking to him. He had made a positive impression on her. Now she wondered if she should have trusted her initial gut reaction.

No question, Charles was a real charmer, good looking and bright, but how much depth did he have? Although she had never felt a physical attraction towards him, many other women seemed to. It appeared to Kitt that relationships with women probably came and went easily for Charles. And what about his deceased wife? As far as Kitt knew, he hadn't mentioned his former wife to anyone, and she hadn't detected any sign of grieving on his part. It hadn't been long after his wife's death that he had moved in with Josie. That, in itself, wouldn't have seemed strange because he needed a place to live while he did his research. Even if his relationship with Josie was only a friendship, it was strange that he didn't seem to be concerned about her whereabouts. Now he was living with Mary and, from what Mary had told her, they had developed more than just a friendship.

Rather than being sobered by his wife's death and Josie's disappearance, Charles seemed upbeat, even to the point of being flippant at inappropriate times. She now thought his comment, "How interesting, a dead body in the cemetery," seemed really odd the night Kitt had discovered the body of Loraine Byrnes. Maybe Charles used humor as a way of cutting through tension.

But maybe he was covering up something.

Then there was Josie's disappearance. If Josie hadn't been able to reach Charles, why wouldn't she have called Eddie? Something wasn't right.

Kitt had other concerns about Charles, concerns that related to decisions he was making as a psychiatrist. Bruno Keppel had been cheeking his Valium and, as a result, had nearly killed another prisoner. Why hadn't Charles followed up with Keppel to make sure he was taking the medication? It seemed strange that a prison psychiatrist would trust an inmate to take medication just because he said would. Certainly Charles knew about the games convicts play with staff.

On top of everything else was her concern about Mr. Hoffman. He was on the way to the hospital, suffering from the side effects of a drug, a drug that maybe shouldn't have been prescribed in the first place. *Was it possible that the respected Dr. Charles McGuire didn't have the credentials she, and everyone else, believed him to have?* The thought made her shudder.

Deep in thought, Kitt stood up and walked over to the window. Her gaze fell on Charles' white Buick pulling out of the parking lot. This was a strange time for him to be leaving. It was only mid-morning and he had a crisis going on with Hoffman.

Kitt had been giving some thought to having an off-the-record conversation with Nancy Mirabal. With Charles gone, this would be a good time to catch her alone.

When she left for the mental health wing, Mary was away from her desk. Kitt left a note on her chair, telling her where she would be.

The wing was quiet until the inmates caught a glimpse of Kitt. "Warden Logan, can I talk to you?"

"Over here, Warden," pleaded another.

She walked past an inmate standing with his hands on the bars of his cell. "What about that guy they took out of here on a stretcher? What's up with him?"

The prison grapevine was already buzzing with information about Hoffman. "He's in the hospital," she said, moving toward Nancy's office.

"Good morning," Nancy said, poking her head out the door of her office.

"Hi, Nancy. I decided to come over and check on Mr. Hoffman's condition."

How strange, Nancy thought, *that the warden would walk over to the unit instead of simply making a phone call.* And as far as Nancy knew, Dr. McGuire had been in the warden's office briefing her less than an hour ago.

"I haven't heard anything more from the hospital," Nancy said.

"Is Dr. McGuire around?" Kitt asked, knowing full well he wasn't.

"No. He said he was going to your office to brief you on the Hoffman situation. I haven't seen him since. Maybe he had a meeting that he didn't tell me about."

What kind of meeting would McGuire have that would take him outside the prison? Kitt wondered. He was working on a temporary basis and would have no reason to be meeting with anyone other than prison staff.

"Do you have time for a cup of coffee, Nancy?" Kitt asked. "I don't get many chances to visit with you."

"Sure. I'd love to take a break. This morning has been hectic, to say the least. The conference room is empty. Let's go in there so we can have some peace and quiet. I'll program my phone in case the hospital calls."

Kitt shut the door of the room behind her. "You've had more stress than usual lately, haven't you, Nancy? Mr. Keppel and Mr. Hoffman have kept you hopping."

Nancy nodded in agreement. "I must admit it has been a bit difficult, especially this morning when I found Mr. Hoffman unconscious."

A red flag immediately went up. Kitt was sure Charles had said he was the one who had gone in to check on the inmate, not Nancy. She watched the nurse's eyes carefully as she restated Nancy's claim to have found the inmate in trouble. "It's a good thing you found him or he might have died. What do you think happened to him? Dr. McGuire said he's on suicide watch. Did he try to kill himself?"

"Heavens, no," Nancy said, a little too quickly. "Mr. Hoffman was very heavily medicated and could hardly walk. He didn't have the physical or mental strength to commit suicide."

"What was the problem with his medication?"

Nancy paused for a moment to wonder why McGuire hadn't explained the problem with the medication to Kitt when he briefed her on the situation. Maybe the warden was double-checking to make sure she had understood McGuire correctly.

"Mr. Hoffman," she answered, "was on an extremely high dose of Haldol, which is a drug used for people with schizophrenia. Normally, a person gets the first dose by IV and is watched very carefully to see how he tolerates the medication. After that, the drug is given orally, starting with a small dose and working up to the amount needed to control the schizophrenia."

"I'm not trying to put words in your mouth, but are you saying Dr. McGuire made a mistake in the way he administered the drug?"

Nancy paused while she carefully weighed her response. "I am very uncomfortable second-guessing Dr. McGuire. He's the psychiatrist; I'm not."

"I can understand how you feel, but I want you to answer me honestly. Over the years you've worked with several different psychiatrists. I'm curious to know how you think Dr. McGuire measures up to the others."

Kitt was quick to notice Nancy was not comfortable with the conversation they were having about Charles, so she added, "Before you answer my question, I want you to know I consider this conversation confidential. What we say to each other stays in this room."

Suddenly the conversation Nancy had with Taza flashed through her mind. The warden was the person who would be asking the questions she needed to answer honestly.

"It might be best if I started at the beginning," Nancy began. "After Dr. Shelton's accident, I had my hands full trying to keep the wing from erupting. I found myself trying to manage an unmanageable situation. Sometimes I had the opportunity to ask Dr. Reynolds for advice, but other times I had to make spur-of-the-moment decisions and didn't have the opportunity to consult with him."

Nancy twisted the coffee stir stick in her fingers. "When Dr. McGuire began working here, I was relieved that a psychiatrist would be making the decisions again, not me."

She dropped the stir stick. "How do I say this?" she asked, more to herself than to Kitt.

"Don't worry about how to say things to me. Maybe if you pretend you're confiding in a best friend, instead of the warden, it will help."

Nancy smiled. "Good idea." She pushed her chair back from the table and crossed her legs. "The first day Dr. McGuire was here, I gave him the list of inmate prescription refills. This was the most urgent matter that needed attention. He asked me if I thought they should all be refilled. I told him yes but I wanted him to check them over to make sure. He didn't. Dr. McGuire took the pile of refills and signed his name without looking at any of them. He said he trusted my judgment, and that he would need to rely on me a lot the first few days. The fact that he had confidence in me made me feel good because Dr. Shelton sometimes made me feel like I didn't know anything about mentally ill inmates."

"That was a big mistake on his part," Kitt said. "Go on."

"It didn't take me long to realize Dr. McGuire was delegating most decisions to me. About the only thing I don't do is have sessions with inmates. Anyway, Dr. McGuire goes out a lot and I'm left here alone, so I still have most of the responsibility to keep things running smoothly."

"Where does he go when he leaves?" Kitt asked.

"I don't have a clue. He never says where he's going. A couple times when he has returned to the office, I have smelled alcohol on his breath."

Maybe that explains why things are going to hell, Kitt thought. *He probably has a drinking problem.* Sheila hadn't mentioned his having a problem with alcohol. It was possible Charles started drinking after his wife's death.

She pulled out of her thoughts and turned her attention back to Nancy. "To be fair, Dr. McGuire does seem to have a way with inmates. They go into the sessions agitated or upset and come out calm and thanking him. I told him he was a miracle worker. I honestly felt that way until the Hoffman incident.

"After Bruno Keppel assaulted Mr. Harper," Nancy said, "Dr. McGuire blamed me for not following up to make sure Keppel was taking his medication. I guess I deserve some blame, but I had my hands full with other things. Dr. McGuire told Captain Mahoney that he had given me the responsibility of making sure Keppel was medicated. I found it strange he would tell Captain Mahoney something like that when it wasn't true. It's like he needed a scapegoat."

"Making sure Mr. Keppel was taking his medication was Dr. McGuire's responsibility, not yours, Nancy. The buck stops on his desk. I'll make sure the captain knows you aren't to blame."

"I don't care what Captain Mahoney thinks. I'm not afraid of him, unlike most staff around here."

A faint smiled creased Kitt's lips when Nancy said she wasn't afraid of Mahoney. "Tell me more about what happened this morning with Mr. Hoffman."

"I've been worried about Mr. Hoffman because he was getting jaundiced and started staggering when he walked. Dr. McGuire didn't seem overly concerned when I pointed out the physical changes in Hoffman last week. He said it was normal for a patient to have side effects when a new drug is introduced into the body."

Nancy's jaw tightened. "I have been making a point to check on Mr. Hoffman every morning right after I get to work. This morning when he didn't respond to my voice, I went back to my office to call Dr. Reynolds and to page Dr. McGuire. That's when he showed up. I asked him to check on Mr. Hoffman. When he shook him and couldn't wake him up, he didn't seem to know what to do. I told him to check the pulse, but he told me to do it myself. After that, I found myself in the position of telling him what to do."

"Anything else I should know?" Kitt asked as her stomach did a flip-flop.

"I've probably said way too much as it is."

"Thank you for your forthrightness. I wanted the truth, and I got it. I told you earlier, what we've said here today stays in this room. And remember, this situation is my problem to solve, not yours. You've always done your job exceptionally well."

"Thank you, Warden. I feel like a ton of bricks has been lifted off my shoulders."

Kitt glanced at the clock on the wall. She and Nancy had been talking for longer than she thought. When she opened the door to leave, Charles was standing in the hallway just outside the conference room.

"What are you two up to?" he asked tensely.

Kitt thought she caught a whiff of alcohol on his breath. "I had a couple more questions about Mr. Hoffman and decided to save you a trip back to my office. I didn't realize you had gone out. Nancy offered me a cup of coffee, and I insisted she take a break with me."

"What questions do you have, or have you asked Nancy all your questions?" he asked.

She glanced at Nancy then met his eyes. "My questions are for you, but they can wait. I'm running late. I'll catch up with you tomorrow."

Your questions better damn well be for me, Sean thought. *I'm the psychiatrist around here.*

Lieutenant Taza, who had positioned himself near the door of the conference room, nodded at Kitt and Nancy as they passed.

31

MARY LOOKED UP AS KITT rounded the corner. "Is everything okay? Your note said you would be in the mental health wing. I was afraid something else had happened."

"No, everything's fine. After Charles left my office, I realized I had a couple more questions for him. Rather than call or ask him to come back here, I decided to walk over to talk to him, more as a show of support than anything else. Charles was out, but Nancy was there. She offered me a cup of coffee, so I visited with her for a while."

"That was nice of you. They've been through a lot these past couple of weeks. While you were gone, you had a couple of calls; nothing urgent. I left the messages on your desk."

"Thanks. Hold my calls, would you, please? I'm going to make a personal call, and I don't want to be disturbed unless it's absolutely necessary."

Kitt closed the door of her office and thumbed through her Rolodex until she found Sheila Frank's direct number. Sheila was in her office.

"Hi, Sheila, it's Kitt. I'm glad I caught you."

"Sounds urgent. What's up?"

"I wish I knew for sure. I need to ask you some questions about Dr. McGuire. You have always spoken highly of him so you may think I'm crazy for asking, but did you ever have any concerns about decisions he made regarding the treatment of mentally ill inmates?"

"Are you asking me if he mistreated inmates?"

"No, I'm asking if he ever misdiagnosed mentally ill inmates or if he prescribed doses of medication which were, well, inappropriately excessive."

"Never. Why?"

"I told you why I had to leave the workshop, didn't I?"

"Yes."

"I believe McGuire has made some bad decisions, and we're having serious consequences as a result of those decisions."

"Really? I don't believe what I'm hearing. What's going on?"

"Well, you already know about the assault. Since then, we've had another incident. McGuire prescribed an inmate a heavy dose of a drug used for schizophrenia, Haldol. The inmate has had a horrible reaction and we don't know if his condition will improve."

"You've had two inmates at death's door in two weeks. That's rough," Sheila said, "but are you sure it's Dr. McGuire's fault? Maybe the pharmacist made a mistake, or the nurse who gave the inmate the medication gave him too much."

"I wish that were the case, but it's not," Kitt said. "There's something else. Charles left the prison for a while this morning. When he returned, I smelled alcohol on his breath."

Sheila gasped audibly. "I can't imagine him drinking on the job. In fact, I don't think Charles drinks at all. At department social events, like retirements and holiday parties, he'd have a club soda or Coke. I know, because I offered to buy him a drink at a holiday party one time and he said something about not having acquired a taste for alcohol. And as for over-medicating inmates," Sheila hesitated a moment, then said, "when we were discussing medications in one of our staff meetings, I distinctly remember his saying he would rather err on the side of under-medicating, if there were any questions about the inmate's ability to tolerate a drug."

"Are you still there, Kitt?" Sheila asked when there was no response on the other end of the line.

"Yeah, I'm here. I'm just wondering how I'm going to get to the bottom of this."

"Listen, I gave McGuire rave reviews when you asked me about him at the seminar, and I stand by what I told you. But I have to agree something strange is going on. When Dr. Sobel and I talked last weekend, I was shocked to hear that Charles had not contacted him to say he was extending his leave of absence. He's a considerate person and I can't picture him not following up with Sobel. It's so out of character for him. Maybe his wife's death. . ."

"I know this sounds bizarre," Kitt interrupted, "but will you describe him to me?"

"Who, Dr. Sobel?"

"No, McGuire."

Sheila couldn't believe her ears. Why would Kitt ask her to describe a man who was working for her? "Excuse me, did you say you wanted a description of McGuire?"

"Just give me the description, please."

"He's in his early fifties; stands about five feet eight inches tall, wears glasses and has a receding hairline."

Kitt's stomach rolled. "Stop. You don't need to go any farther. The man you just described is not the Dr. McGuire who is working for me."

"What? Oh my God, Kitt. What's going on?"

"I don't know."

Kitt could feel her heart pounding. She took a couple of deep breaths.

"If I can do anything at all to help," Sheila offered, "give me a shout. Take down my pager number so you can reach me anytime, day or night."

Kitt scribbled down the number and hung up. Panic was beginning to set in. Kitt needed to get out of the office and sort through what was happening. She opened her office door. Mary was at her desk.

"Mary," she said, "I'm not feeling well. I may have a touch of the flu so I'm going home. Will you call Dale and tell him he's acting warden until I get back? See if he is scheduled to be around the rest of the day. Tomorrow, too, in case it's more than a twenty-four-hour bug."

The deputy warden was in his office. He told Mary he'd come right over to see what needed to be done.

"Can you get home all right?" Mary asked.

"As long as I go now, I should be okay. If I'm still off my feet tomorrow morning, I'll give you a call."

"Hope you get to feeling better real soon. Take care of yourself."

32

CORD WAS IN THE FRONT YARD watering the yucca when Kitt pulled up in the driveway. "Hi, honey. You're home early." He immediately noticed Kitt's face was ashen. "What's the matter? Are you sick?"

"Sick is an understatement. Come in the house. I need to talk to you."

"It sounds serious." He wiped his hands on his Levi's and followed her into the house.

"Serious as a heart attack."

Sitting with Kitt at the kitchen table, Cord listened without interrupting until Kitt had told him everything. "What now?" he asked.

"For starters, I need to clear my head. The guy who is going by Charles is an imposter, no question about that. But who is he? All sorts of crazy ideas are running through my head; what was he doing in Empalme when I met him and is he in anyway connected to the body I found in the cemetery? And what's happened to Josie? She seems to have disappeared into thin air. Charles, or whoever he is, said Josie had to leave for the East Coast to help out her sick mother. Frankly, I'm very uncomfortable relying on any information coming from him."

"I'll make us a cup of tea, and then I'll help you think this thing through." Cord moved toward the stove. Kitt headed for the bedroom to change clothes.

"I'm going to call Sheriff Martinez. If he happens to be in town, I'll ask him to come over," Kitt said when she rejoined Cord.

She took a couple of sips of her tea. "After that, I'll call Eddie to see if anyone has been able to reach Josie."

The sheriff was in his office. He heard the urgency in Kitt's voice. "I'll get there as soon as I can."

In what seemed like only a few minutes, Kitt saw the sheriff's car pull up in the driveway. She met him at the door before he had a chance to ring the doorbell. After exchanging brief greetings, they settled on the couch.

Vinny took copious notes while Kitt talked. After telling him everything she had been able to piece together, she added, "And to top it all off, I'm worried about Josie's disappearance."

"So am I," he said. "I need to get a search warrant for Josie's house. Can I use your phone?"

"Sure."

The sheriff told his dispatcher he wanted a couple of investigators back in Empalme as soon as possible so they'd be ready to go when he got there with the warrant.

"Don't say anything to anyone about your suspicions," Vinny cautioned. "We know McGuire's an imposter, but we don't know anything else. What we don't want is for him to get suspicious that we're onto him. He'll run, sure as hell. It would be a good idea to tell Eddie what's happening, though. Would you mind giving her a call? Tell her I'm on my way and to keep a close eye on things until I get there. We can trust her to keep things quiet."

"The guy is staying with my secretary, Mary. Should I tell her about him?"

"I'd rather not have her know now unless you think he suspects you know his scam. The more people who know, the more likely he picks up on it."

"I don't think he suspects anything."

"Then I wouldn't say anything to her yet. Maybe we'll know more after we go through Josie's house – speaking of which, I need to pick up the search warrant. Use your judgment about if and when you need to tell your secretary," he added, "and if you think of anything else, give me a call on my cell phone."

He handed her his card and started out the door.

"Before you leave, there is one more thing," Kitt said.

He stopped and turned back around to face Kitt. "What's that?"

"You said you found some cigarette butts near the grave where I found Loraine Byrnes' body. I realize you can't tell me what brand they are but, for the record, McGuire smokes Marlboro's."

He nodded his head as if he expected as much, but said nothing.

After the sheriff left, Kitt called Eddie to warn her police tape would be going up around Josie's house.

Eddie could tell from Kitt's voice that it wasn't a social call.

"Something's up. What's going on?" she asked.

"I'll tell you, but you can't talk about it to anyone but Vinny."

"You know you can trust me to keep it quiet."

"Charles McGuire is an imposter."

"What do you mean, an imposter? How do you know?"

"I started to get suspicious after we had a couple of incidents involving mentally ill inmates. I'll give you the details some other time. Anyway, I called the warden in Michigan where McGuire worked before he left his practice. During the course of the conversation, I asked her for a physical description of him. The man she described is not Charles."

The news silenced Eddie.

"Vinny just left the house a few minutes ago," Kitt said. "Investigators will be combing through Josie's house as soon as they get the search warrant." Kitt paused. "Eddie, I'm scared. Since no one knows who Charles really is, it makes Josie's sudden trip to the East Coast suspicious."

"What are you saying?" Eddie's voice quivered.

"I'm not saying anything except that it's time to find Josie or someone in her family to talk to."

"Are you coming down?" Eddie asked.

"When I discovered Charles was an imposter today, I left work saying I was sick. I could take another day off without causing suspicion, but there's really nothing I can do in Empalme. Since no one else at the prison knows McGuire is a phony, I need to be around to keep an eye on him. Until we know for sure what's going on, we're keeping everything under wraps so he doesn't get suspicious and take off."

"Makes sense."

"I'll be in my office tomorrow. Call me and tell me how things are going down there."

Cord had been listening to the conversation. After Kitt hung up, he said, "I think you should do something to make Charles think everything is just fine. Maybe you could invite him to have a cup of coffee with you tomorrow morning. Make it a casual invitation. Better yet, try to bump into him and make an off-the-cuff invitation."

"That's a good idea. I'll wait in the parking lot until I see him pull in."

"On another topic, you're probably not hungry, but I'm starved."

"Dinner is the last thing on my mind."

"I'll defrost some chicken breasts and put them on the grill. You may find your appetite later. How about a glass of wine? It might help you relax," he suggested.

"It's worth a try," she said, attempting a smile. The smile left her face.

"Cord, I can't shake the feeling that Josie's dead."

33

TO BE ON THE SAFE SIDE, Kitt pulled into the parking lot at eight o'clock, even though Nancy had said McGuire rarely arrived at work before eight thirty. She wanted to be there when he drove in so she could make their meeting a coincidence. Kitt took her checkbook out of her purse and began to balance it while she waited for him to arrive.

An hour later Charles swung his car into the spot beside hers. Kitt acted like she was getting some things together, then stepped out of the car. "Good morning, Charles," Kitt called out cheerily.

"Good morning, Kitt. I had an early meeting this morning so I'm a little late getting to my office."

Meeting, my ass, Kitt thought. "I'm later than usual, too."

"How are you feeling? Mary said you went home sick yesterday."

"It must have been a twenty-four-hour bug, or something I ate. I'm feeling much better today."

"Good. I was worried."

"Say, why don't you join me for a cup of coffee? I don't have anything on my schedule this morning and, frankly, I'd like the company."

Charles was obviously delighted with the invitation. Cord's suggestion had been a good one, and Kitt was glad Charles was enjoying a false sense of security. She needed to make sure he didn't bolt.

Mary smiled brightly when she saw them walk in together. "Good morning. You look a lot better today than you did yesterday afternoon, Kitt."

"I feel a lot better, too. Dr. McGuire and I are going to have a cup of coffee. Hold my calls, unless it's something urgent."

"I made a pot after you called to say you were coming in."

"Thanks."

In her office, Kitt poured two cups of coffee. "White and one, as I recall?"

"That's right. You have a good memory."

"I'm glad you have time for coffee with me this morning, Charles. After you left my office yesterday morning, I realized I hadn't asked if there was anything you needed. You and Nancy have had more than your share of stress lately, and I want you both to know you have my full support. I wanted to tell you that yesterday when I stopped by your office but, as you know, I was running late."

Perfect, Sean thought, flashing his most charming smile. "Nancy and I appreciate your concern, but I don't want you to worry. Things will be back to normal in no time. I don't take these things too seriously because difficulties are a given when you're working with mentally ill people. As I've said before, psychiatry isn't an exact science by any stretch of the imagination. On occasion, things go wrong, and that's the long and short of it."

His simplistic approach was so obvious. *Why hadn't she seen it before?* Kitt wondered. *How could she have so misread the man sitting in her office?*

"Are you still planning to go to Empalme this weekend?" she asked.

"Yes. I hope there's a letter from Josie telling me how things are going with her and her mother."

"Me, too."

The two chatted for a while longer, then Kitt said, "Guess I better start through my stack of messages. I'm glad we were able to get a few minutes together this morning."

"Anytime you want to have some company, let me know." *Little does she know that I'll only be available through Friday. After that she'll be without the benefit of my company forever.*

Kitt watched him walk out of her office, and leave her door ajar. He didn't appear to be at all suspicious that she was onto him. She looked at her watch. By this time, Vinny and his investigators would be at Josie's home looking for the names and phone numbers of family members. If only they could find Josie; it would be such a relief.

Curiosity about what was going on in Empalme got the best of her. She lifted the phone and called Eddie. She glanced at the door and decided to leave it open. The door had been closed a lot lately while Kitt made her phone calls; she didn't want to rouse Mary's suspicions.

"Hi Eddie. It's Kitt. I'm at work but I wanted to call and thank you for the nice time we had last weekend."

"You can't talk, right?" Eddie asked.

"You got it. How are things going with you?"

"The investigators are in Josie's house right now." Eddie went on to tell Kitt what was happening.

"Oh, I snagged Charles this morning and invited him into my office for a cup of coffee. We had a nice visit. He's still planning to come to Empalme this weekend."

"So, McGuire's not suspicious. I should tell Vinny. Right?"

"That's right. Now, I better get busy returning some messages."

"Stay in touch, Kitt."

"Okay, talk to you soon."

Mary stuck her head in Kitt's office. "I need to go down to the mailroom. Do you want me to program your phone to the front desk, or do you want to take calls?"

"I'll take them."

No sooner had Mary left than Kitt's phone rang. It was Sheila Franks. "Are you sitting down?" came the strained voice on the other end of the line.

"Yes." Kitt's heart stopped.

"Last night they found Dr. McGuire's car. His body was in the trunk."

"My God, " Kitt gasped. Her mind jumped to one conclusion. The imposter working for her had murdered the real Dr. McGuire. There could be no other explanation; he had assumed the dead psychiatrist's identity.

"A security officer driving through the long term parking lot at the airport got suspicious," Sheila continued, "because the car had been there so long. Yesterday, when he got out of his vehicle to check the car, he smelled an odor coming from the trunk and called the sheriff's office. It's all over the news here. Don't know if it will make the national news or not. I thought you needed to know right away."

After a brief pause Kitt responded. "I really appreciate your call. Who knows what he'll do if he hears about McGuire's body being found. I gotta go. I'll get back to you as soon as I can."

"Be careful," Sheila warned, "obviously this imposter of yours is dangerous."

Kitt looked out and saw Mary was not back from the mailroom. She closed the door to her office and tried calling Vinny on his cell phone. He didn't answer. She dialed Eddie's number.

When Eddie answered, Kitt said, "Is Vinny still over at Josie's?"

"He was there a few minutes ago."

"I need you to tell him to call me right away."

Eddie didn't ask what had happened.

In less than five minutes Kitt's phone rang. It was the sheriff. "Vinny, thank God Eddie found you."

"She made it sound like an emergency."

"It is an emergency. I just got off the phone with the warden of the Saginaw facility. She told me the real Dr. McGuire is dead. A security officer at the airport found him stuffed in the trunk of his car. I'm certain the Charles McGuire I hired is the murderer."

"Well, let's not get ahead of ourselves, but we should assume he's a dangerous man. I'll call the Michigan officials and let them know what's going on down here. In the meantime, if you run into your McGuire, act like everything is just fine so he doesn't get spooked. I'll leave Empalme and come back to Florence right away. I'll arrest him as soon as I get back to Florence."

"What about my secretary, Mary?"

"It's time to tell her what's going on. Can you get her out of there? Take her to lunch or something? I don't want her at work when you tell her about him because she's going to need time to adjust to the shock."

"I'll take her to lunch."

"If she's not at her desk, would it be unusual?" he asked.

"No, her job takes her to other areas of the prison. I'll drive my car in case he leaves the prison. He'd get suspicious if he sees that her car is gone. It won't seem out of the ordinary if my car is gone. I'm in and out a lot."

"After you have lunch, it's important that you both return to work and go about your business as you would normally," Vinny said. "You'll be safe at the prison. I'll make the call to Michigan and leave for Florence right away. I should be able to get there before he leaves work. I'll nab him in the parking lot on his way out this afternoon. After I arrest him, I'll call your office and let you know he's in custody."

"Be advised," Kitt warned, "his hours are sporadic. He often leaves early. Where he goes, I don't have a clue."

"I'll catch up with him one way or the other. In the meantime, stay vigilant and don't leave the prison after you get back from lunch until you hear from me."

Kitt heard Mary stirring at her desk a few minutes later. "You know what, Mary, I'm in the mood to go out for lunch, and I don't want to eat alone. Would you want to come along? It's so seldom we get a chance to go out for lunch with our hectic schedules."

"I'd love to go."

Kitt remembered Nancy saying that Charles often left for lunch around eleven thirty. She wanted to make sure they didn't run into him in the parking lot on their way out.

"Well it's only a few minutes after eleven, but I'm starved," Kitt said, rubbing her stomach. "I didn't eat breakfast this morning. If we go now, we could avoid the noon rush."

"Let's go now, then. I'm hungry, too."

Kitt took her purse out of her desk drawer and locked the door to her office.

"All set?" Mary asked brightly.

"Where do you want to go?"

"Anywhere is fine with me. Do you want me to drive?" Mary offered.

"No, I'll drive. My car is closer."

Kitt drove to the nearby restaurant, keeping the conversation light. The hostess recognized Kitt as she walked over to the two women. "Good morning. I assume you'd like your regular table?"

"Please," Kitt answered with a smile. The hostess guided them over to a quiet table near the back of the restaurant.

During the meal, Kitt chatted about her trip to Empalme and asked Mary about her children. "Can I interest you ladies in dessert?" the waitress asked, as she cleared the dishes from the table.

"Not for me, thanks," Kitt said, "but I'll take a cup of coffee. How about you, Mary?"

"Hmm, decaf with cream, please."

"Mary," Kitt began, "I have some news that will be upsetting for you to hear, and I didn't want to have this discussion in the office."

"What is it?" Mary asked, a look of alarm spreading across her face. "I'm not losing my job, am I?"

"No. It's nothing like that. I couldn't do my job without you. When I say you're my right arm, I really mean it." Kitt took a deep breath. "I need to talk to you about Charles."

The color drained from Mary's face as Kitt told her everything. "I'm sorry to ruin our lunch, but you need to know what's going on. Sheriff Martinez has been in Empalme, but he's on his way back to Florence and will be arresting Charles this afternoon when he leaves work."

"My God. I've been renting a room to a murderer? Please, tell me this is a bad dream," Mary whispered. She leaned back in her chair and tears began to flow down her cheeks.

"I wish with all my heart I could say it's a bad dream, but it isn't. The murder of Dr. McGuire might only be the tip of the iceberg. I pray I'm wrong, but I think there's a good chance he murdered Loraine Byrnes, too."

"Loraine Byrnes?"

"She was the dead woman I found in the cemetery."

"Oh."

"And," Kitt reluctantly pressed on, "remember Josie, the woman Charles was living with in Empalme?"

Mary nodded. Her breathing grew shallow.

"She's disappeared. No one has heard from her in weeks."

Mary sprang up from the table. "I'm going to be sick," she said, as she rushed to the bathroom. A few minutes later she returned.

"I know this has been a terrible shock, Mary. I wish there had been an easier way to tell you. I am so sorry. Are you going to be okay?"

"I'm devastated, but I'll get over it. The worst part is my pride in being a good judge of character just went down the toilet. Literally," she said with a weak smile.

Kitt gave Mary a minute to regain her composure, then said, "I'm feeling terribly guilty because I hired him, but right now we have to concern ourselves with the present. If you happen to see Charles at work this afternoon, you need to act normal. I know it will be difficult, but it is critical. We can't let him know that we're onto him until after Sheriff Martinez apprehends him. Do you think you can pull it off?"

"Like you did this morning when you had coffee with him?" Mary asked. "You must have found out about Charles yesterday and that's why you went home early." Making another feeble attempt at humor, she added, "Guess I now have the same touch of the stomach flu you had yesterday."

Kitt gave Mary's arm a reassuring squeeze. "Yes. During a phone conversation with Sheila Franks, I found out that he was an imposter. I had called her yesterday after my conversation with Nancy, who had shared some things with me about how he had mishandled the incidents with Keppel and Hoffman, and that she had smelled alcohol on his breath a few times. When he breezed in yesterday after I was getting ready to leave the mental health unit, I smelled alcohol on his breath myself. When I got back to my office, I called Sheila. After she told me Dr. McGuire didn't drink and that she had never had a problem with him in any way, I asked her for a physical description of him. Needless to say, the description she gave me didn't match the man we know as Dr. McGuire. Yesterday, I only knew that our McGuire was an imposter. I didn't find out that the real Dr. McGuire was dead until this morning when Sheila called me back, or I would have gotten you out of your house last night."

"I'll try my best to act normal, but it won't be easy." Mary took a deep, wheezy breath. "My lungs," she said patting her chest. "I left my inhaler at home this morning. Stress often triggers my asthma attacks; we better run by my house so I can get it."

34

KITT PULLED INTO MARY'S DRIVEWAY and the two women went inside.

"Okay if I use your bathroom?" Kitt asked.

"Sure," Mary replied, as she disappeared into her bedroom to get her inhaler.

Kitt thought she heard the front door open and close. When she walked out of the bathroom, Charles was standing in the living room holding his briefcase.

"What's going on here?" he demanded. "How did you get in?"

"Hello, Charles," Kitt said in as calm a voice as she could muster. "Mary and I went out for lunch. On our way back to the prison, Mary began to feel a little wheezy and realized she had left her inhaler at home, so we stopped by to get it."

"Strange," he said, "she usually carries her inhaler with her all the time. Oh, well, who am I to talk? I forgot something this morning, too." With a glare, he turned and went down the hall to his bedroom.

After Kitt heard his bedroom door slam shut, she raced to Mary's bedroom. "Charles is here. Think about how you are going to handle it," she said, then quickly walked back into the living room.

Sean threw the briefcase on the bed and sat down. His left leg began to vibrate. He had planned to stop by the house, have a couple of beers and then go back to work. Instead, he had found Kitt and Mary together, supposedly stopping by to get Mary's inhaler.

Yesterday, Kitt had walked over to the mental health wing to see how he and Nancy were doing. Why hadn't she first checked to make sure he was in the office? He had discovered the two having coffee behind the closed door of the conference room. Yesterday, Kitt and Nancy; today it was Kitt and Mary. *Why hadn't Mary called him and invited him to go to lunch with them?* If something fishy was going on, he needed to get to the bottom of it fast.

Did Kitt suspect something? This morning when Kitt had invited him to have a cup of coffee in her office, she had seemed normal.

Sean went over to the dresser, took out the Bowie knife and carefully tucked it inside his belt under his suit jacket. He retrieved the money he had stashed in the bottom drawer of his dresser and put it in his briefcase. After a quick look around the room, he decided to leave everything else behind.

He walked back into the living room just as Mary emerged from her bedroom. Their eyes locked for a moment, then she quickly looked away. Her eyes were bloodshot. Allergies? Maybe, but it looked more like she had been crying.

"So, I understand you had to pick up your inhaler," he said.

"I . . . I forgot it this morning," Mary stammered.

"Are you feeling stressed? You told me once that stress can cause an asthma attack." His voice had a mocking tone to it.

"I'm not stressed about anything I can think of," Mary said, struggling to regain her composure. "It's probably just something in the air."

Sean considered her response as he studied her face for a couple of seconds. She was acting differently towards him. She was no longer the warm and caring Mary he had become accustomed to.

He moved closer to Mary. When she tried to step back from him, he grabbed her arm.

Kitt started to open her purse and reach for her Smith and Wesson, but Charles whipped out the knife and pressed it to Mary's throat.

"Don't do anything stupid, Warden," he hissed, "or you'll have a dead secretary on your hands. I know you carry a gun. Drop the purse."

He was a killer, and Kitt knew he wouldn't hesitate to kill again. When she saw a trickle of blood below the knife blade on Mary's throat, she dropped her purse to the floor.

"Kick it over to me," he demanded.

Kitt gave the purse a hard shove with her foot.

"Now, get me the duct tape under the kitchen sink. Don't take too long or my hand might slip." His voice was chilling.

Kitt knew she had no choice. Mary's life was at risk. She quickly found the tape and returned to the living room.

"That's close enough," he warned. Keeping the knife at Mary's throat, he grabbed a handful of her hair with his left hand and twisted it tightly. "Turn around and put your hands behind your back," he ordered Mary. The knife cut a shallow incision around her neck as she slowly turned.

"Wrap her wrists with the duct tape," he snapped at Kitt.

Kitt gave Mary's cold, clammy hands a squeeze as she taped them together. When she finished, she let go of the tape and stepped back.

He wrapped his left arm tightly around Mary's neck. "Now, Warden, hold some tape out so I can cut it." Mary gasped for air while he slashed the tape with the knife.

The man's pale, icy eyes seemed to have taken on a burning glow. Kitt felt like she was staring into the face of pure evil.

"Tape her mouth shut, and hurry up about it."

"Sorry," Kitt muttered, as she covered Mary's mouth with the duct tape.

"Shut the hell up," he yelled. "I'm doing the talking here."

Kitt cringed when he sliced another piece of tape from the roll. Mary winced in pain. Kitt's eyes met Mary's. *Stay calm*, she silently pleaded.

"Open that door," he said to Kitt, gesturing toward the hall closet. "Get in the closet," Sean barked, giving Mary a push toward the door. Before Kitt realized what was happening, the knife was positioned at her neck and the murderer was standing behind her.

Sean hadn't planned this, but he felt pleased that he had been able to take control of the situation. Mary was bound and gagged inside the closet and couldn't get out. By the time anyone found her, he'd be long gone. Sean slowly edged Kitt toward the closet door then kicked it shut.

With Mary out of the way, he had to figure out what to do with Kitt. If he took her as a hostage, he would probably have a better chance of getting to Mexico. After he was safely out of Florence, he'd kill her and dump her body in the desert. This time, he wouldn't have to waste time digging a grave. By the time anyone found her, he'd be across the border. In the meantime, he had to be careful how he handled Kitt. She was trained in self-defense, and he knew that if she thought he planned to kill her she'd fight for her life.

Kitt realized if she panicked and concentrated on her fear, she'd be at a disadvantage in dealing with the killer who held the knife to her neck. A strange sense of calm came over her as she prayed to God for help.

"Pick up my briefcase," Sean said, as he edged Kitt over to the coffee table, "and don't try anything funny or I'll slit your fucking throat."

Sean pulled his car keys out of his pocket with his free hand. "We're going for a ride," he said. They moved awkwardly toward the front door. "We'll take my car, well, strictly speaking, my mother's car. Rather, it was my mother's car. By the way, you met Mother while you were in Empalme."

"I don't remember meeting your mother," Kitt said, trying to sound confused.

He laughed. "The body you found in the cemetery was my mother's." Kitt recognized the laugh as one of a psychopath.

"Who are you?" she asked.

"Why I'm the esteemed Dr. McGuire, prison psychiatrist."

"A psychiatrist wouldn't do what you're doing," she said. "Tell me who you are. You owe me that."

Sean thought for a moment. He didn't owe her anything, but he'd tell her. He wanted to see the look on her face. Besides, she'd be silenced forever in a little while.

"My name is Sean Byrnes, son of Loraine Byrnes."

This confirmed what Kitt already suspected; he was his mother's killer. She also knew he planned to kill her, too, after they were safely out of town. The contents of her stomach threatened to erupt.

"Where are we going?" she asked.

He ignored her question. No neighbors were in sight as he edged Kitt toward the white Buick parked behind her car.

"Get in on this side and slide over to the driver's seat," he said, giving her a shove inside the door. "Throw the briefcase in the back seat."

Kitt knew she didn't have the right angle to slam the briefcase into his face, so she followed his instructions.

With the knife pressed tightly against her ribs, she slid behind the wheel. Before she turned on the ignition, she buckled her seatbelt.

"What are you doing?"

"Putting on my seatbelt," she said, snapping it shut.

"I would think wearing a seatbelt would be the least of your worries right now," he said with a sarcastic laugh.

Kitt's mind was racing. She believed her life, and the lives of many others, were at stake. She had to stop Byrnes from killing again.

"Turn south," he ordered when she pulled up to the stop sign at the Highway 79 intersection.

She swung onto the highway and stomped on the accelerator. The speedometer climbed to ten miles over the speed limit.

"Slow down," Sean yelled, "the speed limit is forty-five. The last thing we need is to draw the attention of a cop."

That's exactly what we need, Kitt thought, as she continued to accelerate. She felt a searing pain in her side as the knife pushed through her skin and stopped on a rib.

"I said slow down, you bitch," he screamed.

With one final push on the accelerator, she swung the steering wheel all the way to the left. The tires screeched across the pavement and skidded onto the gravel shoulder. The car swerved into the ditch, tore through the branches of a lone paloverde tree, and slammed into an abandoned brick building.

The knife fell away from Kitt's ribs, and everything went black.

35

Through her eyelids, Kitt saw a white light. She heard a voice, a man's voice.

"Can you hear me?"

She tried to answer, but couldn't make a sound.

"Can you hear me?" he repeated. "You're in the hospital."

She struggled to open her eyes. It took a moment for her to realize the man talking to her must be a doctor. Her heart began pounding as she began to remember what had happened.

"Where am I?" she asked weakly.

"In a Phoenix hospital. You were in a bad car accident, but you were very fortunate. Your injuries aren't serious. Other than a stab wound to the rib cage, a concussion and some bruises, you're just fine."

"How long have I been here?"

"Since yesterday. You've been unconscious. Probably just as well, under the circumstances."

"I need to go," she said, trying to sit up. "My secretary is locked in a closet at her house."

"No she isn't. She's here and waiting to see you. So is your husband. If you feel up to having visitors, I'll let them see you now."

Tears of relief began to flow down Kitt's face. "Please, go get them."

Through eyes blurred with tears, Kitt watched Cord and Mary tiptoe into the room.

Cord's face was drawn with worry as he leaned down to give her a kiss.

Mary walked over to the other side of the bed and took Kitt's hand. "Thank God you are all right," she said.

"Thank God you're okay, Mary. I was afraid you would suffocate in that closet."

"It wasn't an accident, was it?" Cord asked Kitt.

"No, it wasn't an accident. I knew Byrnes would kill me after he didn't need me anymore, so I decided to crash the car with us in it. What about him? Is he here in the hospital?"

"No. Byrnes died in the accident. He was thrown out and crushed between the building and the car after you hit the tree. If he had been wearing a seatbelt, he might have survived the crash."

Mary closed her eyes. She was remembering the night she had tried to persuade the man she had thought to be Charles McGuire to wear a seatbelt. At the time she had been a little irritated with him for not heeding her advice. Now, she realized, because he hadn't listened to her, Kitt was alive and he was dead.

"You are one damn smart woman, Red," Cord said proudly. "That crash saved your life and probably saved the lives of other people Byrnes would have murdered."

Kitt smiled at his comment. "I'll remind you that I'm a damn smart woman some time down the road when you don't think I'm so smart."

She looked over at Mary. "How did you get out of the closet?"

"I'll let Cord tell you since he and Vinny are the ones who rescued me."

Cord sat down on the side of the bed. "A dispatcher notified Sheriff Martinez of the crash, but at the time, he had no idea you were in the accident. He sent a deputy to the scene while he went over to the prison to arrest McGuire," Cord explained. "When Vinny got to the prison and found out you and Mary hadn't come back from lunch and that Byrnes was gone, he came over to our house looking for you. On a hunch, I suggested we drive over to Mary's house. Your car was parked in the driveway, but nobody answered the door when we knocked. Since the front door was unlocked, we let ourselves in and called out for you. Mary heard us and started kicking the closet door."

"Does Vinny know the guy's name is Sean Byrnes?" Kitt asked. "And that he's the son of the woman I found in the cemetery?"

"Yes. He has been able to get some history on Byrnes. He was an inmate at Saginaw Prison where the real Dr. McGuire worked.

While Byrnes was under the care of McGuire, he was diagnosed as a dangerous man with psychopathic tendencies. McGuire testified to that effect before the Michigan parole board and, as a result, Byrnes had to serve expiration of his sentence instead of getting an early release. Byrnes obviously carried a grudge against McGuire and must have decided to settle the score after he was released from prison."

"What about Josie?" Kitt asked.

"Her mother isn't sick, and she's not with any family members. No one knows where she is. It doesn't look good. When the investigators were going through Josie's house, they found trace amounts of blood on the floor of the living room. They also found some blood in her yard. "

The doctor came into the room and walked over to the bed. "Kitt needs to rest now."

"Are you going to be okay, Red?" Cord asked.

"Yes."

He nodded as he gazed into her eyes. "We'll be back in a little while," he said, gently giving her a kiss on the forehead. "Come on, Mary, let's go get a beer."

"Bring me one back?" Kitt whispered.

Epilogue

S<small>HERIFF</small> M<small>ARTINEZ</small> <small>HAD CALLED</small> to say he was on his way over to the house.

"Come in," Kitt said, opening the door. "Are you off duty?"

"I will be in a few minutes. If you're thinking of offering me a drink, I'll take you up on it."

"What would you like? We have brandy, wine, beer. . ."

"Brandy, straight up."

"Hello, Sheriff," Cord said, coming into the room. "I'll get the drinks, Red. What do you want?"

"A glass of wine, please. So, what's up, Vinny?"

He took a deep breath. "We found Josie's body."

Although Kitt had feared the worst for some time, it was still a shock to hear the words. "Where did you find her?"

"In a shallow grave outside of Empalme. Her dog was there, too."

"I kept hoping against hope. Does everyone in Empalme know?"

"By this time they do," Vinny said. "Clyde found her body. When he was out hunting rabbits yesterday, his dog suddenly stopped and started digging. Clyde went over to see what was going on and he saw that his dog had found a garbage bag with a body in it. He called me. It was Josie."

Kitt shook her head and put her hand up to her forehead. "How's Eddie doing?"

Cord handed Kitt her wine and Vinny his brandy.

"As well as can be expected under the circumstances. She's a tough lady."

"Your suspicions about Byrnes and the follow-up work you did with that warden in Michigan probably saved many other lives, Kitt. Byrnes was a very dangerous man."

"I get goose bumps when I think of him living with Mary. If anything would have happened to her, I could never have forgiven myself. If only I could do it over again, I never would have hired him."

"Think of it this way. You contained him by getting him to work at your prison. If you hadn't hired him, well, I don't even want to think about what might have happened. Remember, he killed McGuire, his mother and Josie before he started working for you."

"I guess you're right, but he also damn near killed two inmates, Mary and me. Did you ever figure out where the money Byrnes had with him came from?"

Vinny stood up. "No. And we may never know. Well, I better get going. Thanks for the drink." He carried his glass out to the kitchen. "Kitt, you might want to give Eddie a call. She's feeling pretty low about Josie and all."

Kitt and Cord walked the sheriff out to his car. He started to get in, then stopped. He winked at Kitt and said, "If you ever retire and want to earn some extra money, let me know. I could use another good investigator."